Smith's
MONTHLY

Every Month Original Novels, Stories, and Articles

USA Today Bestselling Writer
Dean Wesley Smith

I0554031

TABLE OF CONTENTS

SHORT STORIES

Music in Time — 6

The Tragic Tale of a Man in a Duster — 22

Dreams of a Moon
    An Earth Protection League Story — 40

As the Robot Rubs — 60

FULL NOVEL

Morning Song
    A Seeders Universe Novel — 68

SERIAL STORIES

The Life and Times of Buffalo Jimmy — 32
    Chapters 25-27

The Adventures of Hawk — 52
    Chapters 25-27

NONFICTION

Introduction:
    Science Fiction and Space Issue — 3

POEMS

Memory — 21

So You Want to be a Writer — 160

Smith's Monthly Issue #9

The Writings and Opinions of

Dean Wesley Smith

Introduction
Science Fiction and Space Issue

I FINISHED THE novel that is in this issue, *Morning Song: A Seeders Universe* novel and was wondering what kind of stories would logically fit with the novel. Usually, that's not a thought I would normally have, as those of you who have been following this magazine now for nine issues know. I just put stories in here and keep the reading varied, for the most part.

Granted, I had one issue that had sort of a sex and science fiction theme in a few stories and the novel. But past that, the theme has been that everything in here is my work. Period.

But for some reason, mostly to see if I could do it, I figured this issue, at least the short stories, could have a space and couples theme since that is the major setting for *Morning Song.*

So I started looking at some of my stories that most modern readers in 2014 would never have seen.

First I came across a story called "Music in Time." The story was originally in an anthology called *Love and Rockets,* edited by Martin H. Greenberg and Kerrie M. Hughes. The story is set on a space station. It takes one look at how the future of space flight might be. I loved that story and was really sad it came and went without even a notice.

Why I liked it a lot and wanted it to come back was that it is a story about believing in your art. I believe in the story, so I wanted it back here now.

One story down, three to find. Or write.

Then I found a story I wrote for my short story book challenge last year or so. It's called "The Tragic Tale of a Man in a Duster." It is yet another way of looking at how mankind gets out into deep space and some of the strange Einstein problems of time and speed.

Thanks for the Support

_____

Dean Wesley Smith

If you subscribed to the short stories, you got this story, so you can skip it. But in the last two years, the story didn't sell very well on its own, so since its a favorite of mine as well, I wanted to give it a new life here.

Two stories down.

Then, it just so happened that my *Fiction River* story scheduled to be in this issue was one of the stories that made up the novel from last month's issue of *Smith's Monthly*. It was originally in *Fiction River: Moonscapes* and it is yet another look at space travel.

And again, it has a lot to do with time and speed and is about a couple.

So at this point I had three stories plus an entire novel that were science fiction and couples in one form or another

But now the search got harder, since I now had a pretty clear theme in my head.

It took some searching through old files, but I finally found a story that originally appeared in an anthology called *Alien Pets* back in 1998 in a very altered form.

There is no pet in this version of the story. This is the author's preferred edition. (grin) The other form of this story with the same title also vanished without a trace when it came out.

This story was a forerunner of my Buckey the Space Pirate series. Actually, it was the third Buckey story before I changed him. To be honest, until I looked at the story again, I had forgotten Buckey was even in it.

It's humor (I hope) and is yet another look at how space travel in science fiction can work.

A very tongue-in-cheek look, granted.

So the only two fiction pieces in this issue that are not space science fiction with couples are the two ongoing serials.

I had fun putting this issue together, to be honest. I doubt I will do themed issues that often, but this one sure fit nicely together and brought some of my old favorite short stories to a modern audience.

And I like that. As I said last issue, I hated the old world when I wrote a story, sold it, the book or magazine came out and vanished and the story went into a file drawer, to be forgotten.

I really love this new world much, much more. In fact, the stories that are in the first few issues of this magazine, since I did covers for them, will be coming out shortly in stand-alone form.

I hope you enjoy my first real themed issue as much as I did putting it together.

Dean Wesley Smith
May 8, 2014
Lincoln City, Oregon

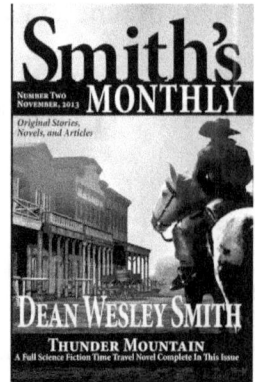

Coming Next Issue in Smith's Monthly
A New Novel Series.
The First Novel in the *Ghost of a Chance* Series

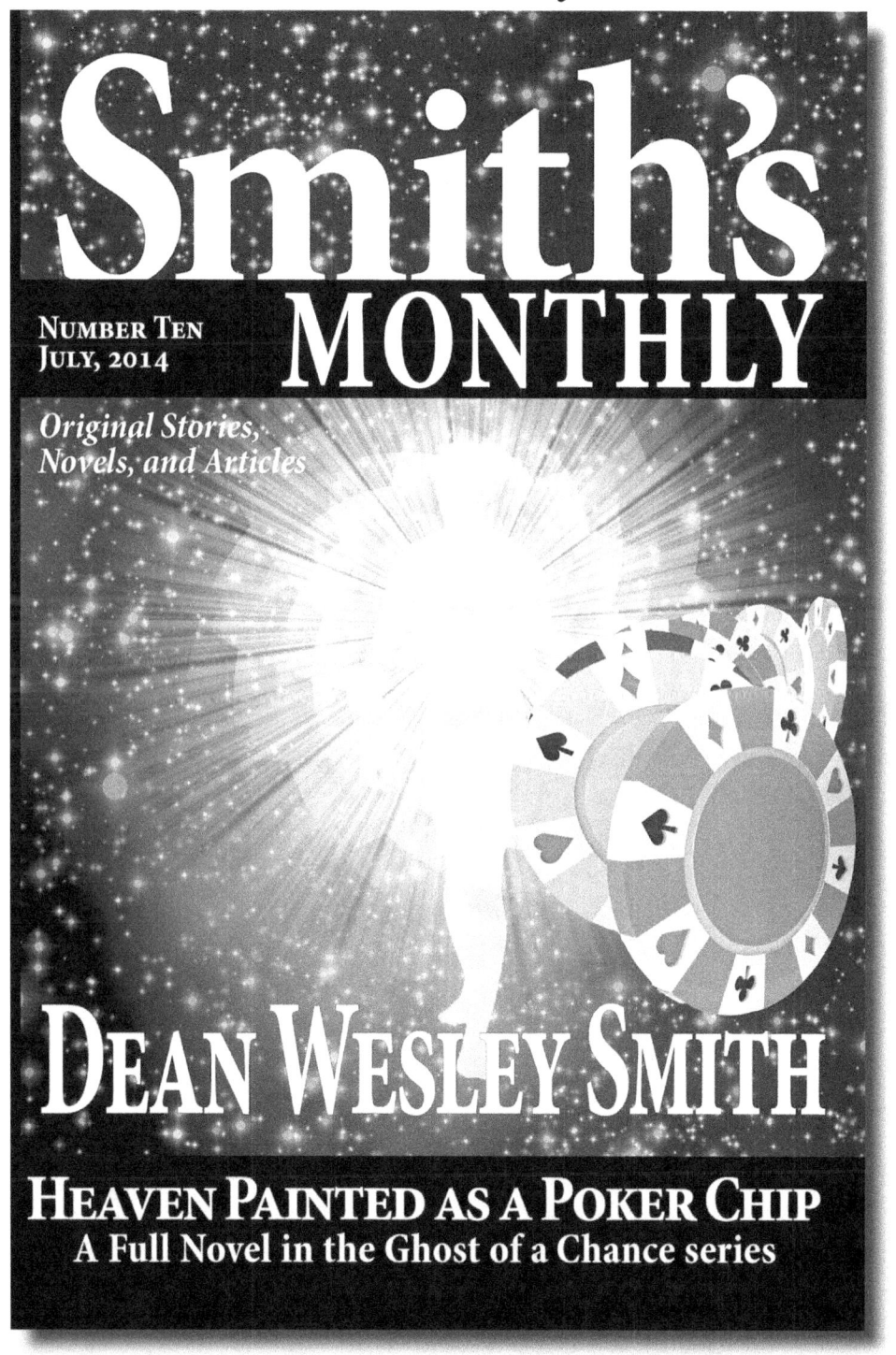

Smith's
MONTHLY

NUMBER TEN
JULY, 2014

*Original Stories,
Novels, and Articles*

DEAN WESLEY SMITH

HEAVEN PAINTED AS A POKER CHIP
A Full Novel in the Ghost of a Chance series

USA Today Bestselling Writer

DEAN WESLEY SMITH

MUSIC IN TIME

Sometimes an Artist's Work is Timeless

"Music in Time" takes a look inside the mind of an artist when that art seems to have left him stranded on a space station.

First published many years ago in an anthology entitled Love and Rockets, *this story remains one of my favorite personal stories. Every artist, in all fields, hits bottom at one point or another.*

I find this great fun to bring back after all these years, now that I have gotten off the bottom.

MUSIC IN TIME

One

THE BRIGHT LIGHT from the Benson Space Station sundeck made the inside of Scott's Tavern as black as the insides of an ore carrier. The thick musty smell of the bar, the comfortable herbal smoke, and the thick, rich odor of beer wrapped around me like a whore's arms, dragging me into the dark. It was cool inside, making sweat break out on my forehead.

A whole lot cooler than that stupid sundeck. Whoever thought of putting a station tube made out of mostly windows open to the closest sun on a space station should be shot. Idiots in bathing suits actually laid out on lounges out there, more than likely frying what little brains they had left.

I let the door slam behind me, closing out the sundeck heat, and stood there for a moment, fighting for my eyes to adjust, letting the cool air relax me. I knew Scott's Tavern wasn't really dark, but until my eyes adjusted, it sure seemed that way.

"Yo, Danny," a voice said from the shadows in the direction I knew the bar was. "Bright out there, huh?"

The voice was Carl's, the owner of Scott's tavern. Carl had bought the place after Scott died in a shuttle accident a few years back.

"Like walkin' on the damn sun," I said.

My eyes had adjusted enough for me to see the tables and chairs, so I started toward my normal bar stool. Carl was already sliding a beer onto a bar napkin just like he had done for me hundreds of times over the last few years.

I could see the shadows of a couple at a table, and one woman bent over her drink at the bar, two stools down from mine. Steve usually sat on that stool later in the night. Steve actually had a real job on the unloading pylons. Middle of the afternoon was too early for him.

I had no job, hadn't found a job in a year of searching, and had basically given up at this point. I was going to die on this stupid space station orbiting a star with a name I can't even pronounce. This morning I hocked my old guitar. I used to think I was going to take the Old Earth Country Music world by storm. I dreamed of selling millions, having fans want my autograph, be in demand by women, the whole deal.

Fat chance that was. I couldn't even find a damn job flipping burgers or cleaning up shuttles or mopping the stupid hallway floors.

I had used the money from the guitar to buy enough food to last for a week, and I had enough money left over to drink myself into a blind drunk tonight. What I would do for tomorrow's drinking money I would worry about tomorrow.

Damn I was going to miss that guitar. It had been like a best friend to me for twenty years. My first and only wife told me I loved the damn guitar more than her, and the bitch had been right about that toward the end of our marriage.

Man, how had I gotten so low as to hawk my guitar for food and drink money?

I shook the thought away, ignored the twisting in my stomach that I had made a fatal mistake, and climbed onto the stool. Coming to this stupid space station had been my fatal mistake. The promise of a gig here fell through twenty minutes after my ship arrived and I've been stuck ever since.

I grabbed the beer and held on for dear life. The glass was cool and wet and felt damned good after the hot sun on that sundeck. Actually, it felt good for a bunch more reasons than just the heat. I downed half, letting the wonderful taste wash away some of the regrets like I had taken a big-ass pill.

I then took out the fifty station credits I had on a chip and slid it across the bar toward Carl. "When that's gone, kick me out of here."

"You got it," Carl said.

He started to pick up the credits when the woman two stools over said, "Hold on a minute."

Both Carl and I glanced at her. Even with my eyes still not completely adjusted to the dim light yet, I could see her well enough.

She had on the traditional space wear business jacket, dark shirt, no tie. Her pants matched her jacket, and I could tell she spent far too much time on her short blonde hair.

I couldn't get the color of her eyes, but I was betting blue.

She was shorter than I was by a distance and looked to be athletic, not extra hyped up like some women were today. She seemed natural and aging normal, just like I was. I liked that.

She didn't look the type to be in Scott's place at this time of the afternoon, let alone picking up some loser like me. I hadn't had a real woman look twice at me in longer than I wanted to think about.

More than likely that was because I had nothing to offer any woman, hadn't cut my brown hair in half a year, and didn't have a non-wrinkled shirt to my name.

"That one's on me," she said, indicating my half-finished beer. "And you may not want another after what I've got to say to you."

Carl and I both just stared at her, then finally Carl just shrugged, as any good bartender would, took the price of my beer from the chip in front her, and turned away.

"And why would something you've got to say stop me from having a few drinks?"

The woman shrugged. "I got a job for you if you're up for it."

My stomach clamped tight at the idea of getting a job, earning enough to get my guitar back. Could something like that actually happen? Could I actually get so damned lucky?

I stared at the woman, her thin face and faint smile. I had never met her before, that I could remember, and I couldn't imagine what kind of job she might have. Or what type of job that would need a drunk from a bar to do.

But damned if she wasn't good looking. Even a loser like me could notice that I suppose.

I turned back to my beer and took another long drink, almost finishing it. My fifty credits still sat on the bar in front of the beer, waiting for me to drink it away. And I had no doubt I was going to do just that, even with a nut-case sitting two stools down from me. But it was nice of her to buy me the first one.

She scooted her stool back with a scraping sound, then reached down into the darkness below her and pulled up a guitar case. She put the case up on the bar between us. "I think you lost this."

I stared at the old case, the once-broken upper latch, the faded sticker from a trip I had taken to the New Mexico Star Cluster for a gig ten years ago. I had figured when I walked out of that pawnshop this morning I would never see it again.

My stomach felt like someone had kicked me.

"My guitar," I said, my voice soft. I wanted to reach out and clutch it like a long lost child, but instead I just turned to stare at the woman. "How did you get it?"

"I bought it out of hock for you this morning, on the assurance to the man in the shop I would take it to you." The woman laughed to herself. "I had to pay him a little extra to let me take it though."

She slid the guitar another few inches toward me. "It's yours. All I ask is you consider doing one job for me in return."

I looked at the case, then back at her. "A few answers first. How did you know I had hocked the thing? And how do you even know I want it back?"

She sort of shrugged and smiled, the smile of an insurance agent.

I was right. Her eyes were blue. I wondered if any of her appearance was actually real. It looked real, unaltered. But with enough money, looking natural could be bought these days and she looked like she had enough money to do just that.

I hadn't had a real woman look twice at me in longer than I wanted to think about.

"I happened to see you coming out of the pawnshop, so I went in and asked what you had sold. When I heard it was your guitar, I knew you could help me."

"And how would you know that?" I asked, doing my best to not get angry at some woman who was trying to give me back my guitar.

She stared at me, then said flatly, "I'll be honest with you. Coldly honest if you can take it."

I nodded and looked her right in the eyes.

"No one with your talent, your former career, would ever give up their instrument," she said, not looking away from my gaze, "without being flat on the bottom, with no hope. And right now I need someone with talent who thinks there is no hope."

I figured right at that moment I had two options. I could let my normal pride make me turn away from this woman, ignore her, or I could laugh. And since my guitar, the special Earth-made guitar I had hocked just a few hours ago, was sitting on the bar in front of me, I figured laughing was the better option.

"Am I right?" she asked.

I finished off my beer and turned on the stool to face her. "Oh, lady, are you right. With the money from the guitar I bought food for a week and that money right there to drink tonight."

I pointed at my last fifty station credits.

"After the food and money are gone, I'm done. I'm about to be kicked out of my room in the workers section of the station since I haven't paid in three months. I've borrowed from every friend and some strangers, and more than likely I'll be sleeping in some station shelter in the outer ring in a week and eating handouts or from garbage before it gets recycled."

I held up my empty beer glass, caught Carl's attention, and motioned for him to bring me another. "Friend, I don't know about the talent part, but you found someone with no hope."

The woman nodded, then stuck out her hand. "Mr. Danny Kenyon, my name is Alexis Pierce. Just call me Lex."

I reached out and shook her head. Her grip was firm, like she had done a few years of good solid work. But at the same time there was a softness to her hand and I held the grasp a little too long as I looked into her eyes.

She didn't look away.

I felt disappointed when I let her hand go finally. I was sure attracted to this woman for some reason.

I stared down into my beer, now feeling embarrassed. "Lex, I don't know what to say."

Carl brought me another beer at that moment, and Lex, bless her heart, bought, indicating that Carl should take the price from the money in front of her on the bar. Lex was going to make my fifty credits last a little longer than I had hoped at this rate.

"Just listen to my offer," Lex said. "You don't have to say anything yet. And no strings attached." She shoved the guitar a few more inches my way. "Better put that under your chair before we spill something on it."

I picked up my guitar and slid it to the floor between my legs. I had sat in many a bar over the years in many a different solar system and space station with the guitar in its case in that same position.

Me and my guitar had seen a lot of bars and a lot of light years. It felt good to have it back.

No, better than good. It felt great. I was whole again. I decided right at that moment I'd head for garbage cans to eat and sleep in the hallways before I pawned the thing again.

"Thanks," I said. "I'd offer to pay you back, but I doubt I'm going to be able to do that any time soon."

"Just considering my job offer is all I ask in return," Lex said. "I'll call it even if you do that."

"Lex, I've been looking for any job for the past year. So I'm more than willing to listen. Fire away."

As I looked into her eyes I felt even more of an attraction. Was she drawing me in with some chemical or some special way she looked? I could see no reason why she would, but I had better be damn careful. Men have disappeared around the systems over far less than a good-looking woman with a fast pitch.

"I need you to play a series of concerts for me."

I laughed again. "For who? I haven't had a gig in three years."

"After I got your guitar this morning I made some calls about you," Lex said. "The information I got is that you're talented and could have made it all the way to the top, but drank it all away."

"That and a few other bad breaks," I said, stung by her words. What did this blonde bitch know about how hard it was to push ahead in the music business day after damned day, sleeping in tiny shuttles, playing in station bars for drunks? It wasn't until everything fell apart that I really started drinking.

Lex shrugged. "What happened in the past doesn't matter to me. I just needed to know you were good, that you could play, and I discovered you can. And that you can write your own songs as well."

I stared at her, then smiled. "You didn't just happen to see me come out of that pawnshop, did you? You've been following me or something."

Lex laughed. "No, not really. I just had some good contacts in pawnshops

---

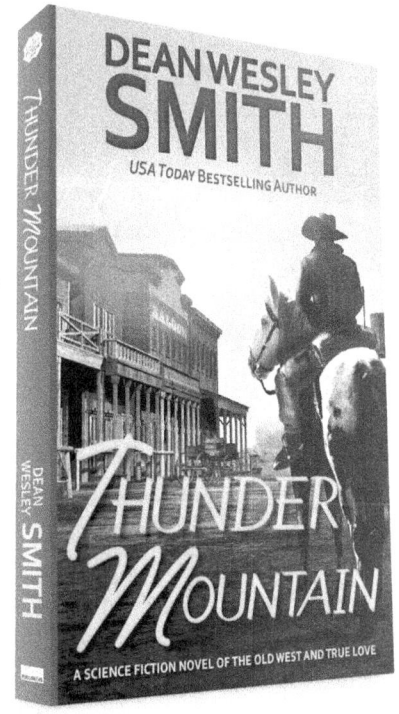

around the stations in this system. The pawn dealer contacted me."

"Why?" I asked.

"I'm sort of a talent agent," Lex said. "My job is to find talented people who have hit bottom, give them one special job, and a new chance in the future."

I kept staring at her, fighting the attraction, trying to not really ignore everything she was saying. Even with my eyes now used to the dim lights of the bar, I just couldn't get a read on her. She looked like an agent, she was sneaky like an agent, and she dressed like an agent. And she tossed money around like an agent. And over the years I had been around enough booking agents to know not to trust them with a mouthful of spit.

"Look," Lex said, scooting over to sit in the chair next to me.

Her wonderful soft smell shocked me. I wanted to lean away and get closer at the same time, so I just stayed centered, holding onto my cold beer like an anchor in a rough sea.

"I'm willing to give you a half million Intersystem Credits for ten concerts over a fourteen-day concert period. I need you to play about twenty or so songs per concert. I don't even much care which songs they are. Covers or your own originals."

"Lady, you are totally nuts," I said, turning back to face my almost empty glass of beer, doing my best to ignore her wonderful smell.

"You promised you'd listen to me," Lex said. "That's all I asked for the guitar."

I moved my right leg and bumped it into my guitar just to make sure it was still there. It was.

"All right," I said, "you're willing to give a washed-out guitar player a half million Intersystems to sing a few songs. What's the catch?"

"The catch is the location of the concert tour," Lex said, glancing at Carl to see if he could hear. He couldn't since he was down the bar cutting up limes for his fruit tray.

"So, I got to go out to the frontier or into the Farms or something like that?"

No way I was going into the Farms. They were the systems occupied by the only aliens humans had run into. The aliens looked like a cross between a black beetle and mass of mud shaped like a deformed cow, which is why humans called their systems the Farms. And from what I hear, they smelled like a sewer. I was fairly certain they had no desire for human country music.

"No, actually, your part of the tour will take just over two weeks each way, all done in a first class luxury cabin. But here in the human systems about ninety years will pass before you come back."

This woman was keeping me entertained, I had to hand her that. I hadn't wanted to laugh this much since I found a hundred credits on the sundeck on the way to the bar three weeks ago.

"I'm a talent agent here in this time period for this section of the Consolidated Planets," Lex said, talking fast and low. "In this time period the Consolidated Planets have not yet been formed, and except for a few high-ranking officials, no one here knows it will even exist in the future. There's a great demand for original old-style Earth music and musicians in the future and this is as far back in time as we talent agents are allowed to go."

I decided to play along with the nut case for a minute. "So how come you just can't beam me into the future and have me back for my next beer?"

"Space and time travel don't work that way I'm afraid," Lex said. "You'll be gone your time about six weeks total, but because of the speeds involved, and a whole bunch of stuff I don't really understand about time travel, about ninety years will pass here. That's why we look for musicians who have nothing to lose and very little family. Of course, it's a help that you are also very talented. Your talent, to be honest with you, is one of the reasons I can offer you as much as I can."

"Thanks, I guess."

"Look," Lex said, leaning forward. "I don't expect you to believe me. I wouldn't believe me if I lived in this time period. But I do want you to think about it. You'll play ten concerts, to audiences as human as I am a very long time into the future. You can stay in the future as long as you would like beyond the tour, maybe never come back."

"Stay?" I asked.

"Sure," Lex said, nodding. "You can stay for a week, or a year. If you stay a year it will be ninety-one years passing here. If you decide to stay in the future and make a career there, your money for this can be transferred forward. But if you do decide to return to here, you won't make it back until at least ninety years into this future."

"And a half million will be worth nothing then, right?"

"Actually, no, with some minor bubbles, money in the systems stays amazingly stable all the way up and into my time period in the Consolidated Planets."

"And I'll be too old to spend it when I get back."

"No," Lex said, shaking her head, "You'll only be six weeks older than the day you leave. Just ninety years will pass here. Again, I don't expect you to believe me, but at least think about it and meet me back here tomorrow."

Before I could say anything, Lex handed me five hundred station credits. "This should help get your rent caught up. Thanks for considering this."

I stared at the money in my hand like it was a snake that might bite me as Lex slid off her stool and headed for the door.

Five hundred station credits was about 50 Interstellar Credits. She was offering me a half million Interstellars. That was a lot of beers.

I watched her walk, wanting more than anything to jump up and follow her and never let her from my sight. But the money in my hand froze me to my stool.

When she opened the door to the sundeck, she was gone into the bright white light.

"Wow, she was a looker. Was she as weird as she seemed?" Carl asked, glancing down the bar at me.

I took another look at the five hundred station credits in my hand, then stuffed them in my pocket. "You have no idea," I said, finishing my beer and motioning Carl for another. "You have no idea at all."

Two

AS IT TURNED out, Lex's offer, my guitar, and the money in my pocket put me right off the idea of drinking the night away. I had one more beer, grabbed a take-home Old Earth style pizza on the way to my room, and then surprised the dump's manager with payment in full for all the back rent.

I was living in such a slum that even after the pizza and rent, I still had enough money left over to last for almost a month if I watched the drinking. Maybe by then

13

I could find a job. A real job, not the crazed thing some good-looking woman had talked to me about. But at least she had bought me some time.

I dropped the pizza on the old scarred coffee table, then brushed some food wrappers aside and dropped onto the couch. I opened up my guitar case like I was standing at the door of a blind date. Inside was my guitar, just as I had left it this morning at the pawnshop.

I held it to my chest for a moment, just letting myself believe that it was actually back in my hands. Then after a few quick adjustments for tuning, I strummed a few chords before putting it back in the case.

How had I let myself get so low?

And why did some woman I didn't know go to the trouble of getting my guitar back for me, not counting the five big she had tossed my way. She couldn't be serious about the job.

There had to be something else going on.

I took a piece of pizza and worked at it, thinking over any possibility of a scam, which was unlikely since I had nothing to take in a scam. After a second piece of pizza, I still hadn't come up with anything that made any sense at all.

I was exactly what I seemed on the surface, a washed-out musician who liked to play in the style of old Earth country. I had nothing to scam. I was worth exactly the amount she had given me and not one credit more.

So, with a quick bite out of a third slice, I went out the door and down to the manager's office to use his com device. I used to know a guy who was one of the brainy types, read a lot, actually had a major education from somewhere. He had done soundboards on a tour I worked

once, and we'd drunk a few nights together. He'd understood this time travel stuff and if it was real or not.

I had to give the manager the fifty station credits I had planned to drink earlier to cover any intersystem charges. I hoped like hell the call was going to be worth that.

"Steve," I said as he came up the com link. He looked about the same, maybe a little shorter hair, and he still hadn't had his lack of chin fixed. "This is Danny Kenyon, from the Country Old-Style Planetary Tour back a few years. Remember me?"

"Uh, yah, sure Danny, how are you?"

I knew he didn't remember me, I could see it in his eyes, but at this point, that didn't matter. At least I didn't owe him money, so he wasn't either cutting the link or asking for his money back just at the mention of my name.

"Sorry to bother you, Steve," I said, "but I got this dumb science question that a few friends and I have been arguing about, and I figured if anyone would know the answer, you might."

"Fire away," Steve said. "I took some science classes back in college." Clearly not talking music or money made him relax a little, even though he didn't remember me.

"Okay, promise not to laugh too hard," I said.

He laughed and said, "Promise."

"Okay, my friend was telling me that time travel is possible and in the future we might actually invent it. Does that sound stupid to you or what?"

"Not at all," Steve said. "Lots of scientists over the years, starting with Einstein back on Old Earth, thought that time travel might be possible. But a lot of factors would have to be solved and we're nowhere near that kind of major breakthrough."

"You're kidding?" I said, shocked. "It might actually be possible in the future?"

"Possible yes," Steve said. "Likely, probably not. Not in our lifetimes anyway."

"Well, damn," I said. "I lost that bet. Thanks, Steve."

"No problem," Steve said, "take care of yourself, Danny."

I shut down the com link and headed back to my room, thinking over what Lex had said. It was possible. How completely crazy was that?

By the time I had finished the pizza and played a few songs, I had decided to go back to Scott's tavern and meet Lex tomorrow. What could it hurt, as long as she didn't ask for her money back?

Three

JUST AS THE day before, it took my eyes a moment to adjust inside the dark bar from all the light in that stupid sun section of the station. I had managed to finally get some sleep and by the time I reached the bar I was slowly getting angry. I might be broke, but I'm not completely stupid, and Lex, for some reason, was trying to get me to buy a huge pile-of-shit story.

I just didn't know why.

As I headed across the dark bar I felt like I needed a beer more than just about anything, especially after the hot sun beating down on me in my walk through that sundeck ring.

I could see through the darkness that Lex was sitting on the stool beside my favorite, sipping on something. Just the fact that she was there again surprised me.

And actually made me happy.

I hated that I was attracted to a nut case. Just hated it.

My former wife had turned into a nut case, swearing there were aliens in every station, on every planet we visited, and that they were watching us every minute. Invisible aliens.

She blamed the aliens for our divorce. She was partially right.

Carl was behind the bar as always, and otherwise the tavern was empty.

"Danny," Carl said, slipping a beer onto a napkin in front of my stool. "Good to see you."

"Give my eyes a minute," I said, "and I might be able to see you back."

Carl and Lex both chuckled at my stupid joke, then Carl moved back down the bar to keep working on the evening preparations.

"Thanks for the loan," I said to Lex after taking a sip of the wonderful, cool beer. Again I'm not sure when I'll be able to pay you back."

Lex held up a beautiful hand. "No need to even think of paying me back. The money was like an option on your time. I wanted you to consider my offer."

"Well," I said, taking another sip of the beer. "I considered it. I even called a friend who confirmed that time travel at some point in the distant future would be possible."

Lex nodded. "It is."

"So how far forward would I be going?"

"A very long ways," Lex said.

"How far?" I asked.

Lex glanced at me, then at Carl to make sure he was far enough away to not hear.

"Fourteen thousand years."

"Not possible," I said, turning back to my beer. "Humans won't be around for that long."

"Oh, they very much are and have a real desire for Old Earth music like you play."

"So why not go back another six hundred years and get real Old Earth musicians?"

"Not allowed to," she said.

"So explain to me how it works," I said. "Since you're asking me to give up my life and climb into something that flies through time, I better know at least some basics about how it works."

Again Lex stared at me for a moment like I was some alien thing. Clearly other dead-end musicians she had offered this to hadn't bothered with any homework.

"I really don't know how it works," she said. "At least not the science of it. Something about folding space." She glanced down the bar to make sure Carl couldn't hear what she was saying.

Damn I just couldn't get the attraction I was feeling toward her out of my head. She had to be doing something to me. I hated agents and she was an agent. I couldn't want to sleep with an agent. That would be like sleeping with some mud-cow alien on the Farms. But I still just wanted to lean forward and kiss her.

Had to be the reaction to the money.

"The Consolidated Planets are a group of about forty thousand systems banded together for safety and trade. The Planets as an organization has been in existence about ten thousand years now."

I was too stunned at the number to say anything since there were only about fifty colonized systems now.

She went on. "Travel between my time and this time is done by only people who have no ties or family because of the time loss issues."

"Okay, that makes my brain hurt," I said. "So you have no family, no husband waiting for you back home?"

"None," she said. "If I did, they would be long dead by the time I returned from one trip. The time lag works both ways I'm afraid."

"Okay," I said, not liking the sound of that either, but deep down happy she didn't have anyone.

Lex went on. "Only two weeks will pass on board the ship, but decades will pass on the planets at either end of the trip, forty-five years on the trip there, forty-five years on the trip back here."

I finished my beer and held up my glass until Carl saw it and nodded.

"I see why you need someone with no ties to here."

Lex nodded and again I resisted the urge to just kiss her. She put her hand on my hand and the soft feel of her skin sent a shock through my system.

"Are you drugging me?" I asked, looking into her blue eyes.

"No," she said, smiling. "Not my style. Just trying to do a job."

"And this attraction I'm feeling to you is part of the job?"

She pulled her hand back and shook her head, looking away. "Never happened before."

I wanted to believe her but I wasn't sure that I did.

Carl slid another beer in front of me. Again Lex bought.

I stared at her, then decided I still needed a few more questions answered. "So, what planet were you born on?"

She smiled. "One named Small Five about two hundred light years from here. It hasn't been discovered or explored yet in this time period."

"So, how many trips have you made to this time period?"

"This is my second."

"Ninety years each?" I asked, staring at her. "How old are you?"

Lex laughed. "Actually, in real time just three years younger than you are. I'm thirty. Time passes normally on either end. I'm still aging just like normal. But if you took my birth date on my home world, I guess you would say I'm a lot older than you."

"We'll just leave it at thirty." I took a big drink out of the beer to try to give myself time to think and also not look at her. The attraction between us seemed to be growing by the minute, at least on my side.

"It's a job," Lex said, clearly feeling she needed to explain even more. "I meet interesting people like you and I do a service. In a few years I'll retire back to my time. There are some beautiful places in the future among the Planets."

"There are beautiful places here in this time, too," I said. "Granted I haven't seen many of them lately, but I know they're here."

"Take this job," Lex said, "live a couple of months like you've never lived before, see planets you can't even imagine exist, play ten concerts and then come back rich, with enough money to see the places you want to see and start your music career over under a new name."

"Ninety years from now."

Lex nodded.

"So why? Why me?"

> *The attraction between us seemed to be growing by the minute, at least on my side.*

Lex actually laughed at that. "Honest question. We want to hear you play concerts. That's all. The Consolidated Planets love any type of Old Earth music, and have gotten very little of the style of music you played before. That's why we're willing to offer someone of your talent so much money. Trust me, we'll make a profit on you."

"You've gotten people to go with you for less?"

"Oh, sure. One burnt-out rocker went out about two years ago with only the promise of a lifetime supply of food and drugs."

"And how did it go for him?" I asked, before it dawned on me Lex would have no way of knowing.

Lex shrugged. "He's still in transit."

"Still in his first day on the ship?"

"More than likely," Lex said. "He won't arrive for another forty-three years this time."

"Oh," I said. I was starting to catch on to how it worked.

"What I told you is the limit of my knowledge about this stuff," Lex said, her voice soft and sincere sounding. "I've been totally honest with you. I just fly in the ships and hope someone somewhere knows what they are doing."

"I know that feeling," I said, smiling at her. "I'm the same damn way with these spaceships that flit from system to system now."

"So you understand?" Lex asked.

"Not a bit of it," I said. "But what the hell difference does that make, right?"

"Right," Lex said. "So what do you say?"

"Give me an hour sitting here alone," I said, "and I'll give you an answer."

Lex nodded and slid off her stool. I really didn't want her to leave, but I had to be outside of her wonderful smell, those driving blue eyes, to think clearly.

A moment later the tavern was lit with bright light as Lex went out onto the sundeck

"The way you two were talking," Carl said, "it seemed important."

I shrugged and finished off my beer so Carl could bring me another. "She's just offering me a gig is all."

"Fantastic," Carl said, his face lighting up like someone had just given him a hundred buck tip. "It's about damn time you got back on the horse."

"Not even sure what a horse looks like anymore," I said.

Carl laughed as he slid another beer in front of me. "Man, I heard you when you opened for Baked Pie in the Princeton System in the Baseline Theater. Trust me, you know the horse."

I stared at Carl, actually looking at him for the first time in the two years I had been coming into this place. "You were at that concert?"

"Sure was," he said. "And I saw you over on Mercer as well, when you opened for Craig S. and the Princes. I even bought a hard disk copy of your first song collection."

"Only collection," I corrected.

"First," he said, smiling at me.

"Man, I didn't even think you knew who I was."

Carl laughed. "I let people in my bar do as they want. But I can tell you I was a huge fan of yours. You were just ahead of your time is all."

"Yeah, ahead of my time playing Old Earth Country," I said, sipping my beer.

It sure seemed that time was an issue a lot lately.

"No man, honest," Carl said. "Things have changed, your original songs would take off now."

"I sure hope you are right my friend."

"Oh, I am," Carl said, smiling. "Take the gig, get back on tour. I'll miss your business, but I can buy the next collection and play it in here on busy nights."

It had always seemed that my songs, the only songs I really wanted to play, were just a little too "edgy" for most Old Earth Country fans a few years back.

"Man, this is exciting that you're getting back to playing," Carl said. "Just tell me when and where your first concert is, and I'll be there, right in the damn front row. I know a bunch of fans who will do the same."

"Well, right now everything's a little up in the air," I said.

Carl smiled real big. "Just let me know."

With that he turned and walked down the bar, going back to his prep work for the nightly crowd, leaving me to my thoughts.

I couldn't believe how much things had changed for me in simply a day. I had an offer for a short tour that I didn't really believe, yet part of me accepted.

And I had been reminded I still had fans, few as they may be, but they were still out there, and they remembered my work.

I glanced down the bar at Carl. I doubted he had any idea how important his comments were to me. Hell, any fan's comments to any artist, in any field were important. When the money runs out, the recording contracts are cancelled, all musicians have are fans to keep them going. Fans. They are everything.

I sipped my beer and sat there, remembering the concerts, the feel of making people happy with my music, the disappointments and setbacks on the business side, and finally all the loneliness, hitting bottom yesterday when I hocked my guitar for money.

Lex had been right. I had nothing to lose by taking her offer.

I glanced down the bar. Nothing to lose except fans like Carl, who still remembered.

Carl's dream had been owning a bar. He'd told me that right after he bought the place. He was scared to death, and at the same time as happy as a little kid at Christmas. It couldn't be easy running a bar off a sundeck on an old space station orbiting a star with a name no one could pronounce, but he was doing it, making it one day at a time.

I shook my head. Man, that was admirable. Maybe Lex was right, maybe I had given up and dove into the bottle a little too soon.

And now I was getting a second chance. Granted, no one like Carl would be around to remember me in ninety years, but it was still a second chance.

Maybe my songs would be dated by then, I would be dated. Wouldn't that be ironic, a musician who was ahead of his time coming back dated?

Again that time thing.

I glanced down the bar at Carl. I hated to lose my fans, even the few who still remained. I hated the idea of coming back and starting over and being dated then. For me it would only be a few months, but I wouldn't recognize most of anything.

There had to be a way to get everything. I was always accused of wanting everything, and I guess this time was no different.

I started to take another drink from my beer, then looked at it and set it back down on the bar napkin. I pushed it to the inside edge of the bar, away from me and said, "Hey, Carl, could you bring me a diet soda of some kind?"

Carl looked up, the smile on his face huge. "Coming right up."

Four

THIRTY MINUTES LATER, when Lex came back through the door and stood for a moment letting her wonderful blue eyes adjust, I had my plan pretty much worked out. It was going to cost me a pretty penny to pull off, but if it worked, I just might get the best of both worlds, Lex's and mine.

And if I got lucky, maybe Lex as well. As I said, I wanted everything.

Lex slid onto the stool beside me and Carl brought her a diet drink as well. I sipped mine, some sort of drink that tasted like lime only sweet.

After Carl moved down the bar, Lex pointed to my drink and smiled, looking into my eyes. "I see you've made a decision."

"I have," I said. "But hear me all the way out like you asked me to do for you. Okay?"

"Okay," Lex said, a puzzled look on her face.

"Your entire problem with finding people here on Earth to play out in the Consolidated Planets is time. Right?"

Lex nodded.

"And Carl said that my songs had been ahead of their time," I said.

"I think he was more than likely right," Lex said. "I listened to your first collection. It's amazingly good."

"So here's what I want to do," I said, plowing on and ignoring her wonderful compliment. "I want to take you up on your offer, but I want to postpone when I leave."

Lex really looked puzzled, but she didn't say anything, letting me go on.

"I want to try to make a comeback right here, right now, first, before I leave. And I want you to be my manager and backer with the money you'll pay me to leave to the future."

With that Lex sort of rocked back and got a distant look for a moment.

So I just went right on talking. "In exchange for you helping me get going again, right now, doing a little bankrolling, I'll help you recruit some top talent for your Planets tours. And if I don't make a comeback here, I'll take less than what you offered me now in a couple of years."

"And if you do make it big?" Lex asked.

"We both get rich and we'll just fake my death when I get as far as I can here, and then head out to the Planets together to make some real money. But the key is time."

"A win-win situation for you," Lex said, staring at me, a slight smile creeping into the edge of her perfect lips.

"For both of us," I said. "Think about it. You get me cheaper if I don't make it, we both make money if I do, and I get not one, but two chances to make a comeback. Now and in ninety years. All that is lost is a little time on this end."

Lex laughed and nodded. "You know, that sort of makes sense."

I looked her directly in the eyes and reached out and took her soft hand. "Eventually, my songs won't be ahead of their time."

"Timing is everything," Lex said, nodding, squeezing my hand softly in hers. "You've got yourself a manager and a bankroll."

While keeping one hand in hers, I held up my glass with my other hand and offered a toast.

Lex picked her glass up, smiling at me.

"To time," I said, "the real solution to everything."

"To time," she agreed, tapping her glass against mine.

Then she put her glass down and with her free hand pulled me close and kissed me.

And for me, right at that moment, time just stopped. And I had no desire to restart it.

—

Some Classic Poker Boy Stories

Available at your favorite booksellers.

Poems by DEAN WESLEY SMITH

Memory

She wrote me a letter
this last Christmas, expecting
me to remember who she was,
what color hair she had,
how wide her smile had been.

Ten years ago, give or take a year,
I gave birth to a story called
"Ghosts of Christmas Future,"
a damned original title
now that I look back at it.

The story found a home in a book
titled "Christmas Ghosts."
I made fifty-five bucks I don't remember spending,
the amount recorded in a book of notes
I don't remember keeping.

I have no memory of writing the story,
not one stinking word of it,
yet with one short letter she expects me to remember her
because we slept together for a few months
twenty years before I wrote the story.

Little did I know during those possibly good,
Possibly bad, nights of sex thirty years ago,
that she would become a ghost of my Christmas future,
walking hand-in-hand with that story I wrote
as I desperately ask myself "What the hell was I thinking?"

USA *Today* Bestselling Writer

DEAN WESLEY SMITH

Space and Time
and Cowboys
Seldom Mix Well

THE TRAGIC TALE OF A MAN IN A DUSTER

Lost in deep space, Reeves knew rescue would never happen. But around him the Western, a supply ship full of a lifetime of living, could keep him alive.

Fresh fish from the hatchery, fresh meat from the stored animals, fresh fruit and vegtables from the botanical gardans. Completely alone, no boss, no one to tell him what to do. What more could a cowboy from Idaho want?

First published in stand-alone paper and electronic book form with a very different cover.

THE TRAGIC TALE OF A MAN IN A DUSTER

One

REEVES KNEW HE shouldn't be frying fish over an open campfire in the ship's botanical garden, but the smell alone was going to make up for all the problems he might face if anyone ever found him. The fire crackled in a rock ring in front of him, the flames casting strange shadows on the trees and brush ringing his little meadow. He didn't care about the extra oxygen consumption and the fire repellant system being shut off. All he cared about was the two fish in the skillet, and how wonderful they were going to taste.

Reeves still had on his deep-sleep jumpsuit. It didn't feel right wearing it out here, while cooking trout, but it hadn't occurred to him to change clothes since he woke up. That would be next, right after dinner. Besides, there wasn't much reason to stay in uniform when there was no one to dress up for.

He kneeled and picked up the skillet, studying the fish for any sign of them being overcooked, then quickly replaced the skillet on the fire before the hot handle burned his hand. His dad back on Earth had showed him how to do this when he was a kid, and he had watched it done a dozen times since. His dad always used to say that fish were never meant to be baked or broiled or steamed. Only fried.

Reeves had to agree. Cooking fresh trout in the ovens they had on this piece of floating space junk would be a crime. No sir, fish were born to be covered in corn meal crumbs and fried quick and hot in a half inch of margarine in a heavy metal skillet while the flames licked the sides of the blackened pan.

And right now the two Rainbow Trout he'd caught out of Danny's stream over in the hatcheries section of the ship were being cooked in exactly that way.

The rich, wonderful smell was almost more than he could take. It covered the faint odor of the pines around him, filling the small meadow with a mouth-watering aroma. He just wished that when the builders had designed the botanical garden they would have made it possible to open some sort of portal so he could sit beside a fire under the stars. He glanced up hoping to see stars, but the roof was black, the light low, simulating night. Maybe at some point in the future he'd go up there and paint some fake stars on that ceiling just to make the feeling right.

He glanced around at the darkened meadow and the trees and brush beyond. He had to do this cooking at night. No other time would be right for cooking fresh-caught trout over an open fire.

The smoke from the fire was swirling upward around the skillet and then on toward the ceiling, lost in the darkness.

He had no doubt the garden was going to smell of smoke for months to come, but he didn't care. Hell, if this worked, and these two fish tasted anywhere near as good as they smelled, he might even fry a couple more fish tomorrow night.

And a couple more the night after that.

Maybe he might even fix up a tent and bedding to sleep nearby. What could it hurt? There was no one to stop him out here in the deep space between stars and jump stations. There was no fixing the ship. He had determined that an hour ago. And if he did happen to get lucky and live long enough to finally reach Jump Base Perry, he'd deal with the consequences then. But in the meantime, he was going to eat freshly-cooked trout.

Two

"BLAME IT ALL to damn!" Canny said, her fingers running over the smooth surface of the tracking board, bringing up images on her screen faster than Fergason could follow.

Canny was in charge of tracking what they called the "pink sector," officially call the "P" sector, following ships and anything else that might be jumping through hyper space in that area. Fergason had never heard her swear in the three years he had worked with the tiny and very competent woman.

Canny was from a colony world around Devan Six, and claimed she was five foot tall. She had typical Devan red hair and light, fair skin. She also had a laugh that sounded like a chime and made him smile.

Today Canny wore a white blouse, dark black pants made out of some new material, and flat-heeled shoes meant for comfort.

Fergason was Canny's immediate supervisor and her exact opposite in just about every way. Where she was short, he was tall, slouching at six-five. Where her skin seemed to glow white in the lights from the screens, his skin was dark, his hair pitch black and short. And he came from Stevens, a planet that had been waging an economic war with Canny's home planet for decades. Yet somehow, over the years, even with the differences, they had become close friends.

And were getting closer every day.

Around them the large General Hyper Drive control room felt hushed as a few of the other controllers glanced at Canny's direction with a look of surprise.

Fergason stood from his supervisor console and moved over beside Canny, glancing at her screen. "Transfer to the wall screen," he said.

She nodded as her fingers moved over her board almost faster than Fergason could follow. He knew she was one of his best, but he had never seen her work at full speed before.

Suddenly she stopped, sat back, and just shook her head.

"Dropped out," she said. "Twenty-six hours ago real time."

Fergason stared at the wall monitor filling a section near Canny's station. It showed three-dimensional representation of the "P" area of space Canny had been monitoring. She had put up a line starting at Jump Base Peanut and ending about halfway to Jump Base Perry.

"What's the ship?" Fergason asked, stunned that he was seeing what she was indicating. He had never had a drop-out on his watch, and the last serious drop-out that had occurred was two years before. Ships, with all the fail-safes, and the nature of the hyper-space tubes between jump points, just didn't drop out of hyperspace in the middle of nowhere.

Yet one just had.

"It's a supply and research ship, a big one called the *Western*. Headed for the lower edge of the "D" section to help supply a new colony there."

Fergason nodded. Nothing unusual at all.

"Seventeen jumps successful, Canny said, "thirty-six more to go."

"So any signal from the ship?" Fergason asked, following procedure.

"Nothing," Canny said. "One minute it was fine, the next it had dropped out of hyper."

"Can you pinpoint its location?" Fergason asked, still following the questions he was supposed to ask a controller in this situation.

"I did," Canny said. She reached forward and tapped her board, changing the image on the screen on the wall.

Fergason just shook his head. The area shown on the map where the ship would have dropped back into normal space was a sphere of over three light years in diameter.

There was one more question on the list that he had to ask any controller in this situation, just for the record. "Could you get a reading on the real-space speed of the ship as it dropped?"

"Fast," Canny said. "Ninety-one-point-three percent of the speed of light."

"Damn," Fergason said.

"You can say that again," Canny said, shaking her head. "The poor guy. He probably isn't even awake yet, with the difference in time factored in."

"Only one crew?" Fergason asked. Usually freighters had two or three. The *Western* must be one of the newer model ships, only needing one man to take the chance on the deep sleep and the hyper jumps with the cargo. And all that one man did was wake up at each jump point, run diagnostics of the systems, then give the all-clear for the ship to make the next jump.

She leaned forward, tapped a key on her board again, and then sat back. "His name is Reeves, from Earth actually."

"What part?" Fergason asked, as if that was going to make any difference at this point.

Canny again glanced at her board. "Idaho region."

One of the old United States areas. Fergason had never been near it on any of his visits to Earth. Maybe next time.

"Alert rescue," Fergason said, glancing at the other controllers who were watching the event. "Tell them to get a ship headed to the center of his possible drop-out area. Make sure you feed them all your data, including his likely speed."

Canny glanced back at him, her green eyes showing surprise and maybe a little something else. "Sir, you know they will veto you. It's not worth risking the lives of a rescue team and ship in an unscheduled hyper-drop."

Fergason knew, but he said nothing.

Canny went on. "Plus the percentage chances of finding one ship in that much area are close to zero, even if the thing was equipped with a newer emergency beacon. The rescue ship would have to stumble within light-days of the *Western* to trace-hear it."

"I know," Fergason said. "But I'm not going to be the one to make the decision to let that poor man die out there alone."

She looked at him harder than she had ever done before. There was a caring and understanding in the look that he hadn't seen before. Finally she nodded and turned back to her board. "Alerting rescue," she said.

Later that night, she asked him to join her for dinner. It had been fantastic, a special baked-trout dinner with all the trimmings. That night she told him how much she admired him and his heart.

And later that night they kissed and kissed and finally talked about being together for the rest of their lives.

The next morning he learned, as they had both expected, that Rescue Control had declined to send a ship.

Reeves from Earth was on his own.

Three

REEVES KNEW, WITHOUT a doubt, that he would grow tired of fresh-caught, freshly-cooked trout, no matter how good they tasted.

He had set up camp with bedding, a tent, and a change of clothes in an area of the botanical garden near where he had cooked the fish the first time. After dinner that first night he had changed into some western-style clothes he had found in supplies for the colonists. Then with the addition of a cowboy hat, cowboy boots, and a duster he felt almost at home. He could almost imagine he was back in the mountains of Idaho, especially when he was near his fire.

He had reset the lighting in the garden so that there was more night, because that was the time he didn't have to think about where he was, and what had happened to him.

After finding the clothes he had gone to a mirror in one of the bathrooms. The hat hid his white forehead and receding hairline, and the duster swung loose and free, giving his body a lean and mean appearance. He had been lucky that the colony this ship had been packed to supply was for a western-based group. He hoped they survived the loss of these supplies long enough to get more.

Too bad there hadn't been something he could have done about saving the ship. He had been in cold sleep, as anyone was going through jump space, when the ship had malfunctioned and dropped out of hyper-space. His last readings before the jump had shown no indication of any problem at all.

The moment he had woken up to the sounds of the alarms filling every inch of the cold sleep chamber, he knew he was in trouble.

Deep trouble.

It had taken him a long time to check all the ship's systems and discover everything was just fine, except for the fact that he, the ship, and all its cargo were no longer in hyper-space. He had no idea what had gone wrong, and didn't have the skills or the desire to find out.

He had set the rescue beacon just in case someone came for him, and actually found him, and then he had sat for hours just staring out of the control room's viewports at the stars and the blackness of space. He had no idea where he was, or even exactly how fast he was moving, or where he was heading.

Hyper-space travel used jump stations, connected to other jump stations. Only close-in system travel used actual real-space movement. It just took too long and had too many troubles with the differences in ship-board time and real time.

While he sat there staring at the stars and feeling sorry for himself, he started thinking about never seeing Earth again, and just generally considering his future death alone in deep space. Then, as if hit by a sudden blast of realization, he really understood his situation. He might die alone out here, but until he did he was now a really free man.

No more worrying about money, or jobs. The ship had more than enough supplies to last him for a very long life.

He no longer had anyone to answer to, to be chewed out by.

He was on his own, in a seven-mile-long space ship full of everything he might need.

With the realization he had laughed out loud, staring at the stars. The entire thing was sort of a glass half-empty, glass half-full sort of thing. Yes, he was trapped in deep space with almost no hope of rescue, yes he had known this possibility might happen, but now that it had happened, he could live any way he wanted.

He could cook fish over an open campfire.

He was a free man who loved fresh-caught fish.

Finally, on the third day of staying in the meadow near his campfire, it became clear he was going to need other fresh foods beside fish. So after finishing a wonderful breakfast of trout, he made a trip through the seven mile-long ship to the embryo stores near the nose of the giant ship.

He felt odd walking in his cowboy boots down the wide halls, his duster swirling around his legs with every step. And his duster was a little warm for the environmental settings, but he didn't care. He was living on a new frontier, just like his ancient ancestors had done when they had gone west in the old United States. There were hardships on the frontier, the least of which was heat and cold.

They had been alone, in a wild and dangerous place.

He was alone in a wild and dangerous place.

They had survived in their way, he would survive in his.

It had taken him hours to finally reach the right area, not wanting to use the ship's directional systems to help him. His ancestors didn't have directional systems to help them out west.

After only a few wrong turns, he found the storage area he was looking for. It was where the animals that were scheduled to be born and raised on the new colony were kept. He pulled up on a screen the animal cargo list and smiled when he saw it was as he had hoped it would be. Cattle, horses, sheep, pigs, chickens, and so on. And there was enough feed on the ship as well to keep the animals well-fed for many years.

And another thing that worked in his favor. The ship was carrying an Accelerated Growth Lab that could take an animal from embryo state to full grown in three or four days.

He studied the list of his choices. He didn't want to raise too many animals too quickly, mostly because he only needed as much as he could use over a few months time, and he wanted to make their feed last as long as possible. So he did some calculations as to exactly how long the feed would last for a certain number of each animal, then went to work taking out a few of the animals and putting them in the Accelerated Growth Lab chamber.

Then, as almost an afterthought, he picked out a horse and put it in the cham-

ber as well. His ancestors rode horses, so could he.

He spent three days there in the lab, eating rations while wishing for trout, sleeping in a bunk room, growing the animals to a decent size. He used that time to set up sections of the ship for each group of animals to live.

The chickens he put in a large storage area with old-world furniture they could nest in, then set the timer on the ship's computer to remind him every three days that he needed to replenish the chicken's food and supplies, and with luck harvest the eggs.

His mouth watered at the idea of eggs and bacon, cooked over a camp fire. What a perfect life he was setting up.

He worked out similar environments for the cattle and pigs, then prepped a slaughter area and then used it to kill a calf, using a colony butchering-machine to package and refrigerate the meat all in one process.

Tonight, back in his meadow, over his campfire, he would cook veal. And then tomorrow he would start changing a few of the areas in the gardens for fruit and vegetable growing. Maybe in a few weeks he might have corn-on-the-cob with a great New York steak. His mouth watered at the thought as well.

Finally, after everything was set up, and his saddle bags were packed with the veal and oat feed for the horse, he led the big, brown mare he had raised into the hallway and back down the miles of corridor to the botanical gardens.

On this trip he felt better walking the halls in his duster, the horse's hooves clopping on the hard surface behind him. He now felt like a true pioneer going into the unknown.

Four

FERGASON SAT AT his desk in his living room and stared at a picture of Canny, his wife of over sixty years. He missed her more than he wanted to admit. Their children and grandchildren were good company, visiting him often, but nothing could replace the closeness that he had had with Canny.

They had had a great life together, happy, and had recently been planning trips back to their different home worlds to visit family. Then, without warning, a few months before she had died of a heart attack at the young age of only 104. He had another thirty or forty years of life expectancy these days, yet he couldn't imagine living those years without her. It was as if everything inside him had been ripped out.

"Grandpa?" a voice said from behind him.

The voice was from his youngest grandson, Steph, standing respectfully in the door to the study. Steph was going on thirty, and was already making a name for himself in Space Rescue Corp.

Fergason took a deep breath and slowly swung around, looking up into the green eyes and pale skin of his grandson. The kid was about the same age as Canny had been when they had started working together. Steph had her eyes and her good looks and fair skin.

"You all right, Grandpa?"

Fergason shrugged. "I guess as good as can be expected."

There was no other answer to that question. Of course he wasn't all right. He had lost the love and meaning in his life.

"Thought you might be interested in this," Steph said, stepping forward and handing a report from Rescue Central to him. "It came into control today after one of the test runs of a new search system."

Fergason glanced at the paper, not really seeing it. Then suddenly a name caught his attention.

Western.

He quickly scanned the sheet, stunned at what he was reading. They had finally found the cargo ship *Western*, over sixty years after it had dropped out of hyper-drive and vanished.

He glanced up at Steph who was smiling. "This is the ship that was lost on your grandmother's watch. I was supervisor that day."

"I know," Steph said, smiling. "You and grandma decided to get married that night, didn't you?"

Fergason nodded as he stared at the report. He couldn't believe the *Western* had been found. He hadn't thought of that ship for decades.

"There was a man on that ship," Fergason asked, trying to find the information on the report that he was looking for, but failing. "What happened to him?"

Steph snorted. "His name was Reeves. Shipboard time only had two weeks passing. But the guy didn't manage to survive that long."

Fergason shuddered. He couldn't imagine the loneliness the man named Reeves must have thought he was facing. Deep space did that to people, sent them over the edge and into insanity, often far quicker than two weeks.

Fergason knew he was facing the same type of loneliness without Canny.

"What did he do, kill himself?"

"No," Steph said, shaking his head. "He broke his neck."

Fergason glanced up at his grandson. "How?"

"From what the investigators could tell," Steph said, "he fell off a horse."

"A horse?"

"A horse," Steph said. "And he had grown cattle, pigs, chickens and who knows what else in an old Accelerated Growth Chamber. He even had a campfire going in a botanical garden. He had reverted to being a cowboy from the old west region of Earth."

Fergason shook his head as his grandson went on, not really understanding how a spaceman could become a cowboy on a hyper-drive jump freighter in less than two weeks.

"You ought to see a picture of the guy. He put on the cowboy hat, duster and all."

"You're kidding?" Fergason asked, knowing his grandson wouldn't joke about something like that."

"Nope," Steph said, "it's the truth. And what's even more amazing is that he'd only been dead for less than an hour when they found the ship. There was even burnt fish still cooking over a campfire."

"Fish?" Fergason asked, remembering the wonderful fish dinner he and Canny had had the night the *Western* vanished sixty-three years before. The dinner that had changed their lives.

"Fish," Steph said. "Burnt fish. I doubt they're ever going to get the smell out of there."

"Fish," Fergason repeated softly to himself, shaking his head and remembering the dinner that night all those years ago.

The dinner over which he and Canny had decided to spend a lifetime together.

He glanced up at his grandson. "He fell off a horse?"

His grandson smiled. "Broke his neck while cooking a fish dinner over an open campfire."

For the first time since Canny had died, Fergason laughed, knowing without a doubt that Canny would have laughed with him.

Now Available
from all your favorite booksellers in trade paper and electronic editions.

USA *Today* Bestselling Writer

DEAN WESLEY SMITH

THE LIFE AND TIMES OF BUFFALO JIMMY

Chapters 25-27

What Came Before…

Nineteen-year-old Boston native Jimmy Gray had been traveling with his parents and older brother, Luke, headed west to find a new home and new riches. Before even reaching Independence, they were attacked and robbed by Jake Benson and his gang. Jimmy's parents were killed, his brother wounded.

In one of the wildest towns in all of American history, Jimmy Gray, a sheltered, educated son of a banker from Boston suddenly finds himself very, very much alone. But then through some luck, he finds other young men about his age and down on their luck who might be able to help him. Together, the five of them head west after Benson.

They end up hunting buffalo as he always dreamed of doing, but then they are hit with a massive flash flood and Jimmy is left alone, his friends more than likely dead. Luckily, they all meet up again and are all safe. So they continue west, knowing that Benson is just ahead of them.

Suddenly they come upon Benson and his men killing a farm family. They manage to get one of the men separated from the others, but in a fall he accidently dies. So they scatter to meet up later at a camp. They managed that but found a survivor of the killings. So one of them had to go back with the kid while the others followed Benson.

They caught him once again terrorizing a small wagon train and managed to scare him and his men off. But then they had to cross the forty-mile desert. And right from the start, things started off deadly.

THE LIFE AND TIMES OF BUFFALO JIMMY

Part Twenty-Five
INTO THE DESERT

FOR THE NEXT two hours, as the sun started to color the sky in reds and browns, they rode in silence, moving at a fast pace across the flat sand while it was still cool. Then, just before the sun came up, Jimmy had them stop and rest and water the horses.

"From here," Long said, "we go slowly."

Long and Truitt and Samuel took care of the horses while Jimmy and Zach checked to make sure all the water was secured, protected from direct sun, and not leaking. With the day they had ahead of them, they were going to need every drop.

C.J. figured they had gone at least twenty-five of the over fifty-five miles to the Truckee River.

The easy half was all Jimmy could think.

The next thirty miles, the sun would bake them as dry as an overcooked biscuit, as Truitt would say.

As the sun crested the distant ridge, they started out again, the horses wading slowly in the soft sand.

The farther they got into the desert, the more bones and remains of wagons they found. Some of the remains had been there for years, others were fairly new. Jimmy had no doubt that by the time the summer was finished, and all the wagon companies behind them had crossed this, there would be many, many more broken dreams littering this nightmarish place.

It seemed that Mark Twain's description of this desert was very accurate.

At one point, C.J. pointed out a pile of bones ten feet off to one side of the trail. It took Jimmy a moment to realize what he was looking at in the hot sun.

Human bones.

Maybe three people, their bones piled like fire wood, their skulls gaping at the sand around them.

And from that point on, they saw more and more human bones. Out here, the people who were still alive didn't dare stop and bury anyone. They just left them beside the trail and pushed on.

They had no choice.

They now stopped every hour to rest and feed and water the horses. Jimmy drank what he thought he should to make the water last, but it never felt like enough.

With the sun moving higher in the sky, the temperatures climbed, making

him feel like he was standing far too close to a raging fire.

The glare off the sand was blinding, and waves of heat just radiated up like the sand itself was on fire.

To Jimmy, the short stops seemed almost worse than moving forward, but he knew they had to do them, to pace this journey.

At one point, about an hour after dawn, they came across a bubbling hot springs, the water so hot that steam filled the air around it even in the dry heat. There was no reason for even trying to cool and drink the water, since it smelled like sulfur.

Josh said that someone reported that there used to be a sign here that said, "If you can't go forward, you won't survive going back."

"The sign is a myth," C.J. said. "But more than likely the meaning is very true."

Truitt said something about now knowing where the devil lived as they went past the bubbling, hot sulfur water.

Chapter Twenty-six
ONE DOWN

JIMMY WATCHED TRUITT sway for a moment side-to-side in his saddle like he was on a boat in high waves, then tumble off his horse and land with a thud in the hot, desert sand.

"Truitt's down!" Jimmy shouted to the others ahead of him, panic filling his gut like a bad meal. He jumped off his horse and scrambled in the deep sand to where his friend lay. He felt like he was running through deep water, the sand was so soft. It fought him every step.

He knelt beside Truitt, the hot sand burning through his pants. Carefully, he turned his friend over and brushed the sand away from his mouth and eyes, moving Truitt's brown hair off his forehead at the same time. Truitt's skin was red and he was breathing shallowly.

"Truitt? Can you hear me?"

Truitt moaned, but didn't open his eyes.

They couldn't lose Truitt. Not now. Not here.

Long ran up with the rest and knelt in the sand. He quickly unscrewed a canteen and poured a little water on Truitt's forehead. The sand and dirt turned to a thin mud and dried in streamers down his cheeks almost instantly in the intense heat.

Long glanced over at Jimmy. "Open his mouth."

Jimmy pried open Truitt's mouth with his fingers and Long poured the water in slowly. Truitt choked for a moment, coughed, then drank.

After a moment which seemed like an eternity, it was as if Long had given him a magic medicine. Truitt blinked, opened his eyes, looked at the five men hovering over him, and then asked in a soft whisper, "What happened?"

Long gave him another drink of water, then stood. "Heat."

He pulled out a piece of buffalo jerky from his belt pouch and handed it to Truitt. "Chew on this and drink."

Truitt made a face, but did as Long said. None of them liked how salty Long's jerky was, but they all trusted Long when it came to anything having to do with survival out in the west. And right now, here in the middle of The Forty Mile Desert, the most dangerous stretch of the California Trail, they really needed his special skills to stay alive.

"Everyone, water and jerky," Long said, taking a drink himself and then taking out a piece of buffalo jerky. Long had spent nights smoking the jerky back after leaving Fort Hall, and Truitt had complained that Long had used a lot of their salt provisions for the process.

All Long had said was, "We will need it salty." He hadn't explained, and no one had asked. It was now, in the heat, that for some reason, Long wanted them all eating the salty jerky.

After they got out of this, if they got out of this, Jimmy would ask him why.

Jimmy moved away from Truitt and stood beside the horses, letting his wide-brimmed hat protect his face from the glaring sun. He then did as the others, working on the jerky and washing it down with water. They had carried into the Forty Mile Desert as much water as they could, but they were going through it alarmingly fast.

Long and Zach gave water to the horses. Joshua and C.J. sat in the shade their horses offered, drinking and chewing on the buffalo jerky.

Truitt had managed to move over beside C.J. in the slight shade of one horse and was looking better by the minute.

Jimmy turned and looked back the way they had come. The drifting sand made it impossible to see anything but the distant low hills. In the other direction, ahead, through the haze of the hot summer day, were the mountains of the Sierras. They looked to be both invitingly close, and impossibly distant.

And somewhere, just ahead of them, Jake Benson and his two remaining men were moving with a wagon company. Benson had killed Jimmy' parents, shot his brother, and then had killed another family back on Goose Creek, on the east side of Nevada.

At night, Jimmy was still haunted by the man they had accidentally killed at that homestead, but during the day, Jimmy just didn't let himself think about it. That man had been one of the men who had killed Jimmy's parents, and the family on the homestead, and who knew how many others. Yet Jimmy still hated the fact that the man had died. That wasn't what they had planned.

And the accident had given him many, many nightmares over the past weeks. He had no doubt, it was going to haunt him for a lot longer.

He pushed the thought away. Right now, Benson and his men were ahead of them, in the desert, pretending to help a small company of wagons. More than likely, Benson was going to rob and kill the fine people in the wagons somewhere in the middle of this horrible desert, but there was nothing Jimmy or any of the others could do about it. They had even tried to warn the people, but had been ignored.

"Keep eating and drinking," Long said. "We'll rest the horses for another ten minutes."

Jimmy nodded. Even though Jimmy was mostly in charge of the group, when it came to the horses, Long was in charge. He knew how to keep them alive and moving west, and that was all that mattered.

Jimmy looked at the distant mountains and wondered if he would ever see them. They had a long way left to go to get across this desert, and their water supply was going down fast. Without water, what happened to Truitt would happen to them all in the intense heat.

Very quickly.

Chapter Twenty-seven
MORE TROUBLE AHEAD

AFTER THEY RESTED and had eaten the jerky and drank enough water, Long said to Jimmy. "We need to walk from here. The horses can't carry us much farther in this deep sand and in this heat."

Jimmy agreed.

Long had warned them all this would happen. It was part of their plan So, on foot, they started out again, leading their horses.

Each step felt to Jimmy like he was sinking in quicksand, as the desert wanted to not let his boot go. He tried to stay in the wagon tracks, but often missed and stumbled, using the reins of his horse to keep himself from falling face down.

Every step drained more and more energy.

Every mile was a torture.

It wasn't even the hottest time of the day yet, yet the air felt like he was inside a hot oven.

An hour later, as they crested a slight rise in the desert floor about three hours after dawn, they could see the seven wagons that Benson had been "helping" across the desert.

They were stopped dead in the trail and there were no signs of people or the oxen and horses that had been pulling them.

Jimmy wanted to stop short, let Long scout ahead and see what was happening, but both C.J. and Josh said, "We can't stop. We have to go past them."

Jimmy glanced at Long, who clearly agreed with C.J. and Josh.

If they stopped, they died.

If Benson was still with those wagons, they were going to have to take the chance and walk right past him.

Jimmy didn't like that idea at all.

In fact, that idea scared him almost as much as this desert did.

"We ride the next mile until we're past those wagons," Jimmy said.

Long agreed and had everyone give their horse a drink.

Back in the saddle, even moving slowly, it didn't seem to take them long to cross the next mile of desert.

Jimmy now wasn't focused on the sun, but on what was ahead. He hardly took his eye off those wagons.

There was no sign at all of life.

Nothing was moving, not even the canvas tops of the wagons, since there was no wind at all in this forsaken place.

The closer they got, the more likely it was looking that Benson and his men had robbed the poor wagon company, killed everyone and left.

Twice so far, in the thick sand, the trail had gone around what had been a stopped wagon company some years before. Those wagons had been weather-beaten and the white bones of stock and people littered everywhere. Now this wagon company had stopped right in the middle of the trail as well, and it didn't look as if those wagons were ever going another foot forward.

There were no oxen or horses left with the wagons to pull them.

As they got close enough to see details, it became clear that what they were seeing was a massacre.

Benson and his men had struck again.

All the men and boys were scattered around the wagons, some laying face down in the sand, others face up. They were clearly all dead. A couple of them had guns in their hands, including the man Jimmy and Long had talked to.

It seemed he had been wrong. He had let Benson get the drop on him.

Jimmy had no idea why they hadn't heard the shooting. Maybe sound didn't carry well over the sand.

"No women," Zach said as they got closer.

Jimmy was surprised he hadn't noticed that. There weren't any women's or children's bodies in sight at all. Maybe Benson and his men had taken them.

Then Long pointed to one man's body and Jimmy recognized him as one of Benson's men. It was the one with the broken arm. It looked like he had just passed out and died right where he lay. Or maybe one of the wagon men had shot him.

Long led them in a wide circle around the wagons, starting what would become the new trail through the sand.

It wasn't until they passed the last wagon in line that Truitt shouted, "The women!"

At first, Jimmy didn't see them. Then, as Truitt turned and rode toward the wagons, Jimmy finally saw movement. It was a child moving his arm.

The women and children were laying in the sand in the shade under the lead wagons. None of them seemed to have been shot, but the heat of the first three hours of the day without water had done its worst on them.

All them moved closer, leading their horses to what little shade the wagons gave them, then dismounted.

Jimmy found one woman who looked to be about his mother's age. She was barely able to talk and he gave her a small sip of water. Her chapped lips struggled with the drink, but after a moment, some life returned to her eyes.

37

"Give everyone else some water," Jimmy said to the others, "see who is alive, who isn't."

"Don't give them too much water at first," Long said. "In their conditions, it will make them sick."

The boys spread out to the women and children laying under the wagons, waking them, giving them water.

"Jake Benson?" Jimmy asked the woman. "Did he do this?"

She nodded. "He and his men turned on us in the middle of the night. They said we were slowing them down. They robbed us, shot the men, then took all the water, stock, and money. They left us here to die."

Jimmy felt sick to his stomach. Benson was the most cold-hearted creature that had ever pretended to be human. How could anyone do this simply for money?

Jimmy gave the woman another small sip, then stood and went to talk to Zach and C.J.

"We have to get these women and children to the Truckee," Jimmy said.

"I can't see how we can," C.J. said.

"But we can't leave them," Zach said, echoing exactly what Jimmy was thinking.

"I know that," C. J. said. "But taking them may mean that none of us make it. We're still a long ways from that river."

Jimmy nodded. The sun was pounding on them. It felt like he had gotten far, far too close to a fire and there was no place to get away to.

"How far?" Jimmy asked.

C.J. shrugged. "From my guess, we are still a good fifteen, maybe twenty miles away from the river, through thick sand."

"And Long is going to want us to walk to save the horses," Zach said.

Jimmy didn't like the sound of that. "Find out how many women and children there are. And have Long check how much water we all have. Then we'll all talk. We're all risking our lives with this, we all need to be a part of this decision."

The rules of the west were that each person took care of themselves, but Jimmy had no doubt that he couldn't let these woman and children just die here. He was going to help them somehow, save them from what Benson had done.

He just hoped it didn't cost them all their lives.

Continued next month...

Now Available
from all your favorite booksellers in trade paper and electronic editions.

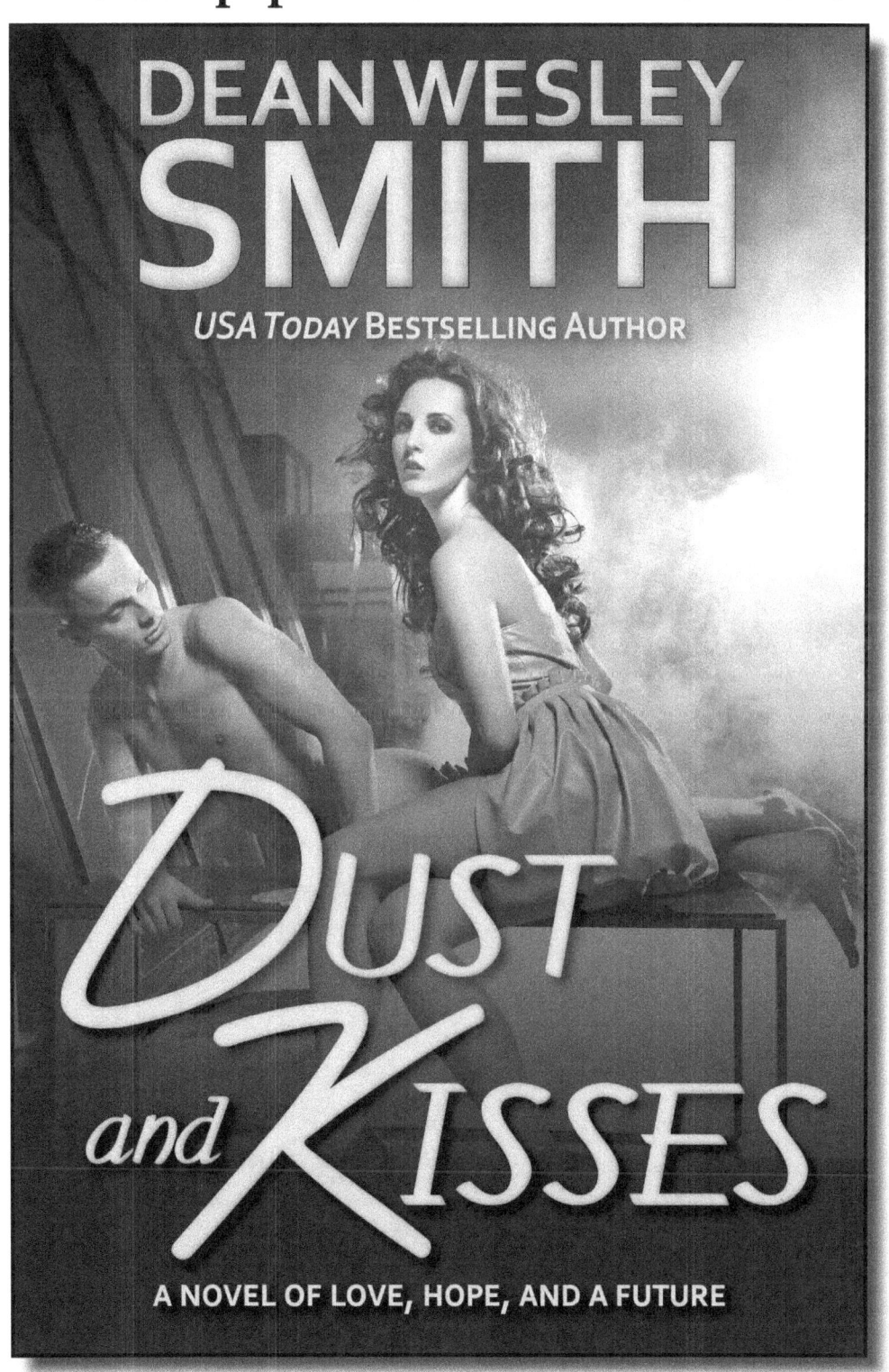

DEAN WESLEY SMITH

They Were Young,
They Were Old,
They Saved the Earth
Between Dances

DREAMS OF A MOON

An Earth Protection League Story

USA Today *bestselling writer, Dean Wesley Smith, returns to the fan favorite universe of the Earth Protection League.*

Once again, Captain Brian Saber and Captain Dorothy "Dot" Leeds must leave their nursing home to fight for the very survival of the Earth.

This story first appeared in Fiction River: Moonscapes. *The story was also incorporated as a number of chapters in the novel last month,* Life of a Dream.

DREAMS OF A MOON

One

THE YOUNG, STRONG lieutenant gently nudged Captain Brian Saber in his nursing home bed, pulled back the blanket and sheet covering him, and then easily picked Brian up with strong arms. His name was Lieutenant Magusson, but he had told Brian one night that some people called him Big Ed.

Brian was going on a mission.

Brian could feel the excitement surge through his old body.

A mission, a chance to live again, to be young again.

He made himself take as deep a breath as he could without setting off a fit of coughing.

The Shady Valley Nursing Home room hadn't changed since Brian fell asleep at 10 p.m. Now his old clock on his dresser told him it was a little after one in the morning. If he survived this mission, he would be back in fifteen minutes. But he might be out there in space for a month or more, if he was lucky.

Big Ed turned for the room's sliding glass door. Behind him Brian saw Captain Dorothy "Dot" Leeds being carried from her room across the hall and through his room. The young woman carrying her was Lieutenant Sherrie and she followed Brian and Big Ed out into the cold night air of a Chicago winter.

The light nightshirt Brian wore to bed was no match for the biting cold air, but he didn't mind. He wouldn't be out in the cold long enough for it to matter.

Overhead he could see the full moon, bright in the night sky. He and Dot were both far too old to ever walk under that moon. But at some point they would be together, staring up at some moon, somewhere.

No one talked.

No one said a word.

They were on a mission for the Earth Protection League. Something had happened on the border a long ways from Earth, which is why the League needed Brian and Dot. The League needed their ships, needed the two of them young and willing to fight.

All over the country right now his crew and Dot's crew were going through the same routine.

Damn he was excited.

He always felt this way going on a mission.

The four of them neared the center of the courtyard of the nursing home. The frozen snow crunched under the boots of the two lieutenants and Brian could see his shallow breath in the dim light.

The full moon was so beautiful on a clear winter night. He hoped he would see it again tonight.

Then a yellow beam struck them from above and lifted all four of them up easily into the big intergalactic transport ship.

The warm air of the ship covered him and behind him he heard Dot say softly, "See you on the other side."

He would have answered her, but he couldn't talk louder than a whisper. He couldn't walk or even lift his arms much at all either. A stroke had taken most of those skills a few years earlier.

She knew that and didn't expect an answer from him. He was eighty-eight, she was eighty-seven. Both of them were captains of major starships for the Earth Protection League.

They had been friends in the nursing home and one night she had seen him being carried out to go on a mission. So the next day he got permission to recruit her, and she had risen quickly to the rank of captain as well, in just under twenty missions. She was that good.

And they were both very much in love. At some point soon they would get married and live out on the frontier, not ever having to return to earth and their old bodies.

But right now they were still frontline fighters. And clearly they were needed.

Big Ed laid Brian down in what looked like a coffin in a private cabin off to one side of the big hallway.

That coffin was a sleep chamber that knocked Brian out during the trip at Trans-Galactic speeds toward the frontier of the Earth Protection League. And during that sleep, because of the nature of space and time and matter, his body would regress to being young and healthy again.

He had no idea how or why it worked that way. A couple of people had tried to explain it to him once. Something about matter being at a fixed point in time and space, so if a person flew faster than light, everyone on board regressed in age in relationship to the distance traveled.

They had figured out a way to help the brain hold the memories of being old, and the experiences during the trip.

Brian was just glad it worked the way it did, because otherwise he would be stuck in that nursing home and in the stroke-damaged body just waiting to die. Now he could actually do something constructive, help defend Earth and its allies.

Big Ed stepped back and snapped off a salute. "Good luck, sir," he said.

Then he lowered the lid until it latched over Brian and the light went out.

Brian would have loved to salute the young man back, but he couldn't.

Instead he just lay there thinking of seeing Dot again in her young and youthful body.

And he thought of them dancing as they always did after a mission.

But first they had to survive whatever faced them in deep space this time.

A faint orange smell seeped into the coffin and Captain Brian Saber dozed off.

Two

CAPTAIN SABER AWOKE what seemed like just an instant later.

He reached up and easily pushed the coffin lid open. Then he levered his young body out of the sleep chamber.

He never got tired of that feeling after being trapped in that wheelchair and bed what seemed like just moments before. The magic of the Trans-Galactic speed had done it to him again; given him his young body back.

He had sure taken this body for granted when he had been young.

He quickly slipped off the old night-shirt and tossed it back in the coffin. He would need that for the return trip back.

If he survived.

If he didn't, his son would be called in the middle of the night and there would be a funeral for a body that was a fake of his. And no one but those in the Earth Protection League would know Brian Saber of Chicago died in space, fighting for all humanity.

And he didn't honestly care if anyone knew. He just loved doing this, getting a chance to be young again.

He quickly dressed in his tight brown pants and tall black leather boots over the pants. He put on a loose white-silk blouse and a brown vest over that with a logo on it that read EPL. He strapped his two photon blasters on his hips with a wide black-leather belt and then looked at himself in the mirror.

This trip they had gone a little farther out. He looked to be about twenty-five. Often he ended up closer to thirty on missions.

So that meant they were very, very close to the EPL border, more than likely the border with the Dogs, one of the nastiest alien races to ever exist.

And a race set on the destruction at any cost of the EPL and Earth.

He turned and left his room, turning right and heading for the command center. He was on his own warship, the *Bad Business*.

Dot would have been transferred to her ship as well, the *Blooming Rose*. He wished he could see her now, kiss her, hold her with his young strong arms. But there would be time for that later.

Right now he had to focus on the mission they faced.

He got to the control room just a few seconds before his other two command crew arrived. Marion Knudson, a striking redhead from Wisconsin took her second chair. The two of them had been a team for a dozen missions now.

She was tough, all business, and smart as they came.

This time she had her red hair long and down over her shoulders. Usually she kept it up tight against her head.

Behind them Kip Butcher dropped into his chair with a "Damn this feels good."

Kip was from Southern California and lived in a nursing home there. When he was young he had been a surfer and now, even in his uniform, he still looked the part with his tan skin and blonde hair.

Back in Wisconsin, Marion lived alone, even at the age of ninety. As Kip had said once, she was too damn mean to die.

Marion had not argued with that, only smiled that smile that let Brian know that at some point Kip would pay for the remark.

"So any news as to the mission, Captain?" Marion asked, her fingers running over the board in front of her. "We are within striking distance of the Dog border. Much closer than normal, actually. No sign at all of Dog warships."

"And there are six other EPL warships with us," Kip said. "One is the *Blooming Rose.*"

Everyone knew about his and Dot's relationship.

"No word yet," Brian said. "But I suspect we don't have long to wait."

He pointed to the board and as he did, a red light started blinking, meaning an emergency message was coming in.

"You creep me out every time you do that," Kip said, shaking his head and turning back to his board.

Brian just smiled at Marion. The brass had a certain timetable that they allowed the crews to get into positions on their ships, and that never varied.

"Message on screen," Kip said a moment later.

General Dan Holmes's face appeared, his frown causing his middle-aged face to wrinkle even more than it already was.

"Captains," he said, nodding. "I'm afraid this is as bad as it gets."

Brian said nothing, as did the other captains of the other six warships, so the general went on.

"The Dogs have launched a moon at Earth."

Brian sat there hoping that General Holmes would take back that statement.

He didn't.

The General just kept frowning.

"The moon is accelerating from deep in Dog space and will be at the border at your position in about six hours."

"Fleet of ships with it, I assume?" Saber asked.

The General shook his head. "They don't think they need ships on this one. The moon they have launched is as big as our moon around Earth."

Brian sat back and tried to imagine what it would take to get a moon like that actually moving, what kind of power and how the moon would even hold together. And how they would even aim it from such a long distance through space.

And how many thousands of years at real-space travel it would take to get to Earth.

"I'm sending all the data we have on it through to you," the general said. "We want you to investigate the moon the moment it crosses into our space, pass on the data to our scientists."

With that he clicked off, leaving the screen blank.

"Why do I think there's something he flat omitted from that briefing," Kip said.

Marion's fingers flew over the keys as Brian sat there, waiting. He knew Kip was right. The General wasn't telling them everything. There was something more.

"Oh, shit," Marion said.

Brian looked over at her. She never swore.

She put up the report that made her swear on the main screen in front of Brian so that they could all see it.

"One hour after the moon crosses into our space," Marion said, "it reaches Trans-Galactic speed and will be protected by the Trans-Galactic shields. Nothing will be able to change its course until it plows into Earth."

"They built a TG drive big enough to power a moon," Kip said, shaking his head. "Wow! That's impressive."

Brian had to admit, it was impressive. But there was only one problem. Once something was in Trans-Galactic drive, it couldn't be stopped. It wasn't in real time and the shields that formed with the drive could plow through anything.

So they had to figure out a way to stop a speeding moon.

Or Earth would be destroyed very, very shortly.

Three

CAPTAIN SABER LOOKED around at his command crew, then shook his head. "Looks like we got seven hours to figure this out. Marion, make sure to get that report to the people on board who understand Trans-Galactic drive physics."

Marion nodded, her fingers moving quickly over the controls as Brian turned his big chair around so he could face Kip on his right and Marion on his left.

"Done," she said.

Brian knew that meant the other 40-some members of his crew all knew the score and were working on solutions as well. When you got that many experienced people working hard on something, results tended to happen.

And Brian knew that everyone on the other ships was doing the same. That was a lot of years experience focused on the same problem.

"Let me kind of think out loud here," he said.

Both Marion and Kip nodded.

"I assume TG space will power the thing once the moon reaches Trans-Galactic speed. But what's powering it now?"

Both Kip and Marion had the report at their fingertips and it was Marion that spoke first. "The moon has a hot core, so the engines spaced around the moon are feeding off the internal core of the moon itself."

"All TG engines," Kip said. "All shielded as would be expected. Nothing we have will knock them out."

Brian knew that and he nodded. He'd been in a lot of fights with Dog warships and knocking their engines out was never an option, just as Dogs knocking out a TG EPL engine wasn't possible either. It was the nature of Trans-Galactic engines and the shields that built up around them.

"Can we dig the engines out of the moon's surface outside the shields?" Brian asked.

Again both his command crew worked on the report, then both shook their heads. "Engines are buried thirty miles deep inside the moon. No dislodging them."

Brian looked at the big screen near Kip with the report and wondered how the EPL got all the information. More than likely a number of people had died for it.

"And I assume no blowing the thing apart before it enters Trans-Galactic speed?" Brian asked.

"They found the most stable hunk of rock I've ever seen," Kip said, and Marion nodded.

"It would take an entire fleet of ships," Kip said, sounding disgusted, "pounding it with all weapons, and I doubt that even that much would make more than a dent."

They all three sat there in silence.

Brian just kept looking around, looking at his young body, at his command crew's young bodies. Somehow they had made it out here, to this exact location in space.

He looked at Kip. "Who is driving the moon?"

"No one will be on the moon," Kip said.

"So who drives us when we come out here," Brian asked. "to exact coordinates, with our Trans-Galactic drives?"

Marion frowned and turned back to her board.

Kip did the same thing.

You don't just send a ship hurtling through more miles of space than Brian wanted to think about without something or someone driving. Even with top shields, you didn't want to plow holes through things along the way that didn't need holes in them.

So that transport ship from Earth had someone driving it, controlling it, from somewhere.

And that moon would have someone driving all the way to Earth. One planet that far away was far, far too small a target

to hit from this distance without a number of course corrections along the way.

"Computers," Marion finally said. "Each transport we take out here is run by a computer to do course corrections."

"Through sensors, the computer is able to see the route ahead," Kip said, "and make corrections to avoid the transport putting a hole in a planet or moon or anything else along the way."

"So there is a computer on that moon somewhere?" Brian asked. "We know where?"

"Buried with the Trans-Galactic drive engines," Marion said.

"Damn," Kip said, clearly getting angry. "They thought of everything."

"Not everything," Brian said, smiling. "Is the moon rotating in any fashion?"

Kip and Marion both looked puzzled at him, then quickly checked.

"No," Marion said. "It couldn't rotate and maintain its TG drive thrust."

"So we blind it," Brian said. "Tough to hit anything without being able to see."

"The computer sensors," Kip said, laughing. "Of course, they would have to be hidden on the front side of the moon to feed the computer."

"And I'll wager those sensors are not hardwired into that computer," Brian said. "Not through that much rock."

Marion laughed, the first time Brian had heard that for some time. "What are you thinking, Captain?"

Brian sat back, his hands behind his head.

"How about we feed those computers in that moon some bad targeting information, something simple such as the location of a Dog military base."

"Oh, that will annoy them something awful," Kip said, laughing so hard tears were coming to his eyes.

Marion informed all the other ships of the idea and then all three of them set to work on exactly where on that moon those sensors would be planted and how to intercept the signal from the surface sensors to the moon's targeting computer.

Four

THE MOON WAS fast approaching the EPL border when Command gave the clearance to try their plan. It had been a scientist on Dot's ship who had finally cracked the Dog computer code between the moon targeting computer and the sensors.

And it had been a scientist on yet another warship who had figured out how to intercept the signals from the sensors.

They would need to have a ship in tight over each of the six sensors on the moon and the intercept signal would have to be sent at exactly the same moment to all sensors.

In essence, the control of the moon was going to be transferred to Brian. He and Kip and Marion were going to turn the moon just before it started into Trans-Galactic drive and fire it at a Dog military base.

And then destroy the targeting computer by feeding it a very nasty virus.

That moon would wipe out that Dog base and then head out into deep space at full TG drive. The engines would have to fail before that moon dropped back into normal space a very, very long ways away from this entire galaxy.

At least that was the plan.

But there was one major problem with the plan that Brian didn't much like. Six EPL ships would have to basically hover in close over the moon to intercept the signal from each sensor and relay the signal to his ship and then, in turn, take the new instructions and feed them back into the sensors.

Dot and her ship would be one of those in close.

And they would have to stay in close during the moon's turn and then somehow get a safe distance away when the moon jumped to Trans-Galactic drive.

It was going to take exact timing. Just a second or two of delay and a warship would be lost.

And if one warship didn't stay in close enough, all six sensors wouldn't feed the computer the right data and there was no telling what might happen.

Brian sat back in his chair, trying to keep his nerves under control as they waited the last ten minutes. He knew everyone was busy checking and double-checking the plan. He had talked with Dot privately thirty minutes before, telling her to be careful and that he loved her.

She just laughed that wonderful, young laugh of hers, and said, "Trust me, I'm not missing the dancing tonight for anything."

Dot loved to dance, more than anything in life it seemed at times.

And he loved to dance with her.

"Moon crossing the border now, Captain," Marion said.

Brian nodded to Kip who opened a fleet-wide communications link.

"Move into positions now."

On the screen in front of him, Brian could see the six other EPL warships with their sleek noses and wing-like appearance move as one, turning toward the large moon and matching speed with it. EPL warships had been designed to look like birds not only to allow them atmospheric flight if needed, but because in so many of the cultures the EPL fought against, birds were feared.

Including with the Dogs.

Brian kept the *Bad Business* outside and above the group, moving with them to match the speed of the moon.

Then, almost as a practiced dance in space, the six ships broke away from each other and moved in over an area of the large moon.

The closer the moon got, Brian could see that it did look a great deal like their moon at home. It had no atmosphere and was covered with impact craters. And it was just about the same size.

Brian took the *Bad Business* in right over the center of the moon and matched its speed and acceleration to stay in position.

"Thirty seconds," Marion said.

"Signal when in position," Brian ordered the other ships.

Each ship had to hover no more than a football field length above the surface where the sensor was, and match the increasing speed of the moon at the same time.

Very, very tricky flying and a slight miss and the EPL warship would crash into the moon's surface, or be too far away to intercept the signal.

Brian could see the *Blooming Rose* turn and settle into its assigned position above the moon surface. Dot would be flying it. She had one of the steadiest hands at the helm of a ship that he had ever seen.

Three other warships signaled ready.

Then Dot signaled *The Blooming Rose* was in position and steady.

"Ready here," Brian said, checking to make sure his people were ready with the computer download and new signal into the moon's computer.

At the same moment the other two ships reported they were in position and stable.

"Hold and be ready to turn with the moon," Brian said.

"Intercept signal," Brian ordered the other ships.

As one all turned green that they had the sensor signal.

Then he turned to Marion. "Feed it."

Her fingers flew over the panel and the new programming for the Dog's computer was fed through all six sensors.

An instant later the moon started to turn off its course for Earth.

"Stay with it, everyone," Brian commanded to the other ships as he moved the *Bad Business* to maintain position and keep the feed to the other ships constant.

The moon kept turning and somehow the EPL warships held their positions.

"We got some swearing and close calls," Kip said, "but everyone is holding.

"Ten more seconds," Marion said. "And the virus will be loaded."

At five seconds Brian counted it down for the other captains.

"Five. Four. Three. Two. One."

Marion signaled cut.

"Get out of there now!" Brian shouted to the other pilots.

As one, the other pilots moved their ships up and away from the rough surface of the moon.

Brian had the *Bad Business* moving with them, pushing the ship as fast as he could to try to reach a safe distance.

Twenty seconds later the moon vanished into Trans-Galactic drive space, headed back into the Dog's territory

"Clear," Kip said.

"All ships made it out of the wash zone from the drive," Marion said.

Brian slumped in his chair, just smiling as both Kip and Marion applauded and laughed.

Somehow, Earth had dodged that moon. Barely.

Five

CAPTAIN BRIAN SABER looked down into the wonderful brown eyes of Captain Dorothy Dot Leeds and smiled. "One more dance?"

She laughed, the sound high and wonderful and something he needed to remember in the long days and nights at the nursing home. "Our bus back to the home is going to leave without us."

"Let it," he said, pulling her close and enjoying the feel of her against him. Since they had turned the moon weapon back on the Dogs, the general had allowed all seven EPL warships to dock at Stevens Base for some well-deserved time off while in younger bodies.

Brian and Dot had spent the first night dancing, then in his room on the base. The next day they had spent in meetings with the general and others, then dancing more that evening, then back to her room for the night.

The General had approved their application to move to Stevens in a very short time, be married, and work frontline there with their ships and any crew that wanted to join them, based out of Stevens.

As the General said, it was about time they had a staffed base full of frontline defenders. He wanted Brian to lead the wing of fighters. The EPL would still bring many in from Earth when needed, but a number based out on the edge of the frontier would be a good idea.

But until that was fully approved, Brian and Dot now had to go back to Earth and the Shady Hills Nursing Home.

With one last dance, they kissed and walked hand-in-hand to the transport, not saying anything.

He kissed Dot one more time at her cabin door, then with a promise from her that she would help him with his applesauce at breakfast, he went to his cabin and took off his uniform, slipping back into his old nightshirt and crawling into the coffin.

The very next thing he remembered, he was being carried by Lieutenant Magusson from his sleep chamber.

His old stroke-damaged body now part of him again.

Dot and Lieutenant Sherrie met them at the transport chamber.

Brian so wanted to reach out to touch Dot's hand, but he could no longer move his arms hardly at all.

The cold air of the Chicago night hit him as the transport beam let them go in the nursing home center court.

Above him the golden moon was full in the crisp night air.

He stared up at it as the Lieutenant carried him toward his room.

"Not so pretty any more, is it?" Dot said.

She was right. It wasn't.

After this mission, he wasn't sure if he would ever look up at the moon in the same way again.

It was amazing how seeing the universe and defending Earth could change a person's perspective on things.

Simple things, like staring up at the moon.

FICTION RIVER: YEAR ONE

Missed a volume from Fiction River's first year?

No problem. Buy individual volumes anytime
from your favorite bookseller.

See why *Adventures Fantastic* calls *Fiction River*
"one of the best and most exciting publications
in the field today."

FICTION RIVER: YEAR TWO

USA *Today* Bestselling Writer

DEAN WESLEY SMITH

Chapters 25-27

THE ADVENTURES OF HAWK

What came before...

Nineteen-year-old Danny Hawk, his uncle, and his best friend Craig, were in Cairo to look for his missing father. Danny had witnessed the death of his only contact in Cairo, Professor Davis, because the professor had Danny's father's journals.

Danny knows that the men who had killed the professor were now after him and the journals. Danny finds the journals and gets his uncle and friend to safety in an airport hotel where he tells them what happened. They decide to keep searching for Danny's father and try to rescue him. Along the way, Danny and Craig find some help from a street kid named Bud and twins from South Africa who had worked with Danny's father.

They managed to escape the men chasing them twice so far; Danny wasn't sure their luck would hold a third time. And it barely did. They finally decided to head out of Cairo. Beyond the headwaters of the Amazon, in the Republic of Congo, after a few more close calls, they hire a guide to take them into the jungle in search of a lost ancient city. And even into the jungle on the Trail of Elephants, they are followed.

Then Danny barely escapes death when he falls through a floor in an old temple. The rest rescue him, but when they reach the bottom the men following them throw down the rope and trap them under the ancient city.

THE ADVENTURES OF HAWK

CHAPTER TWENTY-FIVE

September 17, 1970
Under the Lost City of Ishango, deep in the jungle of the Republic of Congo.

"HAVE I SAID lately how screwed we are?" Craig said, staring at the pile of rope.

Above them the hole in the floor of the temple seemed like an impossible distance away to Danny. Totally impossible.

And the men that had been chasing them were up there, more than likely standing guard.

Before anyone else could say anything, Hassatt held up his hand for all of them to remain silent. "We need to get away from this area quickly," he whispered. "Just in case they decide they need a little target practice."

Danny glanced back up. Hassatt was right. Shooting them now would be like shooting fish in a bowl.

Hassatt pointed to the rope on the ground. "Bring that." Then he motioned that they should follow him.

Danny picked up the huge pile of rope and his torch, and then he followed Hassatt and the others down through the cavern, heading for old stone stairs that led deeper underground. At some point, the stairs must have led to something in the big cavern, but rocks now covered whatever it was.

Danny was glad that at least they were still alive. But they wouldn't be for long if they didn't find another way out of this cavern. Clearly, the two Hydra League men above didn't think there was another way out.

And Danny bet they knew the ruins.

The six of them quickly wound their way down through a series of linked smaller caverns, following the ancient stone path and stairs carved six thousand years before. Danny, on one trip to the Southwest, had gone into Carlsbad Caverns. These caverns seemed very much like those. The deeper they got underground, the more stalactites and stalagmites they wound their way through.

The colors of the stones shimmering in their torchlights were fantastic. Bright reds and blues and greens.

The deeper they got, the louder the sound of the river became, filling everything. If Danny hadn't been so worried about finding a way out, he would have enjoyed the cave exploring a lot more than he was.

Finally, the series of small caverns opened up into a huge cavern with a river running through one corner of it, crashing down over rocks and then disappearing into a wall, clearly going deeper in to the ground than it already was.

The stalactite-covered ceiling of the cavern was a good hundred feet over their heads. And from what Danny could see, there were a dozen smaller caverns leading off in different directions from this one. There was a maze of caverns under the ancient city. A maze that could easily get them lost forever.

Hassatt, who had been leading them down the stone path of the ancient people, stopped in an open area and dropped the pack he had been carrying. "I don't think they can hear us down here."

"You think they're going to follow us?" Bud said.

Hassatt shrugged. "Not for a week or so. Then they'll come looking for our bodies."

"Great," Craig said.

Danny glanced down at the river. "We have water, that's for sure. Anyone bring any food?"

"A day's worth for everyone," Hassatt said.

Everyone else shook their heads no.

"We can stretch that to last a lot longer," Hassatt said. "As long as we can drink that water."

"True," Bud said. "Many times I've gone without food for a week, but I had water."

Danny glanced at his short friend. He didn't want to know what the Cairo street kid had been through while trying to survive alone on the streets, but with comments like that, he was getting a good idea.

"So," Craig said, glancing at Danny, "what's the plan?"

Danny shrugged. "We find the next Hydra Journal entry. Then find a way out of here."

"How about we do both those things at the same time?" Bud asked.

"Seems like a good idea to me," Hassatt said, smiling.

Danny agreed. They needed to find a new way out, since their way in was blocked to them, and more than likely guarded. Clearly, the ancient people used these caverns under their city, so it would be logical there would be more than one way in and out. If those ways were still open after six thousand years.

Ed glanced around, then quoted the third Hydra Journal entry. "Under the teeming masses, the river becomes clear, the path muddy."

"Shall we try to find the muddy path?" Ernie asked.

"As good a plan as any," Danny said. "And the farther we get from those men back there, the happier I will be."

"I'll second that," Craig said.

All six of them glanced back into the dark where they had come, then as one, they turned and headed down the stone pathway toward the loud river crashing over the rocks below them.

CHAPTER TWENTY-SIX

September 17, 1970
Under the Lost City of Ishango, deep in the jungle of the Republic of Congo.

"A PATH," ED said an hour later.

Danny was up on some rocks above the river, climbing to see if he could see anything from a higher position that they had missed. The stone path they had followed down through the caverns had just ended at the edge of the river like a docking port.

But the river was tumbling over the rocks so hard just below the path that Danny couldn't imagine even taking a raft down that river and into the dark tunnel.

Hassatt had suggested that back when the path was built, the river had been calmer, and the tunnel led to other caverns. Maybe, but Danny doubted it. Six thousand years just wasn't that long in the life of a river cutting through solid rock.

"It's a debarkation platform," Ernie had finally said after they had explored the edges of the tunnel below the platform. "The ancient people were coming from up the river to here."

There must be something back in the cavern they had started in that the ancient people would raft to here, then walk the rest of the way. Whatever it was had clearly been covered in cave-ins and rockslides. Danny hoped the next entry in the Hydra Journal wasn't back up there.

That was when they had focused their attention upstream and Ed had found the path.

Unlike the stone path they had come down into the cavern, this path was more natural and wound its way around and past rocks. The spray from the river caused it to be wet and slick and slightly muddy.

"Well," Craig said, "we found all the parts of the third Hydra Journal entry. Now what?"

"We follow the path," both Ernie and Ed said at the same time.

"Might as well," Danny said, glancing back up the cavern to where Bud had stationed himself as a lookout for the Hydra League goons. He waved for Bud to join them, then turned to everyone. "I want us all roped together in case we slip and fall in that river."

All of them agreed, and they waited until Bud joined them to put him in the middle.

"I'll lead," Danny said. "I'm a good swimmer. Dr. Hassatt right behind me. Then Bud and the twins. Craig, you bring up the rear."

They all tied themselves into the heavy rope that they had lowered themselves into the cave with, spacing themselves four paces apart.

"Everyone be careful," Danny said. "Watch your step, but keep your eyes open for any ancient writing."

Danny took a couple of deep breaths, then, holding his torch high over his head to keep it as far from the river spray as he could, he started forward.

The path wound its way along the rocks just above the water. In the tunnel, the river seemed almost calm and very black. Danny had no desire to go in that cold water and find out what lived in there.

He wasn't thirty paces into the darkness of the river cave when he noticed two things. The first was a giant spider web across the path, its web glimmering in the faint light and dampness.

He eased forward and lit the bottom of the web on fire, using the flaring torch to break the web apart. Out of the corner of his eye he saw something move in the rocks, but he forced himself to not turn to look. It was just better to not know what lived down here in normally total blackness.

Then, as he held the torch out directly in front of him, he noticed it was blowing back slightly toward him, the smoke catching him in the eyes.

A breeze.

He stopped and glanced back along the trail where everyone else had stopped waiting for him to move forward. "Notice the breeze?"

"An opening somewhere ahead," Hassatt said, smiling.

"Now if it is only big enough for us to get through," Ed said.

"We'll make it big enough," Ernie said.

Danny nodded, hoping Ernie was right.

Danny led the way along the slick, muddy path beside the river's edge. The path seemed to wind on forever. Clearly, this tunnel was not normally walked. There weren't any rapids in the river, so whoever used this usually floated down from some place up ahead.

"Any idea which direction we're heading?" Craig asked from behind Danny.

"I think we're going west," Dr. Hassatt said. "Toward the mountains beside the city."

Danny didn't know if that was good or bad. He just kept going, moving slowly and carefully through the rocks.

Finally, just about at the point he was going to have them stop and rest, the tunnel opened up into a giant cavern.

Danny stepped a dozen steps out into the huge space, held up his torch, and stopped cold.

From what he could see, the cavern was huge, bigger than even a massive football stadium back home. On one edge, the river had turned into a decent-sized lake, with a high platform right in the center of the room beside the lake.

The platform faced a thousand stone seats that formed an amphitheatre around the platform.

"The Great Council Chamber," Dr. Hassatt said beside Danny, his voice hushed. "We found the ancient's Great Council Chamber."

"There's got to be treasure here," Bud said.

"Amazing," Ernie said.

"A stunning find," Ed said.

"Wow! Big place," Craig said.

All Danny could do was stare.

And wish his father were here to see this.

CHAPTER TWENTY-SEVEN

September 17, 1970
Under the Lost City of Ishango, deep in the jungle of the Republic of Congo.

WHAT IS THE Great Council Chamber?" Danny asked Dr. Hassatt after another minute of all of them staring at the huge cavern in front of them.

"From everything I can gather," Dr. Hassatt said, "the ancient people who lived here and in other great cities around the globe were governed by a group of ten elders. These elders were elected and served like a city government, representing the adults, both men and women, of the city. This is where everyone met to listen to the council debate, act and vote."

Dr. Hassatt pointed to the main platform beside the lake. "The Great Council would meet there and anyone who wanted could watch and listen. The important issues and elections would fill this place I'm sure. I had always hoped to find the remains of a Great Council Chamber, but never in this good a condition."

Dr. Hassatt started off toward the huge platform beside the lake. The floor of the cavern was paved in stone blocks and perfectly smooth. This entire room was an amazing piece of construction.

Danny and the rest followed, moving slowly, staring at everything around them.

Danny almost wanted to hold his breath as he climbed up the stone steps to the giant stage.

A stone table with a polished top filled the center of the stage, but nothing else was left but dust. After six thousand years of being in the open, even in a dark cave, that made sense. No wood or cloth would survive the moisture down here.

Behind the table on the stage was a stone wall. And across the top of the stone was carved hieroglyphs, large enough for everyone in the room to read, even from the top seats. It was the first writing of any type that Danny had seen in the ancient city.

Dr. Hassatt, Ernie, and Ed stared at the hieroglyphs.

"What does it say?" Danny asked.

"Hopefully it's an exit sign with an arrow," Craig said.

"From the greatest city," Dr. Hassatt said.

"No, highest city," Ed said, stopping him.

"I agree," Ernie said. "Not greatest, highest."

Dr. Hassatt studied the carvings for a moment, then nodded. "From the highest city, power flows to the many."

"The forth Hydra Journal entry?" Danny asked, sick to his stomach that it looked like the trail to rescue his father would end right here, in a cave deep under a jungle.

"More than likely, yes," Dr. Hassatt said. "The ancient people wrote very little in stone. This is written in an early form of Egyptian hieroglyph, as the others were.

"Well, that's that," Craig said, sitting on the edge of the Great Council table. "That's not going to lead us anywhere."

Dr. Hassatt looked at Craig, then at Danny and laughed. "Of course it is."

"From the highest city, power flows to the many," Danny said, repeating the phrase. "Assuming we can get out of this cave, how is that going to help us?"

Again Dr. Hassatt laughed and even Ernie and Ed looked puzzled. "Danny, your father and I both believed that this ancient civilization existed, and we both believed that it spanned the globe and was of a high degree of engineering and civilization before it died off for some reason. Many different races are descendants of this first civilization, and many races built in their ruins."

Danny nodded, as did Ernie and Ed.

"That was in my father's notebooks," Danny said.

Dr. Hassatt pointed back at the images carved in the stone over the great stage. "The highest city?"

Suddenly Danny realized what Dr. Hassatt was talking about. "Machu Picchu?"

"Exactly," Dr. Hassatt said.

"But wasn't that an Inca city?" Craig asked.

"Later," Dr. Hassatt said. "The Incas took it over, built new parts, and made it their own. But there is much evidence that the city was older than the early Incas."

"Power flows to the many?" Danny asked.

Dr. Hassatt shrugged. "That's something you'll have to figure out there."

"So the next clue is in the Andes?" Bud asked.

Danny nodded. "Looks that way."

"Great," Bud said. "Glad we found it and figured it out. But right now we're trapped a long ways underground in the center of Africa with bad men stalking us. First things first, I always say."

None of them had an argument for that.

Continued next issue…

Now Available
from all your favorite booksellers
in trade paper and electronic editions.

USA *Today* Bestselling Writer

DEAN WESLEY SMITH

Science Fiction,
Action, Adventure, Lust,
and Sexual Innuendo.
What More Do You Want?

AS THE ROBOT RUBS

Science fiction, action, adventure, lust, and a ton of sexual innuendo. This story hits it all and even more.

Mike Blackmoon, son of the famous story-teller, Howling Blackmoon, tells the story carefully following his father's instructions.

This story inside a story features Buckey the Space Pirate, but not the same Buckey as later stories with the talking oak tree Fred. Who know there were two Buckey the Space Pirates?

A very different version of this story appeared in the anthology Alien Pets *back in 1998. I added in a pet to get the story into the anthology. I like this, the original version, much better.*

AS THE ROBOT RUBS

MY NAME IS Mike Blackmoon. And I got this story.

It might be called a romance, but it's not a romance.

Some folks might call it a mystery. Nope. Wrong again.

If the story were printed, some stupid bookstore owner might stick it in the horror section. Slap that person with rolled up page proofs.

There's just no way this story can be anything but science fiction.

That's right.

Science fiction with sex.

Of course, in science fiction, all the sex is like a Norman Rockwell painting. But it's still sex, so what the hell.

My daddy, Howling Blackmoon, was the greatest storyteller to ever sit beside a campfire. He always said that if you want to hold a listener's attention, you gotta start your story right in the middle of the good part. So that's exactly what I'm going to do.

"Don't stop," she panted.

How's that for a start?

I'll bet right now your mind is skipping right along with pictures of a young, big-chested girl, a must in science fiction — breathing heavily as this young space pirate named Buckey nibbles on her ear while at the same time unbuckling his blaster.

Buckey is a real ladies man in his white tights, white plumed hat, and black boots. He also wears a sabre strapped on one hip and a blaster on the other.

Now, if you're thinking Buckey is going to take off his blaster, you're wrong.

Wrong. Wrong. Wrong.

Buckey is nowhere to be seen. What's really going on is that this woman named Sarah — who is an escaped slave from the horrid Alien prison camp — is telling her fellow escapee, Loreina, the main character of this story, to keep running toward the ancient hidden ship. Sarah has decided that she must stay behind and hold off the prison guards in the narrow desert canyon.

Loreina argues with Sarah for only a moment, then gives her one of those looks.

You know the look.

The same deep understanding look that every mother has when she sees wads of used Kleenex in her teenage son's garbage can.

You know... THE LOOK!

Loreina hugs Sarah.

Only a sparkle of tears form in their eyes. (It's the desert so they can't waste much water.) Then Loreina turns and runs up the canyon while Sarah faces the quickly approaching Alien guards who will for sure either (a) kill her, or (b) torture her, or (c) do whatever else mean and nasty Alien guards do to young women in science fiction stories.

At this point, it is a good story telling technique to jump forward in time. Or, sometimes back in time to explain the good time all the characters had getting to the present time.

Of course, anytime you jump in time, you must let the story listener know you're signaling time out.

In the movies, they do it with fade-outs. In fiction, they use white spaces. In this case I'm just going to pause.

(Pause)

Pause for effect, then hook the listener again, my old man used to say. (He could tell a whopper with the best of them.) So, being a good listener, I'm going to follow old Blackmoon's advice and jump back into this story right at the most interesting part.

"Don't stop," she panted.

I bet I know what you're thinking. Loreina is sitting in the copilot's chair (Right?) of this small space ship (Right?) while the handsome Buckey (the space pirate who rescued her from the prison planet) nibbles softly on her big toe and then starts working his way north.

Right?

Don't you wish.

Remember, this is a science fiction story.

What's really going on is that our heroine (An aside here in the middle of this sentence: My daddy once noted how close the word heroine is to heroin. Heroin is defined as a powerful sedative drug. He told me to think about it. End of aside.) is laying naked, face down, with only a towel over her butt (Don't want to get the story teller too worked up, now do we?) on a massage table back at Galactic Headquarters while a robot carefully works all the soreness out of her muscles.

Leaning against a post (yes they have posts in Galactic Headquarters) is

Loreina's boss and possible future love interest, Jerome.

At least their love might be possible if they don't find out that they are really brother and sister later in the story. (Of course, you might stop and ask yourself why Loreina would be interested in anyone by the name of Jerome. But I wouldn't. It would just complicate the story too much. Trust me that Jerome looks like no Jerome I ever met. Besides, Loreina likes the fact that he doesn't wear underwear under his tight-fitting Galactic uniform.)

As the robot rubs, (Note how swift the title worked in.) Loreina tells Jerome all about how she and Sarah were captured when they were zapped by a Lomax Ray which shut down all their food processing and bar equipment, as well as their main Wild-Blue-Yonder Drive just as they were about to learn how the dreaded Aliens were managing to steal fruit off Eden, the most heavily guarded planet this side of the core.

Jerome just shakes his head, so Loreina goes on to tell him about how horrible it was in the Alien prison and how Sarah stayed back so that one of them could get through with the message and get a good massage.

Again, Jerome just shakes his head.

He knows Loreina likes the strong silent type in her science fiction.

He also read on her job application for heroine that she liked men who didn't wear underwear.

Loreina gives Jerome that serious stare, raising up on one elbow so that she can see him better — and he most certainly can see her better. (The robot doesn't notice. Stupid robot.)

She then tells him, in a very deep tone, that she must return to save Sarah if Sarah is still alive.

She (Loreina) just can't leave her (Sarah) there in that awful place (the Alien prison), she (Loreina) says.

Again, Jerome just nods, never taking his eyes off of Loreina's boobs. (Which means that while Loreina talked, he had moved his face right up against her chest and, as in all good science fiction sex scenes, it is now time to fade out, white space, or pause, and thereby miss all the good description that follows when Jerome removes his eyes from her chest and puts other body parts there.)

(Pause...damn it anyway.)

"Don't stop," she panted.

Take your mind out of the gutter. I am not starting the story back on the massage table where Jerome and Buckey the Space Pirate have drawn a dotted line down the center of Loreina and are having a duel to see who can get their half the most excited.

I wouldn't do that in a science fiction story. Besides, Buckey likes his women whole.

But during all that white space around the last pause Jerome has done the regular man-like, middle class, try-to-take-over-the-story thing and told Loreina that she can't go to rescue Sarah. He has assigned her to a desk job in Galactic Headquarters where he can keep her under his thumb (as well as other parts).

Loreina didn't take kindly to that kind of shit from above, so, not really being a "company" girl or terribly fond of the missionary position, she captures a guard at the space port and is following the guard up a long, circular staircase in the launching tower of the new Bigger, Longer, and Taller spaceship.

The BLT has nifty screens that make the ship almost invisible to Aliens and block out the aliens Zapper Beam. That will allow Loreina to get close enough to the prison camp to rescue Sarah and still have lunch.

This part of the story opens as the guard stops suddenly in front of Sarah halfway up the huge tower. (There's a lot of stairs and they're both out of breath.)

Sarah keeps him going and then, at the top, once she has gotten into the ship, she stuns the guard. As he falls, she notices that he too doesn't wear underwear under his tight-fitting uniform. (The guard, who is a friend of Jerome's secretary, also snuck a peek at Loreina's application.)

Of course, at this point, Loreina is heavily occupied with stealing the ship and getting Sarah out, so, with only one mouth-watering glance at the guard, she jumps into the Captain's chair, straps herself in, and blasts off.

Blasting off should not be noted here with a bunch of noise.

She just floats up through the rain clouds quiet as you please. The drive on the BLT is very silent and doesn't need a match to light it.

Real advanced science fiction stuff.

Of course, out in space, she gets chased by the entire Patrol Fleet, which happened to be home on leave. She doesn't want to Atomize them (or even fire a warning shot across their bows) because she knows The Patrol is on her side, and that some men in those ships may have read her application.

Instead she does a few really nifty moves around the sun, looses about ten pounds when the inside of the ship heats up, then pops off through the Time Warp Instant Trajectory.

When in the TWIT, no one can follow, so she's safe.

Next she goes about getting herself ready for instant sleep to pass the sixty-four days it will take to reach the Alien prison world. She strips down to only her skimpy bikini underwear and a sweat-soaked tee shirt and crawls in.

The last thing you see is her breathing slowing as she passes out and her nipples get hard.

And again, you guessed it, it is time to...

(Pause)

Now where should I open the next part of the story?

My daddy said never let a listener down. If you've got someone's attention, don't disappoint him, especially toward the end of your story. So, following old man Blackmoon's advice once more, I return to the story at a "good" part.

"Don't stop," she panted.

God, don't you just love an exciting story?

I mean, imagine Loreina there with Sarah and Buckey, The Space Pirate on the filthy dirt floor of Sarah's cell in the Alien prison. The three of them are tied up, naked except for Buckey's white hat.

Buckey has one foot between Sarah's open legs and his other foot between Loreina's open legs. He's working on untying the girl's ropes with his toes.

Of course, his heels are making the escape a somewhat pleasurable experience for both women.

Now that you've imagined all that: dirt floor, moldy smell, low moaning, and all, I'm glad you got it out of your system because that's not what is going on. Remember... science fiction story?

I know, I know, I hate repeating myself, too. But sometimes I must, I must.

In the real story, Sarah wakes up after sixty-four days, crawls out, and does the classic yawn. Her little panties seem even smaller and the tee shirt still looks wet, but that's beside the point.

Without dressing, she runs to the cockpit of the ship and checks her instruments. (I won't say it if you don't.)

She discovers she is almost to the Alien prison planet. Now what is she going to do? She looks quickly around nearby space for the intervention-of-the-machine (sounds better in Latin) that will end the story quickly, but she doesn't spot one.

Failing that, the plot must thicken like overripe soup.

Loreina clicks on her screens and sneaks up on the Alien prison world. It just so happens that the entire Alien fleet is circling the prison planet. (Probably on vacation.)

Loreina decides it would be suicidal not only to her, but to her lust for men who don't wear shorts, if she went in alone. Probably get Sarah killed, too.

She thought and thought and wracked her brain trying to figure out what to do. That wasn't a pretty sight, even with her still in her bikini shorts and wet tee shirt.

A smoking, ruined brain is never fun to look at.

Finally, after two issues of Playmate of the Spaceways magazine and a good nights sleep, she realizes the answer has been right there in front of her in the story line all the time: Buckey, The Space Pirate.

She and Buckey go way back. Her first true love.

She loved his sabre.

Only she went corporate and he stayed in the private business sector and it had all ended with a net loss. Why hadn't she thought of him before? She used to think of him often, usually in the bathtub.

She sat there in the Captain's chair and thought about sitting in the bathtub and thinking about Buckey. Pretty soon she is thinking a lot about Buckey and her tee shirt is getting damper and damper and she is panting and it is right at this point, with her eyes closed, that Loreina utters the opening words of this section.

(Bet you thought I'd forgotten, didn't you?)

After a few moments more of thinking, Loreina slowly comes around and realizes (before her hands turn this into a romance) that she's not in the bathtub after all and that Sarah is still sitting down there in that stinking, dirt-floored, Alien prison waiting to be rescued.

Buckey is the only hope.

Loreina brushes her damp hair back out of her eyes, does a few quick calculations, and inserts the ship back into TWIT. Three quick days and she'd be with Buckey, The Space Pirate's fleet.

She did a few instrument checks, then headed for the bathroom. She wouldn't deep sleep this time.

She needed a long, long bath far more.

And, as the door to the bathroom hisses softly closed, this story again does the correct thing and...

(Pause.)

"Don't stop," she panted."

Nice hook to the climax of the story, huh? My daddy would be proud of me.

So, the tension builds.

Where is Loreina now?

Is Sarah still alive?

Does Loreina get Buckey to help spring Sarah from the prison camp?

Does Buckey wear underwear?

Tough questions that must be answered in this section because this is the last damn chance.

That's right.

No more pauses.

If this were a standard science fiction story, this section would have opened with Loreina in the bathtub thinking of Buckey when (suddenly) alarm bells go off all over the ship.

Of course, Loreina would have had time to struggle into clothes before facing the problem of one of Buckey's ships attacking her ship. She would have finally gotten through to Buckey who would have saved her in the last moment so that they could both go rescue Sarah.

Now that's pure pulp storytelling.

But that's not the way it happened. This is a liberated world, remember? Loreina has got to do it herself or it just won't mean anything.

On the third day of Loreina's bath, she gets to Buckey's home base and discovers from Buckey's second-in-command, Fred, (who has a large nose, very white teeth, and a small part in this story) that while on a raiding mission on an Alien world, Buckey's ship blew a warp and Buckey had been captured and was being held on the prison world. (Wow! That explains the entire Alien fleet being around the prison world much better than them just being there on shore leave.)

Fred doesn't know what to do.

But Loreina, after three days in the bathtub thinking about Buckey, has a desperate idea.

She decides to give Buckey's fleet the secrets to the screening device in her BLT so that they can all sneak inside the Alien fleet. Buckey's ships can keep the Aliens busy while she rescues Buckey and Sarah.

Neat plan, huh?

Fred likes the idea (and why wouldn't he?) and so, for the next two weeks, while Loreina takes a lot of baths and she and Fred do a lot of careful rescue planning, the screening devices are built and installed in all sixty-plus ships in Buckey's fleet.

Finally, the fleet is ready, Loreina is well wrinkled, and the plot must go on.

At this point I could go into another pause, letting the three days travel back to the Alien prison world pass quickly. But remember, I still haven't got to the point where the story starts after the last pause. So, let it suffice to say that the three days do pass like a bowl of chili and Buckey's fleet, with Fred in command, sneaks inside the Alien ships and attacks them on their naked, exposed undersides, right where they least expect it.

I could go into long detail about the battle. Blood and violence are okay in science fiction, and in fact are currently fashionable as long as the violence occurs in the future and has a high-tech feel.

You can't make love to someone, but it's all right to kill them.

Even though my daddy was an Indian and my mother was a German, I don't like violence. I like sex.

Luckily, so did my mother and father.

So, if I can't tell all about the sex in this story, I'm not going to give any of the violence, either.

So there.

Trust me when I tell you that except for the loss of two of Buckey's ships, Fred and the crews were completely successful in blasting those mean and nasty Aliens out of the system.

Loreina flew the BLT right down to the prison, landed, and led a raiding party into the cells.

In the human section of the prison, they found Sarah sitting in one cell staring at Buckey in the next cell. Both Sarah and Buckey were fine, except Sarah was a little glassy-eyed from staring at Buckey all those weeks.

That all happened in the last pause.

The last part of the story opens finally with Loreina leading Sarah, Buckey, and the raiding party back through the narrow halls of the prison at a full run. (They don't know that Buckey's fleet is winning the battle out in space.) Loreina guards one side corridor as she tells them breathlessly not to stop. (Remember: great opening line of this section.)

They make it safely back to the BLT and as this story closes with the ending that of course will leave enough open for a trilogy, Loreina sits in the Captain's chair with Buckey kneeling at her right and Sarah standing beside her on the left.

Picture this:

Sarah's hand is on Loreina's shoulder. Buckey's left hand is on his sabre. Buckey's white hat is tipped slightly to one side. His right hand is on Loreina's knee.

Loreina's shirt is still wet.

All three are smiling like damn fools into the view screen in front of them, as if posing for a wedding picture.

Silently, the BLT leaves the nasty Alien prison world behind and inserts itself (with a rainbow of colors) into TWIT, going who knows where.

"Don't stop," she panted.

Loreina gives her last command and, as the story fades to a close, leans back, closes her eyes, and sighs. Buckey's hand moves softly on Loreina's leg.

Sarah glances down and licks her lips.

The end. Except for one loose end. Buckey does not wear underwear. (What do you think Sarah was staring at all that time?)

DEAN WESLEY
SMITH

USA Today BESTSELLING AUTHOR

MORNING
SONG

A SEEDERS UNIVERSE NOVEL

USA Today *Bestselling writer Dean Wesley Smith returns to his fan-favorite Seeders Universe series with a fourth novel,* Morning Song.

A massive rogue ship powers toward the Milky Way Galaxy, threatening to destroy entire worlds. The rogue ship, the size of a moon, seems to have no entrance.

With little time before millions die, Maria Boone and Roscoe Mundy must somehow take a small team into the massive ship to stop it.

A galaxy-spanning tale of adventure and suspense and the humanity that can exist in a vast culture.

MORNING SONG
A Seeders Universe Novel

For Kris
Because she likes this series for some strange reason.

Section One

Prologue

WADE RAY stood calmly, waiting, his hands grasped behind his back as he stared at the huge view screen in front of him. His long gray hair flowed over his shoulders and covered the top of his casual gray silk shirt. He wore comfortable dark slacks and dark leather shoes. He never wore anything else.

He stood only six foot tall, had thin shoulders, and looked fairly young, but his mere presence in the ship's command center kept the other scientists behind him silent, staring at their individual control areas, some using screens, others using holographic heads-up displays.

The command center had three levels. The top level along the back had four stations, all diagnostic stations. The next level one step down had three major stations. Two were ship controls and operations, since the ship was huge, carrying over two thousand people.

The third and center chair was for the chairman of the ship, a term used by many to designate the captain of the ship. Most large Seeder ships like this one, with so many people and families, were for-profit businesses. So chairman was a better title for Wade Ray. Over the centuries, it had always been the standard designation on all Seeder ships.

Ray had stepped down to the area in front of his major control chair to try to get even slightly closer to the empty, black space staring at him on the screen.

Every human on this ship was a Seeder, working to spread the human race over every habitable planet in every galaxy they could reach.

The youngest scientist with him in the command center was only five hundred years old. Ray had told a few who asked that he had lived for just over three hundred thousand years, long enough to see humanity spread over six galaxies, including the Milky Way and its smaller satellite galaxies and now working into the Andromeda Galaxy and all its satel-lite galaxies.

But he was far older than even that.

He hoped to live long enough to see many more galaxies seeded as well, but he had no idea how long he would live. As far as he knew, barring accidents, Seeders could live forever, their bodies constantly renewing. Only boredom or accidents or violence cost Seeders their lives. That's why the mission of continuing to spread humanity from one galaxy to another was so important.

It kept them all sane. And challenged.

From what he understood, there were over fifty thousand major Seeder ships like his, mostly all working in the Andromeda Galaxy on the front lines of the Seeding. There were many, many other Seeders embedded in cultures without ship support working to help newborn human civilizations grow into stable cultures.

Seeders not only planted the human race, but spent centuries with each culture guiding each planet to maturity.

And not only could Seeders live a long time, but many had teleportation

powers over short interstellar distances. It helped those without ships to get around between systems.

He had been embedded in cultures for many, many thousands of years, more than he could ever begin to remember, before taking command of his own ship. Now here, in this galaxy, his ship was one of the trouble-shooting ships who jumped around to where they were needed. He had no more desire to work the frontline of the Seeders. His interests lay with helping the cultures that the front line seeded grow.

Right now, he and his ship were back in the Larger Magellanic Cloud Galaxy, a very long way from the Andromeda Galaxy and all its many satellite galaxies.

There was a problem here.

This Milky Way satellite galaxy had been seeded for a hundred thousand years now and had a stable and growing interstellar culture from which many had been recruited to become Seeders and help out in the Andromeda seeding.

The problem hadn't started here, but right now the problem was here and that's also why he was back across so much space.

Finally, a scientist to his left said, "Now."

As he had expected, a huge ship, thousands and thousands of times larger than his ship, almost unimaginable in size, dropped out of Trans-Tunnel flight, but didn't slow in the slightest as it flashed near the Parson's system near the outer edge of the Larger Magellanic Cloud Galaxy.

The ship was a perfectly proportioned winged ship, shaped like a glider, yet Ray could never imagine it entering any atmosphere since it was larger than most moons. It was normal older-Seeder-ship design, with a command bump near the front and the top of the pointed nose.

It was gray, without a mark or viewpoint or access port on it that anyone on his ship could find. It was as if the surface of the thing was one piece.

There didn't seem to be any engines or thruster ports or anything. Everything on the inside of that ship was hidden.

The huge ship was moving at an impossible real-space speed of over

ninety-eight percent the speed of light.

If it followed its pattern as it had the numbers of times before, Ray knew it would remain in real space for two weeks real time, not ship time, and then jump back into trans-tunnel drive. It would appear again a hundred light years away, remain in real space for two real-time weeks again, then jump again.

Due to time and relativity problems, ship time on that ship was only about two days before it jumped. That was a problem with anything traveling that fast outside a trans-tunnel flight.

The ship had followed the exact same pattern since it was first discovered entering the Larger Magellanic Cloud Galaxy. He had watched it now for weeks.

Luckily, there had been no inhabited planets or systems in its way. It had plowed through a number of red dwarf systems, simply knocking anything aside that got it in its way with force screens of immense power.

Even a collision with a large moon had simply shattered the moon and hadn't even seemed to slow down or alter the big ship's course. That horrified him more than he wanted to let on and he felt responsible.

He knew it should be slowing. It wasn't.

Something was clearly wrong on that big ship and he had to figure out a way to stop it.

Beside him Tacita shook her head. She was feeling the same about this big ship as he was. They had to stop it.

Tacita had been at his side now for more years than he wanted to think about. They were partners in every sense of the word. It seems like they always had been.

She had long black hair that she always wore down and loose and dark black eyes that seemed to see everything.

She was also the smartest human on this ship by far. How she put up with him, he never understood and always questioned.

He could never imagine not having her with him, as his partner in life.

"Has it shifted course at all?" Ray asked, hoping something was changing as he stared at the huge ship on the screen in front of him.

The more his crew and others studied the ship, the more they all became convinced it was Seeder built, but long before any of their time with the Seeders.

He knew it was.

Many wondered if this ship might be from the original Seeders.

That possibility had many on this ship and other ships excited.

He and Tacita kept their silence. At this point they needed to.

"It has not shifted course," Tacita said, her voice clearly not happy with that. "Something is very wrong."

Ray could feel the knot in his stomach tighten even more.

The giant ship was on course for the Milky Way. And in a very short time it would plow through some of the most inhabited systems in the Milky Way Galaxy.

That was assuming it did not alter course, or if he couldn't find a way to alter its course or stop it.

Considering the shields that big ship had, the only way to alter that ship's course was to get inside of it. And at the speed it was going, with the shields it had, he had no idea how to do that.

None.

This was not supposed to be this way.

And none of his smartest scientists seemed to know what to do either.

Standing on the outside looking in was not something he liked or often did.

"Everyone have all the records you need?" he asked, turning to Tacita and the other scientists sitting at stations behind him.

Tacita nodded without looking up at him. He knew that she was scared to death of what the big ship would do when it reached the Milky Way Galaxy, the damage it would cause without ever meaning to.

"We have everything we need," Tacita said, again not looking up, but instead scanning the data on the screens in front of her station.

"Make sure we have two ships taking readings of that ship every time it appears and have them forward that data to us."

He hoped the big ship would start braking, but it should have before now if it was going to avoid disaster ahead.

"They are confirmed and will comply," Tacita said.

Ray nodded and stepped up and sat in his large chair, double-checking all the readings. Then with a glance at Tacita to his right, he said, "Get us to the Milky Way, on the predicted path ahead of this ship."

"Trans-tunnel jump in twenty seconds," Tacita said.

Staring at that big ship one more time, he said, "We got to go find some help. And maybe warn a few billion people to get out of the way."

This entire situation made him sick to his stomach.

"We have candidates that should be able to help," Tacita said.

He nodded.

Then as if he needed just one more look to really make his nightmares even more real, he kept staring at the huge glider-shaped ship until his ship jumped to trans-tunnel flight.

It would take them two days to cross the distance to the Milky Way. It would take the big ship six months.

Six very short months.

Before then they had better have some answers and some help, or billions of humans were going to die.

He was a Seeder. His job was to help start new human life and protect it and nurture it where he could.

There was just no way he was going to let a runaway ship destroy entire civilizations he had helped build.

One

CHAIRMAN MARIA BOONE sat in her office, a dozen images of galaxies and possible paths through them marked in different colors floated in the air around her.

She had a cup of fresh green tea on her wood desk and the remains of a lunch consisting of fried chicken and fries shoved to one side, half eaten. The smell of chicken still filled the space, fighting with the smell of freshly brewing tea.

Beside the desk and comfortable desk chair that molded around her back and gave her perfect support, the other furniture in the room consisted of two chairs so people could sit facing her desk, a soft couch with a quilt tossed up over the back, and a coffee table in front of the couch.

The chairs and the coffee table were covered in data pads and the walls of the office were completely covered with two-dimensional maps of certain areas of space.

Today, she had her long red hair loose down her back and a pink tee-shirt on with the saying, "Don't Mess With the Red Head" on the front below a very large gun. She had a sports bra under the t-shirt and nylon shorts. At some point she planned on doing some exercise in the ship's big gym.

At least when she exercised, her freckles seemed to fade a little.

She was from a cold planet originally, where her light skin, golden eyes, and red hair had become almost the norm.

She hadn't been back there in a couple of centuries, but she kept thinking it might be fun, after all this time, to see how her world was progressing.

But at the moment, she was a couple galaxies away from her home world in the Lesser Magellanic Cloud. For over five years now, she and her crew and her ship had been backtracking the Seeders' route through what was called the Local Group of galaxies.

Over thirty galaxies were in the Local Group, including the three huge ones; the Milky Way Galaxy, the Andromeda Galaxy, and the Triangulum Spiral Galaxy. Over thirty satellite galaxies were gravitationally connected to one of the big three galaxies and the entire Local Group seemed to hold together as well.

Her goal was to find out if the Seeders had come into the Local Group or originated in it at some point in the distant past. That discovery would be worth a fortune to everyone on board. She was known as the top authority on Seeder history, which was why she had been able to organize this business and ship.

Everyone on board was a Seeder, but not one of them had started out that way. She sure hadn't. All six hundred souls on her ship had been recruited to the cause of spreading humanity through all of space at one point or another.

Of course, when someone joined on, they also got the gift of long life and health and a few other great gifts that came in handy at times. She was over four hundred years old now and still looked thirty, if that. Her long red hair still shined and the freckles that covered her face and shoulders never seemed to go away no matter what she did.

She kept wondering why Seeders could start millions of worlds with humans on them, solve the aging and sickness problem, and yet not find a solution for freckles.

All the information she and her crew had gathered in the last few months had seemed to conflict. Some data seemed to suggest that the Seeders had just come into the Local Sector, other data seemed to point to a single home planet where everything started out near the edge of the Local Group.

The problem was that the human planets in these smaller edge galaxies were all very mature and had little or no interest in Seeder history. She got help from them, but not much.

Now her ship was between galaxies, moving farther away from the Milky Way toward the edge of the Local Group. There was a small cluster of about a million stars there that might hold clues.

She was about to call it an afternoon in frustration when Dannie from Communications paged her.

She clicked off the images of the floating galaxies and said, "Yes."

"Chairman, I have a message from Chairman Wade Ray marked critical and for your eyes only."

"Thanks, Dannie," Maria said. "Put it through."

Maria brought the message up on her screen floating in the air in front of her before she even gave herself a moment to worry. She had no idea why Chairman Wade Ray would contact her. If the Seeders had an operating council, which they really did not, he would be the head of it. One of the most powerful of all the Seeders. And one of the oldest humans she knew about.

She couldn't imagine why he would even take notice of her.

The image came up and she could see the famous Chairman Ray smiling at her, but the smile didn't reach his eyes. His classic long, gray hair flowed down over his shirt and he looked thin and young, just as all Seeders did, even with the gray hair.

"Chairman Boone, I am sorry to have to pull you from your mission," he said. "But we have a situation developing in the Milky Way that needs your expertise."

She wished like hell this was an actual conversation so she could ask questions, but alas, it wasn't.

An image of a Seeder ship came up on the screen. It looked old, as some of the early Seeder ships she had studied. And there was something else wrong about the image.

Ray's voice came over the image. "Please note the small dot against the lower right portion of the right wing of this ship."

She leaned forward, staring at what looked like a dot against the hull of the old ship.

Then the image started to zoom in and it took her mind a moment to realize just what she was seeing. That just wasn't possible.

"That dot is my ship, one of the largest ships we have at this time, in comparison to the large ship behind it," Ray said, confirming what she knew couldn't be possible. Space allowed for the building of huge ships, but that huge ship could hold an entire planet's population and have room left over, it was so big.

"The big ship seems to be out of control and it has extremely powerful screens," Ray said. "It will plow through many inhabited planets in the Milky Way,

killing billions, if it can't be stopped."

Ray's face appeared again. "I have sent all the data we have gathered about this ship and its path. We are going to try to board the ship to gain control of it, since we fear it is a ghost ship. We need your expertise on this coming mission."

Then Chairman Wade Ray nodded. "Please help us. Billions of lives are at stake."

At that the message ended.

She sat and listened to it one more time, then did a quick glance at all the data. Maybe, just maybe, she didn't have to backtrack any more to find the path of the original Seeders. Maybe the knowledge had come to them.

She had Dannie send back a short message to Chairman Ray. "Message received. We are on the way."

Then she paged her five senior staff and told them to meet her in the Command Center. At top trans-tunnel speed it would take them almost two weeks to reach The Milky Way and the location where Chairman Ray had asked for them to go.

In that two weeks they had a lot of planning to go.

And research, since that ship's path might point back to the solution they have been looking for on this entire mission as to where the Seeders started from.

But first she wanted to have her senior staff all see the message from Chairman Ray at the same time. She wanted to see their reactions.

And then eventually everyone on board would see the message and data as well. After all, they were all in this together.

But with so many lives at stake, she couldn't imagine a single member of her crew having an issue with returning to the Milky Way and trying to help.

They were all Seeders, after all. Starting, protecting, and nurturing human life was their job.

Two

ROSCOE MUNDY brushed the long brown hair from off his face and looked around, stunned at what he saw. He was alone and he stood in the center of the huge main room of an old lodge.

He had been in some pretty impressive structures over the last few hundred years, especially the last twenty years working implanted as an enforcer with Sector Justice in the third sector of the Milky Way Galaxy, but this building was close to the top in impressiveness of pure comfort of all the places he had seen.

He dropped his small leather pack on the wooden plank floor and took a deep breath of the clean air.

He had on a long-sleeved black shirt with a black leather vest over the top of it and the sleeves rolled up. He had on cowboy boots and jeans and a wide, black-leather belt. The belt buckle was two pistols crossed like swords.

He stood in one place in the big room, just looking around, trying to take in the details.

The walls, posts, and beams were peeled and polished logs that had to be ten feet around in places. A giant, smooth-rock fireplace filled one side of the immense room, a natural crackling fire going in it, giving the room a wonderful, wood-smoke smell.

What looked like a check-in desk, all made out of polished wood, filled the right side of the room near a grand, wood staircase that wound up to a floor above.

To the right of where he had transported in were brown cloth couches and chairs, all facing the huge fireplace and looking very comfortable and deep, with quilts tossed over the backs of a few of them.

He could see pine trees outside the huge windows in a neighboring dining room area that had a good twenty tables with four chairs each. None of the tables were set.

This lodge was very high up in some coastal mountains on a planet that had had a major accident. A stray electromagnetic pulse from a distant nova had wiped out all but a few million of its population. That disaster had happened just over three hundred years before, just after he joined the Seeders and came to the Milky Way to help out.

The population of the planet was recovering nicely, especially in such a short time. In fact, they were almost back into space. They did not know anything about the huge galaxy-wide society of humans growing beyond their system, but eventually they would and join in.

Clearly, this lodge was from the period before the accident, and had been amazingly preserved by someone.

But this planet seemed to be jinxed in more ways than just a freak electromagnetic pulse storm. Now this planet was in a direct line of a speeding monster ghost ship that would destroy it as if nothing were there.

He had been recruited by Chairman Wade Ray to help stop the ghost ship. That's why he was here.

He picked up his leather overnight bag and moved over to one of the big, overstuffed chairs near the left side of the fireplace. He dropped into the chair, enjoying how it felt completely comfortable and natural.

He leaned back and just stared up at the ceiling and the large, wooden logs over his head.

"Amazing, isn't it?" a man said as he came down the staircase.

"Completely," Roscoe said, looking over at the man.

Roscoe had a sudden moment of surprise looking at the smiling, thin guy who looked like a scientist in a brown, pullover sweater and cloth pants and loafers. They guy even wore glasses, even though no Seeder he had ever met needed them.

All Seeder health was perfect. A benefit of the job.

Roscoe couldn't remember the guy's name, but they had met once before about a hundred years ago, trying to stop a war in the first sector. Roscoe hadn't realized the guy was a Seeder at the time.

"Nice seeing you again, Mr. Mundy," the guy said, extending his hand as he got close. "My name is Vardis Fisher. Everyone just calls me Fisher."

Roscoe stood and shook his head. "Just call me Roscoe. Didn't know you were a part of all this when we were back in Sector One."

"I didn't know you were either," Fisher said, smiling and dropping into a chair across from Roscoe. "Maybe they should put bells on us or something."

"Name tags," Roscoe said, smiling. "Never was good with names and after a couple of centuries, that's gotten worse."

Fisher laughed and indicated the big lodge around them. "Like the old place?"

"I sure do," Roscoe said. "All yours?"

"My wife and I sort of met here about three hundred years ago," Fisher said. "This lodge saved her and we were recruited by the Seeders at that point to help out. We've kept the lodge as our home and base ever since."

"Nice," Roscoe said. He had thought of finding a home base at some point, but so far it just hadn't come up since he moved around so much. The longest he had stayed in any one place was with Sector Justice, and he knew that was almost over as well, since he couldn't explain not aging.

But a big lodge like this one with extreme privacy was certainly something he could enjoy. Someday he would find a permanent home.

At that moment, Chairman Wade Ray, his wife Tacita, and two other women materialized in the open area in the center of the room.

Every time Roscoe saw Wade Ray, he was impressed and stunned. Ray was extremely old and powerful among the Seeders. Roscoe had no idea how old he really was and had never had the chance to actually ask. He didn't look old except for the long, gray hair that hung down over his expensive silk shirt.

Both of the other women were stunningly good looking. One had dark, short hair and the other long red hair. The darkhaired one went over and kissed Fisher, so that had to be his wife, Callie.

The redhead just stood there wearing a t-shirt that left little to the imagination and tight jeans and running shoes. Clearly the woman was in amazing shape and her face and neck and arms were covered in freckles that made her look cute and very alluring.

And she had large golden eyes that were amazing. So far they hadn't looked at him, as she was too busy looking around at the lodge. He felt lucky because if she did look at him, he wasn't sure he would be able to turn away.

He hadn't felt that attracted to someone else in a long, long time. He would have to be very careful around her because all he really wanted to do was play connect the dots with his tongue on those freckles.

He forced himself to take a deep breath, clear that thought, and turn his attention to Chairman Ray and his blackhaired wife Tacita. She had done a quick look of the lodge and nodded, then moved over to the couch and sat down, saying nothing.

Roscoe knew her reputation as being cold and brilliant. It was rumored that she and Chairman Ray had been a team for over a hundred thousand years. He couldn't imagine being with one woman for that long. He couldn't imagine living that long, actually. In fact, that number just sort of numbed him, it was so large.

As they all got seated, Roscoe kept his attention on Chairman Ray, but noticed out of the corner of his eye that the redheaded woman had now noticed him and was staring at him. He didn't dare let himself look at her.

He wanted to, but he didn't dare.

"This is our command team," Chairman Ray said. "Welcome. You've all been briefed on what we face, so first let me do some introductions and reasons why I have asked you to be part of this."

He turned to Fisher. "Chairman Vardis Fisher and his partner and wife, Callie Sheridan. Both of them are more educated than most anyone you will ever meet. They will run the science part of this mission, from mathematics to the social sciences. We have no idea what we might find when we get inside that ship, so we need to be ready for anything and they have two of the most diverse and nimble minds I have had the pleasure to meet."

Both Fisher and Callie nodded to that, clearly slightly embarrassed.

Chairman Ray went on. "Their ship and two other scientific ships will be support and they will lead the scientists."

Then Chairman Ray turned to the redhead. "This is Chairman Maria Boone."

Roscoe looked at her, but she had her golden eyes focused on Chairman Ray.

"Chairman Boone is the leading authority on the history of the original Seeders," Ray said, "and she and her ship cut a tracking research trip short and returned from the edge of the Local Group boundary to help. Since that old ship is an ancient Seeders' ship, we're going to need her entire crew of experts to unravel what we find."

Then Chairman Ray turned to Roscoe. "This is Roscoe Mundy who doesn't know it yet, but has become Chairman Mundy of a ship called *The Huntington*. It has just reached orbit above us."

Roscoe managed to not jerk from surprise, but instead nodded a thank-you to Chairman Ray.

Roscoe had had no intention of becoming a Chairman of his own ship this soon. In a few hundred years of more experience, maybe, but not yet. But it seemed he was being given a gift for the moment. He just hoped he was up for the task.

"The Huntington is the heaviest-armed Seeder ship ever built. It was recently finished and stored in the First Sector, waiting for a moment when it would be needed. So Chairman Mundy will be in charge of all military and security forces we might need going into that large ship. He is one of the clearest-thinking military brains we have."

Roscoe nodded to that. He had been briefed on that part of the mission, just not being a Chairman of his own ship. Nor had he expected the compliments coming from Chairman Ray.

"Four other Seeder military ships will be joining us from the Andromeda Galaxy," Ray said, "as soon as they can get here, which will be in about two weeks."

Roscoe nodded, suddenly totally overwhelmed. He had no doubt he was going to have to recruit a few mortals from Sector Justice into the Seeders, with permission, of course, to help on his ship. He had no idea how to do any of that.

Seeders Justice was a fairly new policing organization that had formed in the Milky Way Galaxy. It had a lot of great people in it, experienced people he could trust.

Chairman Ray then patted the leg of his wife. "Tacita and I will be in overall command of this mission. You all will report to me or Tacita."

All four of them nodded.

Nodding right now was about all Roscoe could do. Mostly he kept his focus on the patterned carpet in front of his chair.

"We're going to have to work together if we're going to save billions of lives," Ray said. "The big ship will hit the edge of the Milky Way Galaxy in five months. It will destroy this planet in six months and ten days if we can't stop it or alter its course."

"We have a very real ticking clock," Fisher said.

"Very real," Chairman Ray said, his voice soft.

No one said a word as the fire in the big stone fireplace crackled.

Three

MARIA BOONE had almost melted in her chair when she stopped looking at the incredible lodge they were in and noticed Roscoe Mundy. She had never had a reaction to a man like that before and luckily she had had a few minutes to recover as Chairman Ray introduced them all and outlined their mission.

And watching Mundy get surprised with his own command of a ship was amazing. He actually managed to stay calm, but she could tell from how he shifted twice when Ray wasn't watching, he was trying his best to gather himself.

He was cool and very smooth and stunningly handsome. Wow. Who knew she would be attracted to the military type. His long brown hair sure didn't make him look military.

Finally, it was Chairman Fisher who broke the silence after Ray's announcement of how little time they had.

"Any ideas how we are going to get inside that thing?" Fisher asked.

Maria pulled her gaze from Roscoe, who was still managing to look at the floor in front of him as he gathered himself.

"We have a few ideas," she said, "from plans of other older Seeder ships that have come down through the centuries. But we'll have to work with you to confirm our theories. And from what we can tell from the readings of the shield, teleporting inside isn't an option."

"We have come to the same conclusion," Ray said.

"I am one hundred percent convinced," Callie said, "that this is an old Seeder ship. But in all the records we have ever seen, there has been no real mention of building something this large. So this might be very old, or very new."

Ray nodded to her that she should go on. And Tacita looked up and focused her intense gaze on Maria.

"New?" Roscoe asked, now clearly recovered.

She looked at him and somehow managed to not just stare into those deep, dark eyes. He held her gaze, but he seemed as surprised as she was with the tension between them.

And the attraction.

"It's a possibility," she said, nodding, then pulling her gaze from Roscoe back to Ray and Tacita. "I'm not convinced that early Seeders had this kind of capability. I don't think we do now unless there is something I don't know."

Ray just nodded.

Maria went on. "If the Seeders originated outside the Local Group of galaxies as many think, then their civilization now would be very old and capable of this kind of technology. And might still be using this older design."

Again, Ray and Tacita just nodded.

"It seems there is a second problem in boarding the big ship," Roscoe said. "It's traveling faster than anything I know of when it drops out of trans-tunnel drive."

"With some modifications by my chief engineer, my personal jump ship can match that speed exactly," Fisher said. "My jump ship is small, and can only hold about twenty comfortably, but it can match the speed without a problem."

Maria watched as Roscoe nodded.

"I would like to attempt the first boarding in three weeks," Chairman Ray said.

He then turned to Fisher and Callie. "Thank you for the kind offer of the use of your wonderful lodge as we prepare."

"Feel free to come and go," Callie said.

"We have stocked the kitchen at the bottom of the stairs," Fisher said. "Help yourself."

Maria loved the idea of spending the next weeks coming and going from this lodge. That sounded heavenly after the year she had just spent on board her ship.

Chairman Ray and Tacita stood, forcing all of them to their feet out of respect.

"We meet back here tomorrow for breakfast at 8 a.m. planet time," Ray said. "That is sixteen hours from now exactly."

Maria nodded, as did everyone else.

"Keep your ships shielded and cloaked," he said. "The locals on this planet will detect it otherwise."

Then Ray turned to Roscoe. "Chairman Mundy, come with me and I'll give you a tour of your new command."

With a quick nod, Roscoe smiled at her and then the three of them vanished.

That smile almost took her breath away. Wow, he was something.

Maria turned to Fisher and Callie. "Thank you for your hospitality. I'll see you tomorrow morning."

"You are more than welcome," Callie said. "This is our home we're trying to save so glad this is being taken so seriously."

Maria nodded. "We'll save it."

With that she transported back to her ship, hoping that they actually could.

And hoping beyond hope that she could find time with Chairman Mundy. Private time.

Four

ROSCOE FINISHED THE quick tour of his ship in the Command Center of *The Huntington.* The big Command Center felt at home to him instantly and scared him to death at the same time.

The ship was huge and had firepower that could take down an entire planet if it needed to. Roscoe hoped it would never come to that.

Ever.

But from what he had seen of the big ship coming into the galaxy, nothing *The Huntington* had in firepower would even dent it.

The ship already had a full engineering crew and some basic officers who had gotten it here, but they were not as trained as he would like.

"I have dinner to eat, and you have some core crew in the mess," Ray said, smiling, after he gave him the quick rundown of the Command Center. "They all will head certain areas of your ship and one is your second-in-command. Might want to go meet them to help you get started."

Then smiling, Ray vanished, leaving Roscoe stunned at not only being in charge of such an amazing warship, but that he already had some command crew. He knew the ship needed a basic crew of a hundred to just limp along, which it had now, mostly in engineering and communications, but three hundred would be better.

He had a couple of weeks to get that many in place and no idea how to do that. Now it sounded like he had some help.

He took a deep breath and looked around at the three-level Command Center. His station was in the center of the second level. One entire wall was a giant screen in front of his station. It didn't feel right to go sit in the chair just yet. Maybe tomorrow.

So instead, he took a deep breath and transported to the mess.

Four people were sitting there on the far side of the huge room, around a table near the kitchen door. They were all eating and laughing. Two were men, two women.

The place smelled wonderfully of hamburgers and fries. And they all seemed to have milkshakes in front of them. Clearly the ship had some kitchen crew already. One more detail to not worry about.

Roscoe's stomach rumbled, making him realize he needed to try to eat as well.

He started through the sea of empty tables toward the group of four when he suddenly realized he knew one of them. He would know that shaved head and long nose anywhere.

Jonas Craig, his second-in-command at Sector Justice, the police force that watched over different parts of the Milky Way, sector by sector. Sector Justice knew nothing about Seeders being in their midst. They still believed that all Seeders had done their work and just moved on. Which was mostly true, but not completely.

Jonas was one of the best fighters Sector Justice had and could kill a man with a single finger. They had worked together now for ten years and Roscoe had trusted him with his life. How was that possible that Jonas was a Seeder as well?

"Jonas, you're kidding me, right?" Roscoe said as he moved toward them.

Jonas turned from the others, staring and clearly stunned, his mouth open showing a half-chewed hamburger. Then Jonas blinked twice and closed his mouth.

So Jonas hadn't known Roscoe was a Seeder either. Amazing.

The other three turned and Roscoe recognized them all, even though he didn't know their names. All were from different branches of the Sector Justice force.

It seemed the Seeders were in just about everything when it came to keeping the peace and making sure human populations they had planted progressed in a peaceful way.

Jonas finally gathered himself enough to finish chewing, stand and face Roscoe. "Damn, I'm glad to see you," he said, smiling.

"Not half as much as I am to see you," Roscoe said, smiling. "I didn't know you were a Seeder."

Jonas laughed. "I didn't know the same about you. Go figure."

They both laughed.

The others stood to greet him and with that, Jonas turned to introduce him to the other three. And he started with "Folks, this is Chairman Mundy."

And that once again just shocked Roscoe more than he wanted to admit.

Five

BY THE TIME she finished a quick dinner in her office, alone, Maria managed to somehow get her mind away from Roscoe Mundy and back on the task at hand.

The guy was amazing and she couldn't believe a military type had caught her attention like that.

Yet she so wanted to just get to know him, and maybe a few other things with that incredible body of his as well. It had been far too long since she had a man in her life. She didn't want to think about exactly how long.

Using three-dimensional images projected into the air in her office, she had the big ship's course in a dotted line as it headed for the Milky Way.

In the research on the ship on the way back to the Milky Way, what she noticed about that dotted line was that on short distances, it seemed straight, but over much, much larger distances, it had a very, very slight continuous curve that could be projected backwards.

Every day the course shifted in a slight amount that over hundreds and hundreds of years mounted up to about one percent.

So shrinking down the known area of space to galaxies being nothing more than points in the air in her office, she extended the past course of the big ship.

It would take, at the ship's speed, about three million years for the ship to make a complete circle return to where it started.

Her only problem was that she wasn't sure how long the ship had been going. Any point on the circle could have been its launch point.

So starting with a hundred years ago, she had her computer show her the path of the ship through space.

It didn't come close to any galaxy or even small star cluster at that point, allowing for the speed and direction of the galaxies movements.

She repeated the same over and over and over, taking her time to make sure she didn't miss any detail.

It seemed to always go between star clusters and galaxies as if the course had been carefully planned to have nothing run into the big ship.

It became clear as she went that the big ship's encounter with the two galaxies so far in the Local Group was almost a fluke.

Or planned, one or the other.

She was starting to bet on planned.

In sixty thousand years, the big ship hadn't come close to any group of stars or galaxies at all.

Nothing.

It had traveled in the big expanse between galaxies, missing everything as it went.

That just seemed wrong and almost impossible, so maybe at some point the big ship had changed course. She couldn't imagine the scale she was looking at, yet she knew that the Seeders had been in the Local Group galaxies for about five hundred thousand years that it took to do the twelve small galaxies and the Milky Way.

It had taken the Seeders an amazingly short period of only fifty thousand years to do most of the seeding in the Milky Way. But at around fifty thousand years per large galaxy, and over thirty galaxies in the Local Group, it was going to take over a million years to work through them all and head on outside the Local Group.

No way her brain could grasp living that long, but she assumed it was possible. She just couldn't imagine it.

She had heard that some of the Seeders working the frontlines of the Seeding were older than Chairman Ray if that was possible.

Seeding entire galaxies was such an immense project, she just couldn't grasp it all, even though she was a Seeder and understood every step in the process. Her perspective was still on hundreds of years, which felt stunningly long. A thousand years seemed impossible, and three hundred thousand just wasn't possible to understand, just like the distances of space she was staring at.

So she kept going, trying to change her perspective on time. She tried to make herself believe she understood the scale of space just fine. Time, on the other hand, was difficult for her to grasp.

At eight hundred thousand years back, the big ship was finally in a position to brush past the side of a small satellite galaxy of a larger cloud of galaxies.

But it was only a brush and the ship would have had no reason to leave that galaxy in the direction it had started. So she was pretty sure that wasn't its starting point.

At one million, four hundred thousand years, she finally found what she thought might make sense. The ship went through the edge of a smaller satellite galaxy coming from solidly inside an even larger spiral galaxy.

The ship had completed just under one half of its circle managing to miss everything along the way.

She had the Local Group including the Milky Way galaxy floating on one side of her office in very tiny scale, then she put up this large spiral galaxy in another corner in small scale as well.

Then she had her computer put up all the galaxy formations between the two. Then she asked the computer to show the closest path from the one spiral galaxy to the Local Group and the Milky Way.

She sat back, stunned. There were six major galaxy clusters that consisted of about thirty-five galaxies that formed almost a clear pathway like rocks crossing a pond between the two. Of course there were a lot of other galaxies along the way, but that was the closest route jumping like the leading edge of Seeders expansion did.

The line of the big ship went out and circled back to cross that path here in the Milky Way.

Could that have been the trail the Seeders used? If so, there were billions and billions and billions of Earth-like planets seeded with humans in those galaxies.

Was this big ship sent fourteen hundred thousand years ago as a message through time to the leading edge of the expansion?

And if so, why?

And why wasn't it stopping.

Clearly, if it was meant to come here, something had gone wrong in its braking plans after all those years.

But nothing about any of this made any sense at all.

She recorded everything and then glanced at the time. She only had seven hours before she needed to be on the planet below for a meeting.

She needed to show all of them the data. It might not be right, but if it was, they needed to approach this ship very, very differently than they would approach a ghost ship.

But one thing she was sure of. This Seeder ship was at least one-point-four million years old.

At least.

But from a very, very advanced Seeder culture.

Six

ROSCOE COULDN'T BELIEVE how good a cook Fisher was, and how stunningly beautiful Maria looked in the morning.

He was sitting across from her and eating breakfast in the wonderful café that seemed to fill the basement of the old lodge.

The café had been perfectly preserved over the years and had two u-shaped counters that stuck out into the room with thirty or so bar stools with cloth seats along the counters. The person waiting on them, in this case, Fisher, walked down the center of the counters.

The room had low log ceilings and huge windows that looked out into a vast forest of very old pine trees. The sun was sending rays of light down into the dense underbrush and forest floor that slanted away from the lodge.

Since the end of the counter was curved, all six of them could see each other fine. Ray and Tacita sat on the two chairs at the end of the counter. Roscoe and Fisher on one side, when Fisher stopped serving and sat down.

Maria sat across from Roscoe near Callie, clearly enjoying her eggs and ham as much as he was. She had smiled at him when they arrived and said hello, but nothing else.

Luckily she hadn't said much else. He would have had a hard time talking, since she affected him so much. He really needed to get past that problem if they all were going to work together.

There was an amazing attraction between them, and if they weren't trying to save a few billion lives, he might be trying to get close to her right now. If they did save these planets, there would be time. They were both Seeders, they had lots of time.

But that didn't mean he didn't want to get to know her better. Much, much better.

He had spent most of the time since their last meeting with his start-up crew, working to figure out his new ship and build plans on recruiting.

Since they were all from the Sector Force that consisted mostly of trained fighters that guarded the Milky Way sector by sector, they all felt comfortable recruiting top staff from that. But they would not take so many as to leave Sector Justice depleted.

Some of the most advanced cultures in the first sector, meaning the first sector of the Milky Way seeded, had some top militaries as well. That would be good recruiting grounds as well.

They might not have *The Huntington* fully staffed in three weeks, but they would be able to fly and fight if they had to.

So after only six hours of uneasy sleep in his new command cabin, which was huge and had no personal touches at all yet, he had managed to be on time to the meeting with Chairman Ray and the others.

Roscoe was almost done eating the fantastic eggs, soft toast, and melt-in-his mouth ham when Maria pushed her plate away and turned slightly to face Chairman Ray, who we also just finishing.

"I have something I think we all need to talk about."

Roscoe loved the sound of her voice. It was firm and solid and slightly deeper than he would have expected coming from someone only about five-four and with so many freckles.

"Start us off, Chairman Boone," Ray said, nodding.

Maria set up a small device on the counter in front of her and Fisher, who was standing inside the u-shape of the counter eating, quickly moved to take her plate and dirty silverware.

She touched the top of the device. In the air over the counter between them and the kitchen, an image of the Local Group of galaxies appeared. Roscoe recognized it at once and even knew where in the spiral arms of the Milky Way they were now located and the area of his home world in a small satellite galaxy near to, and almost touching, the Milky Way.

At times he had trouble grasping the size and scale of the entire Milky Way, but he was slowly, over the last centuries, coming to realize how impressive the Seeders were. And how lucky he had been to be recruited into their ranks.

"There are theories that are pretty solid that the leading edge of the Seeders entered the Local Group of galaxies here," Maria said.

She had one of the small cloud galaxies in the group near one side brighten.

Roscoe nodded to himself. That was the theory he had heard as well.

"That was about five hundred thousand years ago," Maria said.

Roscoe noticed that both Ray and Tacita nodded, but said nothing.

Maria went on. "If we follow the pattern of Seeders, we tend to jump as we move forward to the closest next galaxy or star cluster and then move on, like we are doing now into Andromeda and its satellite galaxies, leaving behind many of us to help and protect and guide the forming seeded civilizations."

Everyone again nodded. All basic stuff that Roscoe understood. Clearly Maria was trying to put down a foundation of what she was going to say.

"It takes around fifty thousand years to just do the initial seeding of each normal galaxy, give or take depending on size and numbers of suitable planets."

Roscoe knew that as well, but always had a hard time imagining covering an entire galaxy such as the Milky Way in only fifty thousand years.

"So I extended out the pattern outside the Local Cluster," Maria said, "going from closest to closest galaxy and this is what I got over a one-point-eight million year period of time, assuming the pace of Seeding remained about the same as it has through the Local Group."

The scale of the image of Local Group floating in the air in the diner came down slightly as other galaxies and galaxy groups were added like steps ending in a large spiral galaxy that looked a lot like the Milky Way and Andromeda.

Roscoe had no idea how far that was away and he didn't want to ask. Even if someone said the number, he wouldn't be able to grasp what it meant. He just knew it was a very, very long distance, but yet that galaxy was in the relative neighborhood of the Milky Way in comparison to the entire universe.

Still, the number of years she was talking about just stunned him. Did he really belong to an organization that started almost two million years before?

Chairman Ray was nodding, so Maria went on.

"This is the track of the big ship."

She put a dotted yellow line showing the track of the big ship entering the local cluster.

"The ship is actually turning slightly, but at such a small amount that it takes just at one thousand years to make a one degree shift in course."

"It's turning?" Fisher asked, clearly as surprised as Roscoe felt.

"Not enough to be noticeable over a year, but over one hundred years, yes."

Roscoe looked over at Chairman Ray and Tacita, but both just sat listening.

Roscoe had no idea how far that was away and he didn't want to ask.

"So if we extend out the line the ship is traveling on," Maria said, "we get this. Again, note, in one-point-four million years, the big ship comes near no other galaxy or star cluster until it hit the Local Group here. That had to be planned."

Again the scale of all the galaxies came down as the dotted yellow line went out near the edge of the room, slowly turning until it ran smack into the middle of the big spiral galaxy that in theory the Seeders had come from.

"That's one-point-four million years of travel for the ship," Maria said. "One-point-eight million years ago, the Seeders started on this seeding path, which would be sure to lead to the Local Group and the Milky Way if they continued onward."

Everyone was silent. Roscoe just stared at what she was showing them.

Then Ray spoke softly. "So about one-point-four million years ago, from that galaxy, they launched this big ship to intercept the leading edge of their seeding."

Roscoe didn't know what to think. He was having a difficult time grasping time and the scale of distance.

But he did have one question he needed to ask. "With the time deletion that ship is experiencing, we know from an outside take, it took one-point-four million years if it was launched from there."

He pointed to the spiral galaxy that intersected the path of the big ship.

Maria nodded and Roscoe could see both Fisher and Callie's eyes get big as they caught his question ahead.

"If someone, or a group of people are inside that ship," Roscoe asked, "how old would they be?"

Ray just stared at him, as did those wonderful golden eyes of Maria.

Finally Fisher answered his question. "About two hundred thousand years old, give or take."

"Younger than we are," Tacita said bluntly.

Roscoe just couldn't imagine that, so he pushed the idea of even trying to imagine it out of his mind.

"But why would anyone undertake such a journey?" Callie asked, "assuming there is anyone alive in there and it's not just a robot ship."

That question just hung there in the air along with all the small images of vast galaxies and a dotted line of an impossible journey.

"My question exactly," Maria said. "At our full trans-tunnel speed, going directly from that galaxy to this one would take about nine hundred years is all. So doing this makes no sense."

Roscoe had nothing more to ask or even say. His mind was overwhelmed.

Across from him, Maria sat down and clicked off her device and the galaxies floating in the air vanished.

Ray looked around at everyone, then nodded to Maria. "Great job, Chairman Boone."

Maria nodded, but didn't smile. Roscoe had a hunch his question just tossed in another dimension to the reality of her specialty of tracing back the Seeder's path.

Ray looked at his wife and then at Fisher. "Thank you for the wonderful breakfast. May we impose on you again tomorrow at the same time?"

"Of course," Fisher said nodding.

"He loves cooking almost more than anything else," Callie said.

"Good," Ray said. "I think we need to adjourn until then to think about what Chairman Boone has presented and continue preparing for our first boarding attempt."

Then with a nod to Fisher again, Chairman Ray and Tacita vanished.

"That was amazing," Roscoe said to Maria.

"And that was a great question I hadn't thought about," Maria said.

They stared at each other for a moment and Roscoe couldn't think of a thing to say. The attraction to Maria was more than he could remember ever feeling before.

Fisher and Callie both started to clean up, so finally breaking his gaze from those fantastic golden eyes, Roscoe stood and took his plate and empty orange juice glass and headed for the kitchen.

"I'll be glad to wash," he said.

"And I'll dry," Maria said from behind him.

"And we'll take you both up on that," Callie said, laughing.

Suddenly Roscoe wasn't sure what he had gotten himself into. But he liked the idea of spending a little more time with Maria.

If he could manage to not break any dishes.

Seven

MARIA REALLY ENJOYED the short time she had standing beside Roscoe at the sink in the old lodge. Every so often their hands would touch as he handed her a plate, and each time it felt like a small shock.

He kept glancing at her the entire time as well.

He was so damned good-looking, and it had been so long since she had even allowed herself to look at another man. She didn't dare look at her crew as the Chairman of the ship, and she hadn't spent much time away from her ship in some time.

So maybe she was just desperate. But she didn't think so. Roscoe was handsome and funny and clearly very, very smart.

Callie had excused herself and transported to their ship and Fisher had stayed in the kitchen to clean up the grill, and bring them the remains of the dishes from the counter.

Roscoe had quizzed Fisher on the lodge and then got both of them laughing with his incredible sense of humor.

In a moment when Fisher had gone back into the diner area to make sure they hadn't missed a dish, Roscoe turned to her. "So how far out were you when Chairman Ray recalled you to help with this?"

She laughed. "Far out describes it," she said. "We had gone through three seeded galaxies and were on the other side of the third headed toward a small group of stars at the edge of the Local Group."

"Wow," he said, shaking his head, causing his long brown hair to swirl back and forth on his collar which took her a moment to pull her attention away from and back to the plate in her hand.

"I can't even imagine that," he said, focusing on scrubbing out a pot in the sink like an expert, "yet from what you were talking about, it's a small distance compared to what that huge ship has crossed."

"A very small part," she said. "And it still took us two full weeks at full drive to get back."

"Were the human populations of those galaxies you went through extremely advanced?" Roscoe asked her.

"They were, and very peaceful," she said, remembering some of the encounters. "But we really didn't introduce ourselves as Seeders and none of them had speeds of ships high enough to cross the distances between galaxies. And we didn't tell them we could."

"Wow, sort of trapped in their own galaxy," Roscoe said. "How strange that sounds."

Maria had to admit, it did sound strange. "What was weird was that none of them much cared about the Seeders. They had just come to accept thousands and thousands of years before that Seeders had all moved on and that Seeders couldn't be followed. In fact, the farther out we went, the more Seeders were just myths relegated to deep archives of past religions."

"I don't feel like a religion, do you?" Roscoe asked.

"Honestly wouldn't know what a religion would feel like," she said, laughing.

"I don't either," he said, taking a towel to dry off his hands as he looked at her with a sly smile. "But I'm betting sort of soft and squishy."

She laughed and said, "And slick and hard to hold onto."

He managed to keep a straight face on that handsome face for a moment before breaking into laughter that, if she had her way, she would listen to a lot more of over time.

Eight

ROSCOE SPENT THE next two weeks mostly with Jonas, working with staffing and training the crew for *The Huntington.*

They had decided to mostly stay with Seeders and not recruit too many new humans right out of the blue. In fact, of the two hundred they picked, only ten were non-Seeders. Five couples.

One such couple was the most famous couple in all of Sector Justice, Mattie Silks and Red Kenney. Red owned another organization that worked closely with Sector Justice called Innocence Inc. Mattie was rumored to be the most deadly enforcer in all of Sector Justice and had taken the job as liaison between the two organizations when she and Red were married.

He and Jonas both knew them and had approached them on their private ship. It didn't take long to convince them after showing them the big ship and telling them about the threat they were trying to stop.

Roscoe's highlights of each day had been the morning meetings with Chairman Ray, Tacita, Fisher, Callie, and Maria. Each morning Fisher cooked them

a wonderful breakfast and then after updating on progress and planning the first boarding, he and Maria did dishes.

He was starting to feel more and more attracted to her every day, and more comfortable with her.

And she clearly liked him as well and was flirting back with him. At some point, he hoped to spend a lot more time with her every day besides twenty minutes doing dishes.

It was finally, on the first day of the third week, that Fisher dropped a bombshell on the meeting.

"I think we can board the big ship in trans-tunnel flight."

The statement sort of hung there in the dining room air like a bad odor that no one wanted to comment on. Roscoe just couldn't even image anything like that being possible.

Chairman Ray smiled and motioned for Fisher to go on, then went back to finishing up his eggs.

"The ship's screens won't be active during trans-tunnel flight," Fisher said. "The ship is in the trans-tunnel for only about two hours, so it will be tight, but possible."

Maria shook her head and Roscoe didn't blame her.

"I didn't think it was possible to leave the confines of a ship in trans-tunnel flight," he said.

"It's not," Fisher said. "But we can attach my ship to the big ship near where we think a port is and then board after we come out of trans-tunnel flight. When it drops out, if our drives are off, it will take us out with it."

Again silence.

Tacita looked at Maria. "Chairman, has your team ascertained where the ports might be?"

"Yes," Maria said, nodding. "I believe that Chairman Fisher's option of attachment might not be necessary. We might be able to get the ship to open a port large enough for his ship to enter while in tunnel flight. The ship should have a very large landing deck if the design of this ship matches what we know of older Seeder designs."

"How about we scout this first?" Roscoe suggested, not liking at all what he was hearing. Far too many things could go completely wrong.

"How do you suggest we do that?" Fisher asked.

"You said the shields are off when in trans-tunnel flight?" Roscoe said.

"Scan it then," Maria said at the same time he did.

He smiled at her and her smile made it to her wonderful golden eyes just fine.

"Is that possible for you to do?" Chairman Ray asked Fisher and Callie. "It has been my understanding that scans in trans-tunnel flight are impossible at the moment."

Both Fisher and Callie looked at each other in silence for a moment, then Fisher turned to Chairman Ray. "They have been because no one has had a need until now to do that. Let us talk with our team and we'll have an answer to that in the morning."

Ray pushed his finished plate away and stood. Tacita did the same beside him.

"We are getting close," he said. "Good work, everyone."

With that they vanished.

Callie looked at Roscoe, smiling. "Great idea."

"If we can figure out how to make it work," Fisher said, staring at his wife clearly in deep thought.

"Go get to it," Roscoe said. "We'll handle the dishes and clean up."

"Thank you," Callie said, and an instant later they were gone.

Roscoe stood and started to gather up dishes, not really knowing what to say. For the first time he and Maria were really alone.

And suddenly he felt like he was back about four hundred years in school with a girl he liked and not knowing what to say.

She was gathering plates and cups and silverware on her side of the counter as well when he looked up at her.

She felt him staring at her and looked up, smiling at him with a twinkle in her golden eyes. "This time I'll wash."

He had no idea what that meant.

Nine

MARIA KNEW THAT both she and Roscoe had a lot to do, but she was in no hurry to leave and clearly he wasn't either.

She washed the dishes he gathered up and they talked about the mission. At one point he asked about her home planet and she told him about it, finishing with the fact that it had been a few hundred years since she had been back.

"That would be fun to see," he said. 'Sounds beautiful and cold."

"Cold describes it," she said.

Then she asked him where he was from and he described a standard seeded planet that had gotten into space a little ahead of others in the area. He had gotten a degree in astronomy and physics before joining his planet's military to get out into space. He had been recruited into the Seeders about ten years later.

"Two degrees?" she asked, looking at him, stunned.

"Only way I could get off the planet," he said, laughing.

The more she learned about this guy, the more she was liking.

After a far too short time period, they were done.

They both wiped down the counters last, talking about how great it would be to have a home base like this one.

"Tomorrow morning then," he said, smiling at her and holding her gaze.

She stepped up to him and kissed him for just an instant. Then she stepped back.

She could feel her breath short and she knew she was blushing, but she didn't care. It had been wonderful, even though she completely surprised him.

He also had the decency to be blushing as well.

"What was that, Chairman Boone?" he asked, smiling slightly.

"A promise for the future," she said, smiling back. "Until tomorrow."

And she transported back to her ship before she couldn't hold herself back and jumped him.

Or before he made a move to kiss her.

She had a hunch that neither of them would get anything done if that happened.

It took her a good half hour in the gym working off the excitement of being with Roscoe before she went back to a meeting with her team.

Two hours later they had worked out a computer generated list of a few million standard entrance codes that an old Seeder ship might use for its landing deck, if there was a landing deck.

They were all convinced there was, and that it would be large enough to hold just about any ship.

After that she had a small lunch and then went back to the gym to try to get Roscoe from her mind. Even a hard workout didn't do it.

It had been just too damned long since she had been with a man. And she had a hunch, the way she was feeling, she had never been with anyone like Roscoe.

Ever.

Ten

THE NEXT MORNING at breakfast, Maria was cheerful and smiling. He had worried about her kiss and how she would react today. All fine in that department. He had worried for nothing. She was as stunning and alluring as ever.

And even more friendly.

He had thought about her the entire day yesterday, trying to keep as busy as he could to cut down the time daydreaming of her.

It had worked a little, but not much. He pretty much had everything in place and ready to go.

About halfway through breakfast, Chairman Ray asked them about all their progress.

Maria told him how her crew had come up with a few million codes that might open the docking area if there was one like most Seeder ships. Then she said she and her crew were as ready as they ever would be.

Roscoe reported that *The Huntington* was ready and the other four warships were also in position and standing by. He was ready as well.

Callie and Fisher then reported that their team had figured out a way to get limited scans inside trans-tunnel flight, and had worked out exactly how to match the speed inside the trans-tunnel of the big ship.

The ship would only be in trans-tunnel flight for two hours starting tomorrow, then be in regular flight for fourteen days.

Fisher looked at Chairman Ray. "We're ready now if you want us to try to get a scan."

Chairman Ray nodded. Then he turned to Roscoe. "I want you and four of your best team on Chairman Fisher's ship."

Roscoe nodded, surprised, but it made sense in case something went wrong.

Ray turned to Maria. "I need you and four of your best scientists on the ship as well."

She nodded and said nothing, clearly understanding what Ray was doing.

Ray then turned to Fisher. "Only take the crew you need to get the scans. Leave all your data and most of your crew in one of the other science ships."

Fisher nodded as well. "We'll just need five also."

Roscoe was impressed. Chairman Ray had decided to move, but had reduced the risk down to painful, but not disastrous levels if something went wrong.

"We'll need to depart in one hour," Fisher said, "to be in position and at speed for the big ship's jump."

Roscoe nodded to Ray and stood. "Thanks once again for the great breakfast," he said to Fisher. "I'll be glad to do the dishes when we get back."

Ray laughed. "You all go. Tacita and I are not too old to do dishes."

"Thank you, dear," Tacita said, smiling at her husband.

They all laughed.

"My people will be ready and on board your ship in forty-five minutes," Maria said to Fisher.

Then she vanished.

"As will my people," Roscoe said.

Then he left, jumping back to his ship to get to Jonas and his command crew. He planned on taking the four of his top command crew, leaving *The Huntington* in the hands of Red and Mattie until they got back.

They were going to scan a very old and very advanced ship. There was going to be no telling what they would find or trigger.

And that had him both scared to death and excited at the same time.

Eleven

MARIA LIKED WORKING with Roscoe and felt comfortable with him. He and his top command crew were in a secondary control room on Fisher's small ship called *The Lady*.

His crew stood against the back bulkhead, armed and ready to go. The room was a high-ceilinged room that Fisher said had been used as an exercise room. He had converted it for this mission, along with other rooms.

His ship had a very comfortable feel and she had liked it the moment she stepped on board. The carpet in the hallways and rooms was soft, but not thick. Colors were tan and all chairs were form-fitting.

Fisher and Callie had decorated the hallway walls with various paintings and images from different planets. Often the images were changing, showing fantastic beauty from varied worlds. Maria bet that if she asked Fisher and Callie, each image and painting would have a story from the last three hundred years they had been together.

Fisher had said that most of the time the ship was on one of the big landing decks of his large Seeder research science ship. But he and Callie lived on this ship as their own personal apartment and always kept it at the top performance and with top equipment for all tasks.

Maria's crew stood near her on her right, watching the big image screen on the wall and the heads-up displays in front of Fisher's three crew members.

She and Roscoe stood side-by-side. At one point she had moved so that he almost touched her left arm. She wanted him a lot closer than that at some point.

They had talked a bit while boarding about how excited they were for the coming mission. Now, as they waited in the last few seconds, she shifted from foot to foot, but he stood rock still. How he could do that was impossible for her to grasp in this situation. This was too exciting to not move.

The large screen on the wall kept them all informed as to what Callie and Fisher were doing in the small ship's Command Center.

The big screen also showed the huge old Seeder ship flashing through space at near light speed.

The big Seeder ship was so large, no perspective was possible. It was impossible for her to grasp that someone had built something that big.

"Matching speed now," Fisher said.

She also found it hard to believe that this ship could move this fast. Nothing she knew of had near-light speed.

"Jump to trans-tunnel flight with the big ship in ten seconds," Callie reported.

"Here we go," Roscoe said, glancing at her and smiling.

She smiled at him. He seemed so cool under pressure situations. She wanted to just clutch something. She liked more and more about him, she had to admit. She forced herself to go back to watching the monitors. She couldn't let herself get distracted at this moment by his incredible looks and dark eyes. She was tempted to reach out and hold his hand, but she didn't.

"Two, one," Fisher said from the control room and the small ship jumped to trans-tunnel.

The stars streaked and everything on the screen went from clear to gray as it always did in fast trans-tunnel flight.

The big ship was right beside them, also in trans-tunnel flight.

Fisher had matched the jump perfectly. Amazing. She didn't know this was possible either, for two ships to be inside the same trans-tunnel flight.

Wow, Fisher and his team were really something.

"Ready for scans," Callie said.

In front of Maria, the three crew members from Fisher's team worked their boards quickly. On the big screen, and on the heads-up displays, was where they all hoped the scan results would start appearing.

"Nothing seeming to block the scans," Fisher reported from the Command Center.

Maria now wanted to jump up and down she was so excited. She was about to see inside a million-year-old Seeder ship. Beside her Roscoe didn't even move. He had some amazing control.

"Ready," Fisher said.

"Now," Callie said.

Nothing.

Screens showed the same image of the big ship in trans-tunnel flight.

Maria was disappointed for a moment, then suddenly everything changed.

The trans-tunnel streaks and grayness vanished.

And what appeared on the screen was something Maria couldn't comprehend in the slightest.

Fisher's ship now sat like a tiny dot on a vast plain of decking of some sort. Distant ceiling lights illuminated the vast space that looked like it could easily cover a large city.

The ceiling was so far overhead, it almost couldn't be seen.

"Oh, shit," Jonas said from behind her. "We triggered something."

Beside her, Roscoe snapped around. "Full alert. Jonas, to the control room."

Without looking around, Maria knew Roscoe's military crew snapped instantly into action, weapons at the ready as each took up a position near assigned members of the other two teams.

Roscoe had his pulse rifle off his shoulder and ready, standing beside her, his attention now on the screens as well as everyone in the room.

She glanced at him and then took a deep breath to calm herself and get back to thinking, just as Roscoe was doing.

"Seems we are inside the big ship," Fisher said from the control room, his voice sounding impossibly calm.

"It would seem that way," Maria said, shaking her head. Then she said to Fisher with more authority. "Can we get a signal out to Chairman Ray?"

A moment later Ray's face came on the screen.

She was never so happy to see a face in her life. She released the breath that she had been holding.

"We are inside the big ship," Fisher reported to Ray. "Our scans triggered a transport of some sort."

Ray just nodded. The man had ice in his veins just as Roscoe. "Everyone safe?"

"We are, and still scanning," Fisher said. "Transmitting data to you now as it comes in."

Ray glanced to his right for a moment, then nodded. "Continue as long as you can."

Maria was even more excited that Ray was getting their scans. That was a very, very good sign.

"I'm assuming," Fisher said, "that if we are still here when the ship drops out of trans-tunnel in an hour or so and goes behind its screens, our transmissions will be cut off."

"Understood," Ray said, nodding.

"Suggestions?" Fisher asked.

Ray stood silent for a moment, then shrugged slightly, his long gray hair bouncing on his shoulders. "Find a way to turn or stop that ship before it destroys those planets," Ray said.

"Understood," Fisher said.

Then Ray said simply into the camera. "Roscoe, take care of those people in there."

"Understand, Chairman," Roscoe said from beside her. "We will."

"Good luck," Ray said and cut off.

"Scanning data still pouring out and being received," Fisher said. "Chairman Mundy, Chairman Boone, meet me in the kitchen."

"Understood," Maria said.

Beside her Roscoe nodded and then followed her out of the secondary Command Center and down the short hall toward the small ship's kitchen.

She was inside an ancient and more than likely very deadly Seeder ship.

A dream come true for her life's work.

And a nightmare at the same time.

Section Two
The Past Controls

Twelve

ROSCOE HAD BEEN worried right from the start about their scans triggering a defense mechanism. They had prepared Fisher's ship with supplies and other needed items for just this contingency. And everyone on board had brought a week's worth of clothes that could be washed if needed. From the looks of it, Fisher's wash machine was going to get a workout before this was all settled.

But so far, nothing seemed deadly.

So far.

But he was going to take no chances that didn't need to be taken.

Fisher smiled at them as Roscoe and Maria arrived in the kitchen. Roscoe had his pulse rifle over his shoulder for the moment, but he could get to it quickly. His team was going to be close to any of the other team members at all times in case a group were transported out of Fisher's ship. He wanted one of his armed team with the others.

Roscoe glanced around at the kitchen. It could hold about six sitting around a nifty wooden dining table secured to the floor and the cooking area seemed state-of-the-art from what Roscoe could tell. He wasn't much of a cook, but he tried at times.

Roscoe could see a pantry stocked completely full just beyond one side of the kitchen. He knew that in other places on the ship there were enough supplies on board to feed the fifteen of them for a year, at least.

He sure hoped this mission didn't take that long, or a lot of people on those planets ahead of them were going to die.

Maria seemed calm now, not as excited as she had been before they jumped into trans-tunnel flight. Her excitement had been almost infectious and he loved that feeling of looking at the good things in something instead of always the bad. She balanced him well.

"This sure feels familiar," Fisher said, smiling, seemingly not at all concerned about the situation as he opened the fridge and offered them water or something else to drink.

Both Maria and Roscoe declined, so Fisher took out a bottle of a pink fluid and sat down at the kitchen table, indicating that they should join him.

"Familiar?" Maria asked as she sat across from Fisher. "How?"

Roscoe went over and leaned against a bulkhead near Maria, preferring to stand at the moment. It was going to take him some time to relax at this point.

Fisher took a drink and sighed. "When my friend and I first ran into a large ship coming to rescue the population of the planet where we have the lodge, our ship, this ship, in a much more primitive state, was teleported inside a huge landing deck. It was a smaller deck by a long ways from what we are in now, but still huge by our little ship's standards."

"Is it something about this ship that makes people want to do that?" Roscoe asked.

Fisher laughed and Maria shook her head and smiled at him, which he appreciated more than he wanted to admit. The tension in the room seemed to ease

a lot from his joke question and he loved it when those golden eyes of hers looked fondly at him.

"Must be," Fisher said.

"What happened that first time?" Maria asked.

"Scared to death, we just went outside to introduce ourselves. Seeders, by their very nature, are a peace-loving group. We didn't know that at the time, but we do now."

Roscoe had to admit, that was true. But as Sector Justice forces knew so well, they still needed to know how to defend themselves. This huge ship clearly had good defenses.

"So are you suggesting we go introduce ourselves?" Maria said.

"Can you think of another option," Fisher asked, "after we study what we are getting from the scans, of course. They sure know we are here. I have nothing on this ship that could even pretend to block a scan, even if we wanted to."

Roscoe nodded at that. "How long until preliminary scans will be done?"

Fisher shrugged. "This ship we are in is bigger than many moons, so it's going to take some time to really cover it. But honestly, we'll know if we're alone and the focus of our mission in two hours."

"Can you feed the scans to my people in a place in the ship where we could work?" Maria asked.

Roscoe knew the answer, since he had checked out and helped Fisher set up the ship before the mission. But he let Fisher answer.

"We can," Fisher said. "We retrofitted our second exercise room with ten work and scanning stations before this mission."

He looked over at Roscoe. "I assume you are going to want to look at all the scans as well."

"I am," Roscoe said. "And my second-in-command, Jonas, will as well. We'll study monitors in the room with Chairman Boone's team. The rest of my team will remain on guard with each group in case a group is transported off the ship without warning."

"Very good thinking," Fisher said, nodding. "So in three hours, after the big ship drops back into real space, the three of us will meet here and decide how to proceed next."

Maria nodded and smiled at Roscoe as she stood. She patted him on the arm. "Let's go to work."

Roscoe could tell she was clearly back to being excited, and since the history of Seeders was her passion and life's work, he could certainly understand that.

His passion was to keep everyone safe. And he needed to know what was inside this monster old ship to even begin to do that.

And secondly, he needed to keep them all focused on one task: Stopping this ship before it killed millions of others on defenseless planets.

Thirteen

THE NEXT THREE hours went by quickly, too fast, as far as Maria was concerned. The former exercise room turned second scanning room was long and fairly narrow. Fisher had set up ten stations down one wall. The other walls were covered in art and some of the exercise equipment had been pushed together in a back corner.

The floor was covered in a comfortable mat-like substance that felt soft and warm to her feet. It was a comfortable place to work, but she wouldn't have cared. She could have done this work standing in a closet and she wouldn't have cared.

The scans they were getting of the big ship were amazing.

It had become clear after the first hour that there was no one alive here, even though the ship had been designed for millions of humans to live comfortably for very long periods of time.

And she had a hunch that was a very, very low guess as to the number this ship could actually hold. She just couldn't imagine a ship holding more, so her brain stopped her there.

All of the scans from the three areas of the ship, the main scanning room, the control room, and this room, were being fed into a central image and slowly in that three-dimensional image, pieces of the ship were coming together.

Part of this ship was nothing more than a huge city, plain and simple, with housing that went from small apartments to five bedroom suites. It had what looked like schools, shopping, large areas that would be parks when planted, and so on.

The ship also carried a good five hundred other huge ships on one landing deck. All those ships were also empty of human life, but designed to hold thousands of humans per ship comfortably.

In fact, each ship was bigger than Chairman's Ray's ship, one of the biggest the Seeders had working right now in any of the Local Sector galaxies.

The big ship was also riddled with massive warehouse rooms stacked full of who knew what. Every warehouse looked completely untouched and her scans could not seem to tell what was in any of them. They were just too far away.

And from what she could tell, there were thousands of science labs and other areas for unknown reasons. Offices and work areas she guessed.

Roscoe was at the screen beside her, his rifle over his shoulder. She noticed he was amazingly good at running scans and comfortable on the heads-up board. He seemed to be focused on different areas of the ship than she was.

She liked having him that close and had stopped herself from excitedly showing him something at two different points. It seemed she just wanted to share things with him.

She had always been a loner by nature. This kind of desire to share and be close to another person was different for her and she honestly liked it more than she ever thought she would. And she had no idea why he was bringing that out in her. No other man she had known ever had.

Roscoe's second-in-command, Jonas, had focused his scanning on the Command Center for the big ship.

After three hours, Fisher came in and motioned for her and Roscoe to come talk with him in the kitchen again.

"We're going to need to feed people pretty soon," Fisher said as he entered the kitchen and took a container of water from the fridge and sat down. "We've set up a room as a dining hall and we have a meal already prepared and ready to just heat and serve when we call dinner. After this first meal, we're going to need to do more cooking."

Maria nodded, sitting down at the table across from Fisher again. Roscoe once again stayed standing and close to her.

"How about a group of one person from each team be in charge of a meal," she said, "and we rotate around."

She hadn't given a thought to eating, but knew they had to in order to keep everyone fresh. She also knew that Fisher's ship had been set up for enough sleeping quarters for all of them before the mission in case something like this might happen.

"I think we need to keep at least three people on the scans at all times," Roscoe said, "sort of as a guard. We can set up a rotation on that as well."

"Agree with both," Fisher said. "Even though all of us have been scanning for hours now, we still really don't know what's out there."

"I'm not really wrapping my mind around the size of this ship," Roscoe said. "I figured that if we set off walking from here to the Command Center, it would take us two weeks time if we covered about twenty kilometers per day."

Maria had done similar calculations. "I agree. I'm having trouble with the size as well. I did a calculation on a ten kilometer per day pace that it would take over a month simply to get from here to the other side of that huge hanger deck with all the large ships on it."

"So we can't be doing much walking," Fisher said. "The ship must have some sort of transport system like our big ships do."

"I think we're better off just transporting ourselves for the moment," Roscoe said. "Not sure how much we want to trigger into this ship's systems until we can get to that Command Center and see the path and the mission the ship is intended to accomplish."

Maria smiled at him. "I agree. In fact, I suggest we just stay here for the next forty-four hours until the ship drops back into trans-tunnel flight and we get information from Chairman Ray and his people. They will have had fourteen days to analyze what we sent them in those first two hours."

"I was going to suggest the same," Roscoe said, smiling at her. "Better we know where we are headed before we go wondering around and get lost in this huge ship."

"Any early theories as to what this ship is?" Fisher asked Maria.

She took a deep breath and for the first time since Chairman Ray had sent her the first data, she decided to mention her theory.

"I think this is a Seeder Mother Ship," she said.

"A what?" both Fisher and Roscoe asked at exactly the same time.

"There is one theory in history that Seeders have been seeding for more millions and millions of years than we can imagine," Maria said.

Roscoe and Fisher nodded.

Maria went on. "One theory is that a wave, a direction of seeding from galaxy to galaxy starts with a Mother Ship. Maybe this very ship has started many waves, then been restocked and sent ahead again. We don't know, or maybe this is a new ship, if one-point-four-millions years is new."

Roscoe sat back and looked at her, his dark eyes intense. Fisher was just looking puzzled.

"Remember," Maria said, "that I showed you the big spiral galaxy that I think this ship came from. And that our branch of Seeders left that galaxy and started off in this direction."

She could tell that Roscoe was starting to understand. In the short time they had been working together, she had come to realize he was really smart, maybe one of the smartest people she had ever met.

"They sent a wave of Seeder ships off toward here," Maria said, "then launched this ship so that it would meet the front wave, allow us to staff it and start off in a completely new direction as well as going to Andromeda."

"What made you think this?" Fisher asked.

"I've thought it right from the start," Maria said. "But it was only speculation. Now that I've seen early scans of the inside of this ship, I'm fairly sure."

"Why?" Roscoe asked, his dark eyes focused on her like she hoped they would be for a long time to come.

"That hanger deck full of ships, to start with," she said. "They are front-line seeder ships almost identical to the ones working Andromeda Galaxy right now."

Again both men nodded.

"Noticed that," Roscoe said.

"And because Seeders always just move to the next closest galaxy," she said, smiling at Roscoe's wonderful eyes as he intently stared at her. "And the closest galaxies were not in this direction from that huge spiral galaxy. In fact, taking this route to our Local Group of galaxies might be the third wave of Seeders that left that galaxy."

"Oh," Roscoe said, shaking his head.

"Do we Seeders ever do anything small?" Fisher asked.

"No, even my headache is large trying to grasp this," Roscoe said.

At that, Maria wanted to just stand and kiss him as she laughed. But somehow, she managed not to.

Barely.

Fourteen

TO ROSCOE, SPENDING that first night on Fisher's ship seemed almost like camping back when he was a kid on his home planet.

He could feel the pressure of the huge ship around him like he was in a deep forest a long ways from any city.

And he could really feel the responsibility of the safety of the fourteen people in the ship with him. So far nothing at all had seemed threatening, and the more they learned about the big ship, the more he doubted there was much to worry about as far as attack.

But even still, for the moment, he and his men had set up a rotating guard. And Maria and Fisher both had one of their people each stay on the scanning duty, running as many scans as possible continuously.

So at any given point, three of the twelve of them were awake.

He wasn't scheduled for a two-hour guard shift yet, but there was no chance that he could sleep. He normally didn't need much sleep, but he knew at some point he would have to get some. However, just lying there in the small room they had assigned him and staring at the ceiling wasn't going to work, and he knew himself enough to know that.

So, he took a shower, then changed clothes into a white t-shirt and comfortable slacks, then with his pulse rifle over his shoulder, he wandered back first to the dinner area and picked up a container of water and a piece of dark bread that had tasted fantastic and slightly sweet at dinner. Then he went down the wide hallway to the big scanning room.

Not only were the two there that had shifts, and Jonas standing against the wall near them on guard duty, but Maria was there, hunched forward, staring at something in her heads-up projection.

Obviously, she couldn't sleep either, although her red hair looked damp like she had also taken a shower, and she had on what looked like a form of cotton pajama bottoms with blue flowers and a sweatshirt and slippers of some sort.

Her red hair was pulled back tight and he could see the freckles on her neck.

She was unbelievably attractive, even hunched forward over a work station like that. He just wanted to go up and rub her shoulders and kiss her neck, but now was far, far from the time.

"Couldn't sleep either, huh?" he asked about halfway across the room after he nodded to Jonas.

She turned and smiled at him, her smile beaming, clearly glad to see him. He liked that a lot.

"Far too excited," she said. "Take a look at this."

She turned back to her board and the image floating in the air in front of her.

He stared for a moment, but couldn't make any sense of it. It seemed to be some sort of writing. "What am I looking at?"

"I think it's the name of this big ship," she said.

Her fingers were running over her board faster than he had ever seen anyone move. The freckles on her shoulders almost moving in a dance as her arms and hands flashed over the controls.

"I'm working on language programs," she said. "As with all human cultures, languages all have certain basics and when I hit on the right combination, I'll have the language. We've been loading language into our language program from around the big ship since the first scans. From signs on doors to warning signs in engineering to this."

"Will we then be able to internalize it," he asked, "so we can understand it when we read anything on this ship?"

She nodded. "Easily. Just as we do with any human culture, I can have all of us speaking and reading this ship's old language once we crack the pattern."

"Got it!" one of Fisher's people named Dan said from beside Maria. "Transferring it to you now."

"Wonderful," Maria said, almost jumping in her chair with excitement. Roscoe had to admit, it was impossible around her to not be excited.

"Got what?" Fisher asked as he came into the room, clearly also not able to sleep.

"Language," Maria said. "Dan cracked it."

Fisher came up behind his team member and gave him a congratulatory pat on the shoulder.

Then Maria clapped her hands and started laughing as she stared at the projection of the words.

"What's so funny?" Fisher asked a moment before Roscoe could.

"You folks want to know the name of the big ship we are sitting inside?"

"Very much so," Fisher said, smiling back at the infectious excitement from Maria.

"This ship is called *Morning Song*."

All Roscoe could do was shake his head.

A giant ship, that if not stopped, would destroy planets and kill billions, was named *Morning Song.*

He flat wasn't sure what to think of that.

Fifteen

THE FIRST TWO days were nothing but one exciting discovery after another on the scans of the big ship. She hadn't slept much, but that didn't matter. This was the find of a dozen lifetimes and sleeping seemed to be an inconvenience.

And she loved spending time around Roscoe and he didn't seem to sleep much either. She loved his smile, his intense questioning eyes, and his dry sense of humor.

And he seemed to want to be around her as well, which pleased her more than she wanted to admit.

Now, all of her team and Roscoe and two of his team were in the big scanning room, waiting the last few minutes for the ship to jump to trans-tunnel flight. Fisher and Callie were back in the Command Center with a guard from Roscoe's team and the rest of Fisher's team were in the first scan center with another of Roscoe's team on guard with them.

She had no idea what was going to happen next. She hoped nothing but getting in contact with Chairman Ray.

In real time, Chairman Ray and his people had had fourteen days to go over those first scans. She hoped they had a lot more information. The possibility of that had her really excited.

But she could feel her stomach twisting in slight worry as well. No telling what would happen next when the ship jumped back to trans-tunnel drive. It might dump them back into space and not let them back inside.

Anything was possible.

"Ten seconds," Fisher said from the Command Center.

Maria glanced away from her screen and up at Roscoe's serious face. She was really starting to admire him and like him more than she wanted to admit. But right now he was focused and on guard, standing close to her. And she actually felt far safer with him close by.

That surprised her as well, but she liked it.

She had a scan running of the *Morning Song's* big Command Center to see if anything changed when the jump to trans-tunnel happened. She didn't expect to see anything, but she had decided to scan there even so.

"Two. One. Now," Fisher said.

After a few seconds of waiting, Fisher said, "Chairman Ray, do you copy?"

It took another moment before Chairman Ray's voice came back strong. "Strong and clear."

On a center screen in the room, Chairman Ray's smiling face appeared. He was clearly relieved and Maria could hear applause around him over the communications link.

Maria let out the breath she was holding. Beside her she could feel Roscoe relax and exhale as well.

"Sending data we have taken in the last two days on the *Morning Song*," Fisher said to Ray.

"Receiving," Ray said after a moment. "And you got the language figured out I see."

"We do, Chairman," Fisher said. "But we will need to access the big ship's command systems and other systems to figure out the *Morning Song's* mission. We will be doing that next unless your data bring up something we have not yet discovered."

Maria watched as Chairman Ray shook his head, his long gray hair moving on his shoulders as he did. "We have found, in searching carefully everything you sent us at first, no real threats from the ship itself."

"Besides getting lost," Fisher said.

Ray laughed. "There is that. That ship is impossible for most to comprehend the size."

"It is," Fisher said.

"So, I assume Chairman Mundy and Chairman Boone are on this link," Ray asked.

"Everyone on the ship is listening and on the link," Fisher said. "We seem to all be in the belly of this beast together."

Ray nodded. "Chairman Mundy," Ray asked Roscoe, "Do you see any obvious dangers in exploring?"

"Nothing, Chairman," Roscoe said, "after two days of scanning, it seems clear."

"Chairman Boone?" he asked.

"No dangers that my team has found, Chairman," Maria said, agreeing with Roscoe. In two days she and her team had found nothing that seemed even slightly dangerous.

Ray nodded, then asked Maria, "Do you think this is still a Seeder ship?"

"I do," Maria said, her stomach twisting in excitement. "I'm convinced this is a Seeder Mother Ship and the mission of this ship is to find a large crew and leave the Milky Way in a different direction from Andromeda and the path of the current leading edge of seeding that is going on in Andromeda."

Chairman Ray nodded. "We have come to that same conclusion."

Maria felt her heart race. These Mother Ships had only been a distant and faint myth of Seeders. Now she found herself inside one.

Then Chairman Ray's face became very serious. "We have exactly 161 days before the big ship plows into a populated system and takes out a moon and a number of other bases. We might be able to get those evacuated in time and have started that preparation now."

"Good," Roscoe said softly beside her.

Ray went on. "But the *Morning Song* plows into your home base world, Fisher and Callie, in 167 days and destroys it completely. We are mounting preparations for an emergency evacuation if it comes to that, but will only be able to get a few million out of the billion now on that world."

"We'll get it stopped, Chairman," Fisher said, and Maria found herself nodding in agreement.

"Your timeline is much shorter, you understand," Chairman Ray said.

"Twenty-two days and four hours," Fisher said. "We will stop it, turn it, or destroy it in that amount of time."

Maria again felt her stomach twist. This ship was the greatest treasure from the history of the Seeders. They had to stop it, she understood that, but if she had anything to say about it, they would do it without destroying it. They flat had to.

"Get started and dump data with each trans-tunnel flight," Chairman Ray said. "We'll do what we can in helping from this side."

"Thank you, Chairman," Fisher said.

"Good luck," Chairman Ray said and the screen went blank.

Maria did her best to just let herself breathe.

"Chairmen Boone and Mundy to the kitchen," Fisher said. "Five minutes."

Roscoe smiled at her as she stood. "Looks like we get to go exploring very soon."

At that she actually smiled, pushing back the ticking clock and letting the excitement of exploring an ancient ship the size of a large moon come forward.

"I love exploring new places," she said, smiling at him.

"Actually," he said, "so do I." Then he smiled and raised one eyebrow.

She wasn't at all sure what he meant exactly, but she liked the idea either way.

She laughed and said, "Why does that not surprise me."

Sixteen

ROSCOE KNEW THERE were two major points of danger for the crew. And about fifty million minor ones. But those he couldn't deal with. But he could take a few precautions on the major danger moments.

His first major point was when they first left Fisher's ship. If the big ship had a defense system, leaving the ship would be one place they all would stand no chance of any defense.

Of course, the big ship could have taken them off of Fisher's ship at any point, but it had not.

Their scans showed that when they had arrived, the big ship powered up all environmental systems. After two days, every room and area in the ship had breathable atmosphere and was heated. Even the warehouses.

But no other systems seemed to be running at all. And that told him they were going to have to turn them on.

Fisher's science team had informed him that the ship had maintained vacuum atmosphere interior and extremely cold temps before they arrived. Maria had confirmed that through her team.

So it seemed the ship was welcoming them by at least turning on the lights. Roscoe wasn't so sure if he liked that or not.

At least it allowed them to explore easily.

Maria and her people had also discovered that the ship had repair units that replicated and replaced any near-failing part during the long voyage. Some of those were on tasks now in various places in the ship.

Roscoe just found it all stunning.

So now, they had done all the scans they could. They had to step out of Fisher's ship and onto the decks of the big hanger.

He and Jonas were going to be the two to do it first.

And he had convinced Fisher they needed to do that one act while still in contact with Chairman Ray and send him all scans of the result.

So one hour after they had gotten in touch with Chairman Ray again, and with just under an hour left in trans-tunnel flight for the big ship, Jonas and Ray stood side-by-side, rifles over their shoulders, ready to go. They had decided to not seem threatening in any way, which was why they had their guns on their shoulders.

"See you in a moment," Roscoe said to Fisher and Maria.

She smiled, but he could see the worry in her eyes.

"I'll jump us," Roscoe said to Jonas, who nodded.

"Do your thing, boss," Jonas said.

The next moment Roscoe had them standing on the big deck about a hundred paces from Fisher's ship.

The air smelled sort of stale, but not bad, and had a slight chill to it.

Roscoe looked around, not sure what to expect.

The monster room around them was too large to grasp. Like a distant sky, the ceiling overhead seemed to be full of lights. To his right, Roscoe could see a wall of some sort, but he had no idea how far that was, or even how tall that wall might be.

Scale was totally lost in a space like this, so much so, it almost made him dizzy.

"Wow," Jonas said, slowly turning to look around. "Scans don't even come close to showing the immensity of this place."

"Any problems?" Chairman Ray asked, his voice clear to Roscoe.

Roscoe knew that about a thousand people were watching their every move and monitoring all data they were sending back from their sensors. Roscoe hadn't wanted them wearing helmets, so they had on communications links with implanted mikes and ear buds. And about three ways to track them if the ship took them somewhere else.

Anyone stepping onto this ship would have those communication methods and tracking devices.

Maria answered him. "All scans of the *Morning Song* are showing no alarms or activity at all."

"We ants out here on the big field see nothing either," Roscoe said, slowing turning and admiring the massive hanger deck.

"Seems the ship doesn't mind us," Maria said.

"Coming in," Roscoe said.

Roscoe jumped him and Jonas back to a special decontamination room on Fisher's ship and the two of them were scanned at levels Roscoe didn't want to think about.

"Clear on the decontamination," Fisher said.

"We agree from here," Chairman Ray said.

"A clean ship that has warmed up the place and turned on the lights," Fisher said.

"Seems we have some exploring to do," Roscoe said.

And after being out there in that huge space, that idea actually excited him for the first time.

Seventeen

ONE HOUR AFTER the big ship dropped back out of trans-tunnel flight and they lost communications with Chairman Ray because of the ship's shields, Maria found herself sitting beside Roscoe in the kitchen of Fisher's ship.

He had on a tight black shirt and black slacks with the same wide belt buckle he always wore. His long brown hair was pulled tight behind his head. For the first time since they had been inside the big ship, he had no rifle with him.

She wanted to just touch the muscles that were clear under the tight black shirt, but she didn't. Instead she let her leg sort of rest casually against his under the table. Being this close to him made her feel so much better in so many ways she wasn't sure she understood just yet.

Fisher and Callie were both there as well. All of them were sipping on containers of water and she had one in front of her as well, but hadn't touched it. Besides sitting so close to Roscoe, she was so excited about going out and exploring

Morning Song, she almost couldn't sit still.

Fisher looked at her. "Do you have opinions of the most important areas to explore first?"

"Command Center, of course," Maria said. "We need to get control of this ship in some fashion or another and that has to be priority."

Beside her, she could see Roscoe nodding in agreement.

Fisher looked around at his wife, then back at Maria. "You won't get any disagreement on that at all. Second most important?"

Maria just shook her head. She wanted to see the entire ship, but she knew they had to prioritize right now. "Engines, then secondary control rooms, then living areas, then those big ships on that docking bay. We really need to see how they are outfitted and if they can function after all this time. On second thought, those should be right after the engine room."

Fisher looked at Roscoe. "Your list?"

Roscoe looked at Maria. "I can't disagree with that list at all."

Callie agreed and so did Fisher.

"So there are fifteen of us," Fisher said. "How would you suggest we split up or should we?"

Maria looked at Roscoe who nodded for her to go ahead.

"My suggestion," Maria said. "One from each team remain here on the ship running scans ahead of the three groups that are out. Three groups out at a time, four members in each exploring group. We need at least one member from each of our teams in each group."

"That feels right," Roscoe said.

Fisher turned to his wife. "Would you mind remaining on board this first time?

The Third Seeders Universe Novel
now available from all your favorite booksellers in trade paper and electronic.

I need someone in command here who knows how to fly *The Lady.*"

"I was going to suggest that," she said.

Fisher turned to Maria again. "Who on your team knows the most about the Command Centers of older Seeder ships?"

"Hudson," she said, without hesitation.

Hudson was one of her youngest at three hundred years, but looked far older than he should because of his long black beard and shaggy hair. He had made it his passion to study and fly in reality and in simulations all old Seeder ships she could get him near. He could take apart old Command Centers with his eyes closed.

"So the three of us and Hudson head to the Command Center," Fisher said.

"Jonas could take a team to engineering," Roscoe said. "His passion is engines of all types."

Fisher nodded. "Two of my team are engineers as well. Perfect."

They spent the next half hour detailing out who would go first and so on. They decided that Maria had been right and the third most important place to explore was the big ships on the hanger deck.

Then there was nothing else to talk about.

Maria was almost floating off the deck as she headed for her cabin to get what she might need in the Command Center of the *Morning Sun.* This was all a dream come true.

But in the back of her mind, something was nagging at her. She felt completely home inside the *Morning Song.* Completely, and that felt both good and worried her. She had no idea where the feeling was coming from.

But in her excitement, she decided to just think about that later. Right now she got to explore a Seeder ship that was so ancient, she couldn't believe it actually existed.

And she was going to get to explore it with a man of her dreams.

It didn't get better than that.

Eighteen

ROSCOE HAD LEARNED very early on that when something was going smoothly, something ugly was about to happen. It didn't always work that way, but his voice was telling him that was the case this time.

This ship had made him feel like an ant crawling somewhere on a planet's continent. The builders of this ship were far, far beyond the knowledge and years of the Seeders now or ones working Andromeda.

Sure, the ship had been built by humans. Seeders. But not humans like them at all. Humans far, far advanced. So why did ants like him think they could get control of something this big?

That thought just kept nagging him and he had no idea what to do about that at all.

And he felt completely at home on the big ship at the same time and that feeling worried him even more and kept him even more on guard.

He had insisted that each group only jump with line-of-sight as much as possible. That way the ship would be able to know they were coming and they wouldn't trigger alarms without warning.

He hoped.

"Ready?" he asked the three standing around him in the big former exercise room with the scanning stations. This room would be their jump base. Jonas's group had the main scanning room, and the third group was using a back open area in the dining room.

Fisher, Maria, and Hudson all nodded as one that they were ready. Maria's excitement for the moment had turned to serious worry. He wanted to hug her and tell it would be all right, but damned if he knew it would be.

"I'm going to do the jumping. I'll take us about a kilometer away across the deck along the path toward the Command Center."

Again they all nodded.

So he jumped them.

The incredible open space of the huge deck surrounded them.

The air did smell slightly stale this second time out, and the temperature was slightly under what Fisher kept his ship, but not too cold to be a worry.

Fisher's ship looked like a tiny toy sitting in the middle of a huge room from this distance.

"Stunning," Hudson said softly as if whispering wouldn't draw attention to them.

Roscoe turned to Maria who was slowly turning, trying to take it all in, her large golden eyes even wider than normal.

"How do we look out ahead?" Roscoe asked her after giving her a moment to be shocked and look around.

He then moved over next to her as she fumbled to get her scanner out. Her scanner gave him a clear image of where they were jumping to, and a clear path to the Command Center.

It was going to take him about thirty minutes of quick jumps to get them there, mostly down huge hallways that appeared to be the width of a two-lane highway and up through decks into more hallways.

She checked the scan and then showed it to him, her shoulder brushing his arm. "We're clear."

He jumped them again.

"Scans are clear," Maria said.

"Triggering nothing," Callie's voice came across clear in their ears. The three back on the ship were there to scan ahead and make sure no team triggered anything. "Second team leaving the ship."

"Understood," Roscoe said as they looked around.

He had jumped them right into the middle of one of the huge hallways. Fifty people could walk side-by-side in this hallway and not even touch shoulders. And the ceiling was high and the lights were hidden, but clearly there.

Hudson kneeled and touched the carpet under their feet. "I don't think this is fabric," he said. "I think it's the decking surface itself formed to be soft and slightly flexible."

Fisher pointed to regularly spaced panels about every twenty paces. The panels were dark. "Seems like they might have a ship-wide transport system like our own."

"Ours is like this one," Maria said, smiling. "This ship has been in flight since before Seeders came into the Local Group."

"Yeah, that," Fisher said, smiling back at her.

"Amazing," Roscoe said. "But glad we're not hiking. What are these rooms around us?" He pointed at the closed doors that lined the hall every fifty feet or so and seemed to blend perfectly into the wall.

"Offices of some sort," Maria said, looking at her scanner.

"So how are we on the path ahead?" Roscoe asked Maria, moving over again to stand beside her and look at her scanner.

"Clear," she said.

He nodded. "I'm going to pick up speed now until we get near the Command Center. We jump, check scan, and jump again. So stay close to me."

Twelve jumps through identical hallways later, they were sixty-five decks higher in the big ship and in the hallway outside the *Morning Song's* big Command Center.

So far, so good.

And that worried Roscoe far more than he wanted to admit.

Nineteen

MARIA STOOD ONE hundred paces from the big door that led into the Morning Song's Command Center. She couldn't decide if she was more afraid or excited. Both emotions seemed to be warring with each other.

Roscoe seemed very worried, but he didn't say anything. Fisher also looked worried and Hudson just looked excited.

"This is where we discover just how friendly this ship really is," Roscoe said.

"Callie?" Fisher asked into the air, "any signs of anything coming to life around us or in the Command Center?"

"Nothing," Callie said.

Maria studied her scans. It just showed the big room, nothing more. "Clear here as well," she said.

Roscoe nodded and handed Fisher his rifle. Fisher nodded and put it over his shoulder.

"Back in a moment," Roscoe said, striding down the hallway toward the big door. "Stay there."

Maria held her breath, watching him walk. More than likely he was scared to death, but he didn't show it in the slightest. He was more amazing than she had even known.

She didn't know what she expected when he approached the door, but nothing didn't seem possible. Yet that was exactly what happened.

Nothing.

He walked right up to the door and stopped.

The door didn't slide open. She watched as he looked around for a way to have the door slide open, but clearly he didn't find anything. So he looked back at them and shrugged.

And then vanished.

Clearly he had transported somewhere. Inside the control room, she hoped.

A few seconds later he was back beside her and she actually was so glad to see him, she reached out and grabbed his arm.

"Did I trigger anything?" he asked.

"Nothing," Callie said.

Maria checked her scanner as well, as did Hudson.

"Nothing," she said.

"Callie, watch us closely," Roscoe said.

"Understood," Callie's voice came back strong.

Roscoe jumped them inside the Command Center, just inside the door.

And the sight took Maria's breath away.

Just as with everything on this ship, the Command Center was huge. It had the classic three levels, with a good thirty stations and chairs around the top half-circle level, most facing the wall back, some facing the monster screen on the front wall that was massive.

The air smelled faintly of fresh roses and the floor was a light tan color and soft.

The second level had ten chairs on it, all facing the big front screen. All clearly had heads-up displays that were powered down at the moment.

And in the very center, slightly ahead of all the other stations, two huge chairs towered over any person that might be sitting in them. They were a soft white and dominated the center of the room. They seemed to be linked, form-molded out of one piece of material.

Everything in the room was a brown tone except those two huge molded chairs. The white made them stand out and gave them even more importance.

As Maria moved around the room, she could see that one-half of the two huge chairs was clearly labeled for a man, one for a woman. And between the two chairs was a natural place for the two people to hold hands molded into the chairs.

"You have triggered nothing," Callie said. "But having you in that room clearly gives some perspective to the size of the room on the scans."

"It's huge and amazing," Fisher said.

Maria was just too stunned to say anything. With Roscoe at her side, she slowly moved down and stood in front of the two big command chairs.

Finally Roscoe glanced at her. "Anything like this in the history of the Seeders?"

She slowly shook her head. "Nothing that I have found."

Nothing in anything she knew had prepared her for the sight of those two locked command chairs.

They simply took her breath away.

Twenty

THEY SPENT a good half hour exploring the large room without touching anything before Roscoe recovered enough to ask the question that bothered him a lot.

"Why aren't these stations powering up?" Without the control stations powered up and the big screen working in front of them and all the other wall screens working as well, a Command Center was just sort of a plain room.

And those two molded-together command chairs made no sense at all.

Both Hudson and Maria shrugged that they had no answer, which bothered him more than he wanted to admit.

"We're going to need to touch a panel," Fisher said. "Just see what happens."

Roscoe agreed and hated that idea, but the only hope they had of this ship getting under their control was to do just that.

He moved over to a panel closest to him on an upper deck station and touched it.

It did nothing for a moment, then a screen came up with ancient Seeder writing on it.

"Maria. Hudson," he said softly, but clear enough for them to hear.

Both of them scrambled to his side. Fisher was right with them.

"Does that say what I think it says?"

"Oh, shit," Maria said, staring at the screen.

"We need a damned password," Hudson said. "Are you kidding me?"

On the screen the clear letters that Roscoe could read thanks to Fisher and Maria's people cracking the language problem.

Welcome to the Morning Song.
Please enter command permission code.

After a moment the screen went dark.

"What happened?" Callie asked from the ship. "Scans show a tiny energy signature and then nothing."

"We touched a panel," Fisher said as Roscoe turned away. "We need a command permission code to take control of the ship."

"Oh," was all Callie said.

Roscoe looked at Maria who was standing staring at the big blank screen on the front wall.

He moved over beside her. "How can the Seeders expect us to know a command code after a million plus years? They clearly do."

"I honestly don't know," she said, her voice soft.

He looked around at the stunned look on Fisher's face. Hudson had dropped to the floor, sitting cross-legged with his head in his hands.

"I'm jumping us back to the ship to get some food," Roscoe said. "We can work there on this."

Maria nodded and a moment later he had them back in the slightly warmer and far more comfortable interior of Fisher's ship in the scanning room.

"Come on," Roscoe said, taking off his gear and stashing it near a wall and then helping Maria out of her pack and taking the scanner from her hands and

putting her stuff next to his. "It's our turn to cook."

Fisher nodded. "I'll talk with Callie for a few minutes and join you both."

"I'm just going to sit here for a while," Hudson said, dropping into a chair at a screen.

With that, Roscoe took Maria's hand in his and led her slowly out of the big scanning room and down the small hallway toward the kitchen.

He loved the feel of her hand in his. It felt right and very natural.

She gripped his hand tightly, like he was saving her.

When they finally reached the kitchen, she let go of his hand and then faced him. "Thank you."

Before he could ask for what, she kissed him for the second time, and for the second time caught him by surprise.

But this time he kissed her back.

It was wonderful and they fit together. Her lips were firm and her body felt wonderful pressed against his.

The kiss lasted far, far too short a time before they broke apart and smiled at each other.

"That was great," he said. "Another promise for the future, I hope."

"A very near future," she said, smiling at him.

Then side-by-side, they went to work preparing dinner for fifteen people.

That felt wonderful.

And wonderfully natural to Roscoe.

Pretty soon they were both laughing.

He had a hunch that if they kept working together, they could solve even losing a million-year-old-password to control a machine that was about to kill millions.

Twenty-one

FOR THE REST of the day and all the next day, teams jumped all over the *Morning Song* exploring everything they could in that short amount of time. Maria spent almost as much time out exploring than back in Fisher's ship.

And all the time Roscoe was at her side. He wasn't leaving it, but he was letting her decide where they go. He knew that she needed to work and didn't push her at all.

All teams reported back the same thing with every mission. All systems except environmental were dead on the big ship, waiting for someone to enter a command code.

And Maria felt like it was her problem, her mistake, that she didn't know the command code. After all, she was the expert on the history of the Seeders.

They had fourteen hours remaining until the big ship again jumped to trans-tunnel flight and they could contact Chairman Ray.

She was feeling more and more exhausted and discouraged, but about to jump out again after a light dinner when Roscoe took her by the hand.

"We need to rest."

She looked up into worried intense eyes of a man she had come to respect a great deal. And one she was more attracted to than she could ever imagine.

"We've been going now for twenty-nine hours," he said. "A few hours sleep might help get the answer to this."

She nodded. She had known she was getting tired, but hadn't realized it had been that long.

Hudson, who had come into the room at that moment and heard the last part of the conversation said, "Oh, thank the heavens. I'll be in my room sleeping if you need me."

"Seven hours," Roscoe said as Hudson turned and left.

Maria laughed. "Guess we do need to rest."

Roscoe tapped the communication link with Fisher. "We're resting the team for about seven hours."

"Copy that," Fisher said. "Thanks."

Roscoe took Maria's hand and led her down the hall to her room. "We'll meet in the breakfast area in seven hours."

She yawned and nodded, then looked up at him, smiling. "Not going to kiss a girl goodnight at the door?"

Part of her really wanted the sleep, part of her wanted him to kiss her and make her forget everything.

He smiled back and kissed her lightly. Then pulled back.

"Sleep," he said.

She pretended to salute and then turned and went into her room, closing the door behind her on a man she really wanted to have join her. How silly was that?

She put on her comfortable night cotton pants, a light t-shirt, washed her face and dropped onto her bed.

Three hours later she woke up. Screw it. She wanted to sleep with Roscoe, even if they might not sleep the entire time.

She slipped on her slippers and went out into the hallway and down two doors to his room. She opened it slowly and stepped inside.

He was snoring lightly on his side, facing the wall.

She crawled in behind him, put her arms around him and snuggled close. He smelled wonderful, like a fresh forest, and he felt even better. He was only wearing boxer shorts and his strong muscles and smooth skin felt fantastic under her arms and hands.

He stirred and she said softly. "Sleep."

He reached around and put a hand on her butt and pulled her even closer to his back. Then he said softly, "This is nice."

"Sleep," she said.

He nodded and a moment later he was back asleep.

In all her long life, she had never felt so comfortable and safe with another person in her bed.

How was this even possible?

And before she could even think about that question, she was asleep again.

Twenty-two

ROSCOE AWOKE SLOWLY, enjoying the feel of Maria pressed against his side. He was on his back and his arm was curled around her. She was snuggled up against him, her red hair fanned over his arm.

She smelled of a light maple syrup and her skin under his hand was stunningly smooth and her muscles were firm. He knew she worked out, but he had no idea she was in such good shape.

He managed to turn his head enough to not wake her to see the time on a small dresser beside the bed. It was an hour before they needed to be showered, have some breakfast and make another few jumps before *Morning Song* jumped to trans-tunnel and they could talk to Chairman Ray again.

"You awake?" she asked softly, her voice husky as he turned back.

"Starting to," he said.

"This is nice," she said, snuggling against him. "You sleep all right?"

"Wonderfully," he said, "except for this red-headed pixie waking me up sneaking into my room. Nothing but a great dream I'm sure."

She laughed and ran her hand back and forth over his chest. She then tipped her head up and kissed him.

And that kiss was one he would remember for a very long time. Slow, but intense.

Finally she pulled away and snuggled back with him again. "How much time do we have before we meet the team?"

"Not much," he said. "Time to take showers and get something to eat."

"Seriously?" she asked. "I haven't slept that long in years."

She pushed herself up and sort of half-crawled on top of his chest to see the clock beside his bed. "Damn," she said. "We're going to have to be quick and quiet then."

With that, she crawled completely on top of him and pulled off her t-shirt. Her breasts were perfect and firm, with dark pink nipples. The upper half of her chest was completely covered with freckles.

Then she stood up, one leg on each side of him, balancing herself on the bed.

She pushed down her pants and slipped them off, one leg at a time until she was standing over him, straddling him, totally naked.

"Wow," was all he could manage to say. It had been a long time since he had been with a woman and he could never, in all the decades, ever remember someone as open as she was about being naked.

Staring up at her would be an image he would never, ever forget for as long as he lived.

"Don't move," he said.

He quickly sat up and kissed her crotch softly as he kicked off first the sheet over him and then his shorts.

She looked at him and how excited he was and smiled down at him. "We need to be quick and silent."

"After looking up at this wonderful sight," he said, stroking her wonderful body, "quick won't be an issue. Silent on the other hand..."

She came down on him, spreading out over him and kissing him hard, holding his penis between her legs.

Then she sat up slightly and slipped him inside her.

"Yeah, silent is going to be a problem," she said.

Then, as she started to move on him, she smothered him in the most wonderful kiss he could ever remember.

And somehow, that long and intense kiss kept them from being too noisy.

At least he hoped it did.

He honestly didn't care.

Twenty-three

FISHER WAS COOKING breakfast for him and Callie and Hudson when Maria and Roscoe walked in. She was holding his hand and she didn't care who saw it. It felt right and perfect. In all her life, she never thought that walking with a man holding hands would be something she would ever do, but they had walked from her room to the kitchen that way and she wanted to keep going.

The room smelled like cooking eggs and toast and made her stomach rumble.

Their quick lovemaking had been fantastic, and now they were both showered and refreshed. She had wanted them to take a shower together, but Roscoe rightly told her that if they did that, they wouldn't be on time.

But he made her promise him a shower check, like a rain check, only inside, just as wet, and a lot more fun.

She had laughed all the way through her own shower at that.

"You two manage to get some sleep?" Fisher asked without looking up from the stove.

Callie smiled and covered her mouth.

Maria let go of Roscoe's hand and sat down at the dining table. "Refreshed and ready to go," she said, winking at Callie, who damn near burst out laughing.

Hudson had his attention buried in a portable scanner and seemed very intent and didn't notice a thing.

Roscoe just shook his head at her and smiled. Then he said to Fisher, "Wow, does that smell amazing."

"Two more minutes is all," Fisher said. "Your timing is perfect."

"What are you looking at?" Maria asked Hudson.

The unshaven man looked up at her and blinked. Clearly he had showered and gotten a little sleep, but if she knew Hudson, it hadn't been much. His full head of black hair and full beard was as much of a mess as she had ever seen it.

"I've been researching into every myth and history we have about Seeder Mother Ships," Hudson said. "I've found two references to the dual command chairs."

Maria almost went across the table at that. She had never found a one.

Even Fisher turned from the stove at that statement, but then went right back to tending to breakfast.

"What are they?" she asked. "Did you find out their purpose?"

"They are referenced as 'The chairs of knowledge' both times," Hudson said, doing air quotes around the chairs of knowledge part. "The myths say that the reason they are joint command chairs is because the human race can't exist without both men and women."

"Symbols," Callie said, nodding. "A Mother Ship like this one takes a joint command."

Maria looked at Roscoe. Then back to Hudson. "Chairs of knowledge?"

Hudson nodded. "Both references. All I can find so far."

"And from what we can tell," Fisher said, "every screen and system on the ship needs the command code password to activate. But it seems everything on the ship is also hooked in a fashion to the Command Center and in a way to those two chairs."

"After breakfast we jump back to the Command Center," Maria said, nodding and looking at Roscoe. "I think we may have just solved the command code problem."

"And what's that," Fisher said.

"Roscoe and I have to sit in those chairs."

She looked at Roscoe, who nodded, clearly agreeing.

"Oh, yeah, good idea," Hudson said, shaking his head in disgust.

"Do you think anything will happen?" Callie asked.

"More than likely it will just ask for the command code," Maria said. "But those chairs might be set to sense Seeders and descendants of the Seeders sent in this direction."

"So you are saying," Roscoe asked, "that this ship needs a way beyond basic scanning to tell we are descendants?"

"I think so," Maria said. "But I don't think we have anything to lose. And right now we need to take a few chances."

Roscoe nodded. "After breakfast we'll give it a try."

She smiled at him and wanted to kiss him, but right at that moment Fisher started serving wonderful-smelling eggs and perfectly browned pancakes and light toast made out of that wonderful sweet bread.

After the long night's sleep and the wonderful session with Roscoe, she was hungry.

And once again excited about exploring this incredible huge ship. They would figure out a way to stop it from hurting anyone.

She believed that now.

Twenty-four

ROSCOE WASN'T VERY fond of the idea of them sitting in those two big command chairs. But if Maria thought it might be the solution to getting control of this monster ship, he would do it with her. As she had said, time was clicking down and they had to take some chances.

He doubted much would happen when they sat down, but who actually knew.

Clearly, the chairs were designed for two people. And he certainly wasn't going to stand to one side and let her sit in those chairs with anyone else.

After breakfast, the four of them gathered in the scanning room that was their base. Roscoe made sure all four of them had the supplies they were going to need, then looked at Maria. "Ready?"

She smiled that wonderful smile of hers that reached her golden eyes and said, "As I'll ever be."

Fisher and Hudson both nodded, so Roscoe jumped them all to the Command Center.

They stored their gear against a wall next to the door that wouldn't open, then all four of them moved down in front of the two big command chairs.

They were clearly molded to fit a human body, not just something to sit in, but something that allowed the head to rest back like a half helmet, and the arms to rest partially surrounded by the material of the chair.

Hudson and Maria both took scans.

"As dead as everything on this ship," Hudson said.

Roscoe knew that if they hesitated at all, they might not try this. They had to get this idea out of the way before they could move forward.

He reached over and took Maria's hand.

She smiled at him and nodded.

"Callie, keep a sharp eye for any changes," Fisher said to his wife back in their ship.

Roscoe knew that Callie and two others would be watching every detail of the equipment around them.

"Together?" Maria asked Roscoe.

"Together," he said.

Then holding hands as the form of the two chairs showed, they sat down and scooted back into the tall white chairs.

Roscoe could feel the softness of the chair as it seemed to mold to his body.

"Anything?" he asked Maria, not wanting to turn his head to look at her.

In front of them both Fisher and Hudson had worried looks on their faces. Fisher was watching them while Hudson stared at his scanner.

"Nothing yet," Maria said. "But it's sure comfortable. I think it's moving and fitting to my form."

Roscoe could feel the chair finish adjusting and supporting him.

"Mine as well," Roscoe said.

Then suddenly everything changed. Everything.

A blue translucent display screen appeared in front of him and Maria, between them and Fisher and Hudson. He could still see them through it.

And Roscoe could feel far more going on. He could feel his awareness expanding.

It was as if he could suddenly see everything about the ship.

And understand it all.

He could feel the connections in the ship to this chair.

And most importantly, he could sense and feel Maria beyond her hand he was holding.

She had become just sort of part of him.

He couldn't read her thoughts exactly, but he could sense how she was thinking and feeling and her excitement about what was happening.

He was sort of blended with her. He had no other way to put it.

And he knew she was blended with him as well.

"This is kind of strange," he said softly.

"Very," she said. "But it feels right."

"Very right," he said.

He suddenly realized he wasn't afraid or on guard at all. This did feel right.

Almost being blended with Maria's mind felt natural as well. He wanted to know what she was feeling, have her beside him at all times.

"Odd," she said out loud. "I like this."

She had been almost thinking the same thing he had been thinking.

"Any idea what's going on?" he asked.

On the other side of the blue screen, Hudson said, "The entire ship has activity."

Maria squeezed Roscoe's hand and said, "Look at the screen."

The message on the screen was clear.

Welcome Chairmen.
The command code for Morning Song *is Sunrise.*

"Thank you, *Morning Song*," Maria said.

The first message faded and a second message appeared.

You are welcome.

Roscoe could feel himself being drawn down into understanding areas of the ship that he had no idea even existed. The ship was teaching him in a much more advanced way than language was taught to Seeders when they first came into the organization.

He was learning and understanding and completely comprehending what he was learning.

All in seconds.

"Shall we get the ship stopped?" he asked.

"What?" Fisher asked from the other side of the blue screen that he and Hudson clearly couldn't see.

He could sense Maria turn her attention back from learning.

"It's our ship now," she said.

He knew instantly that was true. *Morning Song* was their ship, jointly. "Let's get it stopped and repaired from its long journey."

"Perfect," Maria said.

Fisher stepped toward them. "Can we ask what you two are talking about?"

Roscoe looked through the blue screen at Fisher. "Get every member of our team here quickly. No need to leave anyone on your ship. We need them here."

"To do what?" Fisher asked.

"We need to get this ship stopped," Roscoe said.

"Oh," was all Fisher said.

As Roscoe and Maria waited, together, holding hands between the chairs and in their minds, they learned about their new ship, every detail of their new ship.

And so much more about each other.

Twenty-five

MARIA COULDN'T BELIEVE the freedom and the lightness she felt sitting with Roscoe in the big chairs of knowledge. Now she understood why the legends called these chairs by that name.

Seemingly instantly, she knew Roscoe, knew his life, his dreams, his immense intelligence. And more importantly, she knew that he truly cared about people and loved being a Seeder.

She couldn't read his mind, but she sensed it all and knew what was right.

And she knew how much he cared for her, far more than she could have hoped, because she cared for him in the same way.

They were blended sitting in the big chairs.

Still individuals, yet blended as a team, working as a team.

It felt amazing to her. Just amazing.

And they were quickly learning every detail of the massive ship, from how the engines worked to the shields to the labs to the hanger bays. In her mind, she could see clearly Fisher's small ship sitting like a tiny bump in the big landing bay.

And she could even see the problem as to why the braking program hadn't kicked in and why the ship was still at full speed. It would be an easy fix, she knew that.

Her and Roscoe's eyes could see every detail, every room, every closet, of this wonderful big ship.

Through the ship's sensors, she could see the big Seeder fleet waiting for them at a point where the *Morning Song* would jump to trans-tunnel drive.

She even understood the physics now of trans-tunnel drive. Before, that had always baffled her.

And she knew that the intelligence that was *Morning Song* was very much an entity, a complete life in its own way that had kept this ship alive and moving and repaired as much as possible through a voyage in deep space of one-point-four million years.

Now, as their teams gathered around them in the big Command Center, Roscoe took charge of assigning each a station in the big room.

"Command code is Sunrise at each station," he said as they quickly moved to their stations.

"Put in the command code," Maria said, "and then put your right hand beside the image where indicated."

"What will that do?" Fisher asked as he moved to a position beside Roscoe on his right.

Callie moved to a position on the left of Maria.

"*Morning Song* will give you a quick training in the station's use," Roscoe said.

"Perfectly safe," Maria said.

He squeezed her hand and as they felt each of their friends come on line and spend a moment learning the station, she and Roscoe kept learning, taking in every detail of the big ship.

Before she could not imagine the scale of the ship. Now it all seemed clear and logical and useful.

"Notice we have no mission statement or history," Roscoe said as they waited the few moments it was taking for everyone to get trained.

"I did," she said.

On the screen in front of them, *Morning Song* replied to his statement.

That information will be supplied after you have control of Morning Song and have all safe.

Your training will take some time.

"Thank you again, *Morning Song*," Maria said.

Again the first message faded and a second message appeared.

You are again welcome.

"Everyone is now on task," Roscoe said a moment after Maria sensed that the stations in the big room were manned and functioning.

"Please monitor your stations carefully," Maria said. "Big screen is coming up."

The entire wall beyond their thin blue monitoring screen became a screen showing space ahead of *Morning Song.*

Then Maria had the blue monitoring screen lowered and both her and Roscoe's heads-up displays appeared.

They were still holding hands, but Maria and Roscoe both knew that would not bother them in the slightest. In fact, it was critical to them staying in contact and working as a unit. All of their commands and actions would be through either *Morning Song* or the crew around them.

"We're going to flip *Morning Song* 180 degrees," Roscoe said. "Fisher, stay with me on this. Everyone, monitor your stations. Shout if the slightest thing gets out of line."

"Understood," Fisher said.

"Morning Song," Roscoe asked. "You understand what is needed?"

Yes.

Maria said, "Callie, please contact Chairman Ray. Tell him we are in control of *Morning Song* and to have all ships stay out of the way until we are finished. Link him into the monitors in here, but please do not put through his audio. Tell him of that restriction so he won't worry."

"Understood," Callie said.

Maria watched and monitored everything closely as Roscoe and *Morning Song* took the big ship and eased her over so that her engines were now facing in the direction of flight. *Morning Song* itself did most of the maneuver, but it could not

have done it without Roscoe's mind and skill as a pilot.

Maria could see Fisher watching closely from his station.

Maria knew that this wonderful ship had taken almost four hundred years to climb to this rate of speed. Now they had to slow it much, much faster if they had any hope of saving millions of lives.

Any hope at all.

"We'll get it done," Roscoe said, clearly sensing her worry.

But they both knew that the *Morning Song* was not meant for such intense braking. They would not have it stopped before they plowed into Fisher and Callie's home world.

But they had other options.

Twenty-six

"COMPLETE," FISHER SAID. "Engines are now facing in the direction of travel."

"Engines coming on line," Maria said.

"Bring the engines up to full power slowly," Roscoe said. "Everyone, monitor your stations closely. Take your time."

Roscoe couldn't believe that he and the intelligence that was *Morning Song* had just done a very difficult maneuver. He had always considered himself a good pilot, but flying this ship would have been far beyond him. You don't just flip a ship the size of a moon 180 degrees without chances of tearing it apart.

Maria squeezed his hand and he could sense her worry as well. And her excitement.

He could almost feel her monitoring the engines as he was, beside him completely in all areas of the ship.

The engines were powering up, slowly at first, then as they stabilized after such a long voyage, their power increased.

"Full power and stable," Fisher said.

Roscoe had known that a moment before Fisher spoke.

Around the room everyone cheered.

"At full power," Roscoe said, "how long until we reach full stop?"

"Seven months and three days," Hudson said from his station.

The cheering stopped as the situation that both Roscoe and Maria knew already sank in.

"*Morning Song*," Maria asked. "May Chairman Mundy and I leave the chairs and possibly the ship and still be in contact with you?"

Yes.

Roscoe instantly knew that in the arm of his chair and Maria's chair was a small needle that would implant a device to allow them to keep in contact with the *Morning Song*.

"Please insert the device," Roscoe said.

"Yes, please," Maria said.

Roscoe felt a slight sting.

"Everyone please do a full check of the systems attached to your panels," Maria said.

Roscoe and Maria both did the same, going over every detail of the ship to make sure that *Morning Song* was stable and slowing.

Then Roscoe took the final precaution.

"*Morning Song*, is the ship stable and slowing?"

Yes.

"Do you see any signs of weakness in any system or engine?" Roscoe asked.

No, but repairs need to be made after full stop.

"We understand that," Maria said. "And they will be done. Thank you."

"We are planning on taking a break now and working toward getting more help on board," Roscoe said. "Do you see any problem with that?"

No.
Please return to the command chairs as soon as possible to continue your training and education.

"We will," Maria said.

With that, Roscoe stood and pulled Maria gently to her feet. He could still feel he was connected, melded in a way with her in so many ways, ways he didn't yet fully understand.

She stood, still holding his hand.

He could sense her reluctance to let go. Her beautiful golden eyes were almost swirling with all the new information.

Around them the big Command Center was silent as everyone watched them.

Finally, he nodded to her. And together they let go of each other's hand.

He could still sense her, still felt meshed with her, and could still feel all the systems in the big ship around them.

She looked around, then smiled at him. "Seems you're stuck with me for a while."

"For a lot longer than a while, I hope," he said.

At that, everyone in the big Command Center broke into cheers and applause and together, they turned to the crew and took a bow.

Twenty-seven

"WE'RE GOING TO need to talk to Chairman Ray," Maria said after the cheering died down.

"He and everyone on his ship have been watching," Callie said, smiling. "As best they can with the time deletion. We've been moving in real fast motion as far as they are concerned."

Roscoe laughed at the idea of that.

Maria really didn't want to just talk with Ray out in the open. And she could sense that Roscoe did not either.

"*Morning Song*," Maria said into the air. "Can we personally transport away from the ship and return?"

On the wall-sized monitor in front of the room the word "Yes" appeared.

"Will we still be in contact with you and the systems of the ship?"

Again the word "Yes" appeared.

"Thank you, *Morning Song*," Maria said.

Maria knew from everything she had learned that normal procedure for a *Morning Song* crew was to leave at least five in the Command Center at all times.

A pilot, a person at security, and three engineers.

Roscoe knew that as well and turned to his second-in-command, Jonas, who had been assigned the security main post. "Stay at your post until I return."

Jonas nodded.

Maria looked at Hudson. "Please stay at your station."

Hudson nodded, his eyes wide from all he had learned in the quick training. He was so eager to learn all the time and all this sudden knowledge must really be messing with his balance.

"Callie, you have command while we are gone," Roscoe said. "But please avoid those chairs."

She laughed and pointed down at her station in front of her. "Right here is just fine."

They picked two other engineers to stay as well, then Roscoe told the rest of them to jump back to Fisher and Callie's ship and get something to eat and rest. Until they got help, all of them would be doing long shifts.

Then Maria turned to Fisher. "You are with us."

He nodded.

She then turned to Roscoe. "Do the honors, partner."

He smiled, took her hand, and jumped all three of them to the bridge of Chairman Ray's ship.

Chairman Ray was sitting in his command chair, watching the big screen in front of him that showed the Command Center of the *Morning Song*.

As they appeared, he and Tacita both jumped to their feet. Then they both did something that Maria would have never imagined them doing in her entire long life.

He and Tacita both bowed to her and Roscoe.

And everyone else on the bridge bowed to them as well.

"Welcome, Chairmen," Chairman Ray said.

She looked at Roscoe who clearly was as shocked as she felt. She could sense his shock and how really deep it ran. Somehow, Roscoe managed to speak. She wasn't sure how. She would not have been able to.

"Can we talk in a private area?" Roscoe asked.

An instant later the five of them were in a large meeting room. It was filled with a long conference table with a white top with a dozen cloth office chairs around it. A large screen, now blank, filled one wall.

The lighting was indirect and bright and there was no smell at all.

A completely sterile-looking room and Maria wondered why anyone would have a room like this one.

Chairman Ray and Tacita took the chairs near one end on the far side of the table, Fisher took the chair in front of him across from Ray and Tacita, clearly just as puzzled as she and Roscoe were.

She and Roscoe took the chairs at the end of the big table.

"So what was all that about?" Roscoe asked.

Maria let her knee move against his leg and could feel his strength and energy just from the touch.

"You both have been chosen for a very honored position among Seeders," Ray said. He looked at Tacita and she nodded.

So Chairman Ray looked back at them and leaned forward. "This was why you were picked for this mission. We hoped that if we figured out a way to get inside, *Morning Song* would accept you both."

Maria sat back and just stared at Ray.

They had known about Seeder Mother Ships. She couldn't believe that. Why hadn't they said something?

"They have not had time for the history of the Seeders," Tacita said, touching her husband's arm gently. "They do not understand, but they will. They have much to learn, as I am sure *Morning Song* told them."

Ray nodded. "You are right, we have a more pressing problem to deal with first."

Maria just sat there, staring at Ray.

Again it was Roscoe who seemed to find his footing a little faster than she did. "We need to save millions."

Now it was Ray's turn to look puzzled. Then he laughed. "You already did that."

Roscoe looked at Fisher, then at Maria.

Maria sat forward. "And just how did we do that?"

"By taking control of the ship, stopping the malfunction, turning the ship around, and starting to brake," Ray said.

Suddenly Maria understood. "We are not letting the ship jump to one-hundred-light-year trans-tunnel flights."

It took a moment, but Roscoe started to laugh and then Fisher followed.

"It's going to take a few hundred years or more at this sub-light speed," Ray said, "for that ship to even reach the edge of the Milky Way, even without braking."

"Oh, thank the heavens," Maria said, leaning back and staring at the ceiling. She couldn't believe how completely relieved she felt. And she could sense Roscoe beside her feeling relieved and happy as well.

They had accomplished their mission.

"So what's the pressing problem we need to face now?"

Ray started to speak, but Tacita touched his arm and shook her head.

Then Tacita sat forward and looked directly at Maria with a dark intensity that Maria had never seen before.

"You need to go back to *Morning Song* and continue your education. Then we can talk."

"Can we at least get help manning the big ship?"

"In four weeks," Ray said, "your speed will be slow enough for us to match with our normal ships and start sending crew aboard. And you will need to pick most of them and a command crew. Until then, I'm afraid it's just the fifteen of you. You will do fine. *Morning Song* is a very good ship."

Then Ray and Tacita stood and bowed slightly to her and Roscoe.

"Please excuse us," Ray said. "Time is short and we have a lot to do."

With that, they both vanished, leaving Fisher, Roscoe, and Maria half out of their chairs.

Maria had no idea at all what just happened.

None.

Twenty-eight

ROSCOE JUMPED THEM back on board *Morning Song* and into Fisher's ship inside the big scanning room. He instantly felt better.

"That's amazing," Maria said. "I feel like I'm home."

"I think we are," Roscoe said, smiling at her.

"So either of you have any idea what just happened?" Fisher asked. "If you do,

you can explain it to me as I get us something to eat."

They followed Fisher into the kitchen and Roscoe sat down at the dining table and Maria sat beside him, her hand resting on his leg, keeping the connection between them. That connection seemed to be growing stronger by the moment and Roscoe liked that more than he wanted to admit.

He wanted her to be a part of him. And he had a hunch that if she wasn't close, he would no longer feel whole.

Just as being away from *Morning Song* didn't feel right.

"I think that Ray and Tacita knew right from the start what the big ship was," Maria said.

"I agree," Roscoe said. "But I have no idea why they didn't tell us."

"And how do they know?" Maria asked. "My sense is that they have sat in a joint command chair at some point in the past."

"Could they really be that old?" Fisher asked as he pulled out bread and some cut turkey to make sandwiches with.

"Nothing stopping any of us from getting very, very old," Maria said. "*Morning Song* promised us history and far more education. Seems we need that."

"I agree completely," Roscoe said. "Maybe after that we will understand why they didn't tell us what this ship was in the first place. And what they were in such a hurry to go do."

Then he sat back enjoying the feel of Maria beside him as they planned crew rotation onto the *Morning Song* Command Center.

About halfway through the quick lunch, Roscoe suddenly had a thought. "You can't count Maria and me as part of that rotation."

She looked at him and then nodded, clearly understanding.

"We're going to be in school," Roscoe said.

"And at times we might not actually be on board," Maria said.

"That's possible as well," he said, nodding. "It's up to you to just keep this big ship braking and stable while we learn what we can about what we are up against and what comes next."

Fisher just shook his head and said, "I'll do my best."

Roscoe smiled at Fisher. "She's a good ship. She'll help you."

"I hope so," Fisher said.

After they finished, Roscoe took Maria's hand, enjoying the feel and the energy running through it to him.

"Ready to go to class?"

"As I'll ever be," she said, smiling at him and then quickly kissing him.

This kiss surprised them both because even more energy flowed between them and a lot more caring and feeling.

It was so passionate in just a slight kiss, it took his breath away.

"Well, that's going to be interesting," she said, touching her lips and then smiling at him.

She was flushed and breathing hard.

"And that's an understatement," he said.

"What just happened there?" Fisher asked, frowning at them.

Maria laughed. "More information than you want to know."

Fisher blushed and turned away to clean up the dishes. "Meet you in the Command Center."

Roscoe and Maria both laughed, then holding hands, jumped back to the heart and soul and brains of *Morning Song*.

Twenty-nine

MARIA STOOD IN front of the two command chairs, holding hands with Roscoe. A tiny part of her was worried about sitting down again, but honestly, she felt excited about the learning she knew was coming.

"How did it go with Chairman Ray?" Callie asked.

"Interesting describes it," Roscoe said. "Fisher will explain. He'll be here in a moment."

She nodded.

Maria pulled Roscoe toward the two chairs. "We have some lessons to learn."

"Looking forward to it," he said, squeezing her hand.

Then they turned and sat down, scooting back into the form-fitting chairs and making sure they had a solid hold of each other's hands.

Again the blue heads-up screen came up in front of them and Maria could again feel her mind expanding even more.

She and Roscoe both did a quick check of all the ship's major systems.

"Everything seems to functioning fine," Maria said.

"Better than can be expected after such a long trip," Roscoe said. "*Morning Song*, you have done a great job over the long voyage."

Words appeared on the translucent blue screen in front of them.

Thank you, Chairmen.
Are you ready for the next stage?

"We are," Maria said.

The form of the chairs shifted and encased them quickly in a tight but comfortable shell. She still held Roscoe's hand, but could see nothing at all.

There was no sense of movement at all, but within just a few seconds the big chairs opened back up.

They were now sitting in a large circular room, their two chairs on a higher level looking out over what looked like a comfortable living room. Five steps led down into the round center of the room.

Long couches, large overstuffed chairs, coffee tables, all formed in groups in the large room like a lounge, or a very comfortable waiting area. The floor seemed to have a carpet of some sort on it and everything was in brown tones.

Maria guessed that the room might hold a hundred people without trouble, and there were enough couches and chairs for more than that. It was an immense round room. But at the same time it had numbers of areas where just a few people could talk and feel private.

The ceiling was far overhead and the light indirect. The only thing she could smell was a faint scent of bread cooking.

Maria knew that they were supposed to stand and just make themselves at home. So they both did stand, looking around, but keeping their hands together.

Maria was amazed. The huge room, even for its size, felt very, very comfortable.

Maria had a sense where they were, but she didn't want to think about that being possible.

Roscoe pointed at the wide area where their two chairs sat. "Landing areas for a good fifty sets of chairs around the room. See the marks on the floor?"

She did and she agreed. This is where the Chairmen came.

At that moment another set of command chairs shimmered into existence about a quarter turn around the circle away from them.

Maria remained holding Roscoe's hand as the new command chairs opened and Chairman Ray and Tacita stood, smiling.

Of all the people she had expected to see here for their training, it was not them. Not after the way they had acted on their ship just a short time ago.

Chairman Ray, his long gray hair flowing behind him, stepped down into the main part of the room with Tacita at his side.

Roscoe glanced at her, then led them down the five steps.

"Where are we?" Maria asked as they got near Chairman Ray.

"Earth," Ray said, smiling.

"All human cultures name their home world Earth," Roscoe said, annoyed at the dance of an answer.

But Maria knew what Ray meant. She had to just let him say it.

"The first Earth," Ray said, still smiling and indicating they should sit on a comfortable-looking couch. "This is the home world of all the Seeders."

Maria just couldn't breathe.

It felt like something heavy was on her chest.

It wasn't possible.

She knew that the Seeder home world was just a myth. She never expected to be here.

Yet she knew, with her connection to *Morning Song*, that Ray was telling the truth.

She was on Earth.

Not her Earth or Roscoe's Earth.

The first Earth.

Thirty

ROSCOE COULD SENSE how upset Maria was and squeezed her hand some and guided her to sit down beside him on one of the soft-looking couches.

As they sat, the couch shifted slightly and molded perfectly to their forms.

Ray and Tacita sat across from them, both smiling.

"We are sorry about our deception on my ship," Ray said. "We knew you were going to go back to the *Morning Song* and immediately jump here for your training and we needed to get to our ship to get here as well to greet you and help you get started and answer questions we couldn't answer with Chairman Fisher present."

"Where is your Mother Ship located?" Maria asked.

"In the spiral galaxy that is named The Sevens by the residents there," Tacita said, her voice soft for the first time that Maria had ever heard. "It's the same spiral galaxy that *Morning Song* originated from."

"It is our base," Ray said. "Our ship is called *Warm Night*. We built the *Morning Song* there along with her sister ship, *Morning Breeze,* who is coming into the Milky Way in about forty thousand years on the same path."

"You built them?" Maria asked, trying to wrap her head around how old the two sitting across from them really were.

"We did," Tacita said, nodding.

"Maria and I are the first Chairmen of the *Morning Song*?" Roscoe asked, clearly as surprised as Maria felt.

"The only ones there will ever be unless there is an accident or you have a desire to step down," Ray said. "She is your ship and your companion from the moment you sat down and she accepted you."

Maria had nothing to say.

Neither did Roscoe it seemed.

Ray smiled. "I assume since you had just gotten here you have eaten before coming?"

"We did," Maria managed to say.

"Good," Ray said, standing. "We will jump back when your first training is complete to help in answering any questions you might have."

"Just stay seated," Tacita said as she stood beside Ray.

Then they turned and moved toward their command chairs.

And at that moment a simple bubble surrounded Maria and Roscoe and collapsed in skin-tight on them.

Maria only had a moment to even think about it before the images came flooding in.

And for the first time, she started to really understand that even though she had been an expert, how little she had known about Seeders.

And their history.

Thirty-one

AS THE BUBBLE that had wrapped around them dropped and Roscoe let the last of the images fade away, he shook his head. It felt like he had had so much information crammed into his mind, it would be impossible to remember it all.

But somehow, it felt like he did.

Around them the large circular room hadn't changed at all.

He was still holding Maria's hand and he turned to face her.

"You all right?"

"I think so," she said, blinking her wonderful golden eyes. He could feel so much more of their attraction now and all he wanted to do was hold her in his arms.

She moved over and leaned into him and he put his arm around her.

"This feels perfect."

"It does," he said.

They sat there silently like that for a good minute, just not talking. Roscoe was lost in all the information he had been given, and in his incredible feeling for Maria.

Two command chairs shimmered into place and again Chairman Ray and Tacita got out and came toward them.

"How long were we in that information flow?" Roscoe asked, describing what had happened to them in the best way he could.

"Three hours," Ray said.

"Food will be brought in for all of us," Tacita said, "and we can answer questions as you have them."

"I'm not sure what I know and don't know," Maria said.

"That feeling will pass with time as your mind organizes everything," Ray said.

Roscoe nodded.

"Can you help me," Maria said, "if possible, understand a timeline structure for the Seeders."

"Of course," Ray said. "It was your passion before this, I would have assumed it would remain your passion."

Roscoe was just going to let her lead on this. He needed the same thing, a way to organize the vast amount of information that had flowed into his mind in the last few hours.

"The Seeders originated on this planet?" she asked. "The first Earth as it is called."

"Yes," Ray said.

"And as they managed to make it into space and discovered trans-tunnel drive, they spread out and discovered they were alone in the universe."

"They were alone in this galaxy, yes," Ray said.

Roscoe was following all of this and having Maria talk it out loud really was helping him organize his mind as well.

"And as they spread out, they developed the techniques the frontline Seeders use now in terraforming appropriate planets," Maria said, "and then seeding them with human life and plant life from their original home world."

"Yes," Ray said. "But in those first few hundred thousand years in this galaxy, they learned the hard lesson about the falseness of non-intervention in growing human civilizations. It was not a smooth road to galaxy-wide stability."

Roscoe nodded, remembering all that very clearly now as Ray put it in clear form.

"After this galaxy stabilized," Ray said, "and became very advanced, faster ships were built from a series of really lucky inventions and we were able to jump to a nearby galaxy. We again found no other intelligent life."

"So they seeded it," Maria said, nodding.

"Yes," Ray said. "And continued on until in one galaxy the explorers ran across alien life, a young civilization they called The Ants because of their heritage."

Roscoe could see The Ants clearly in his mind. Very close to Earth ants, only the size of small dogs and with advanced hive minds. When humans had discovered them, The Ants had managed to get into space, but only barely.

"We left that galaxy alone and moved around them," Ray said, "not bothering them."

"They are now extinct?" Maria said simply.

"Sadly, yes," Ray said. "But we have not touched their galaxy in any fashion in case some of their members have survived."

"Seven alien races, seven galaxies skipped," Roscoe said, clearly getting the images of each alien race. None of them felt threatening in any fashion in his teaching. And four of the seven were now extinct. None of the four had yet to make it out of their own home system.

Roscoe knew there was an entire branch of Seeders who did nothing but study and look for new life forms. They always moved ahead of any Seeder frontline into a galaxy to make sure there were no aliens in that galaxy anywhere.

"That is correct," Ray said, answering Roscoe's statement about how humans skip entire galaxies with hints of alien races.

Tacita finally added to the discussion. "To answer the next question, no one really knows exactly how many galaxies humans have spread over. The galaxy this original planet is in cannot be seen from the Milky Way."

"That far?" Roscoe asked, again not being able to comprehend the distance.

"That far. No number really describes the distance," Ray said.

"How many Mother Seeder ships are there?" Maria asked.

Roscoe was surprised he didn't have that information in the giant information load they had taken in.

"At the moment there are twenty-eight of us," Ray said. "Counting your ship. Fourteen more ships are in transit as the *Morning Song* did, but we hope without the programmed braking problem. Ten more are under construction in various galaxies."

"We need many, many more," Tacita said.

Ray only nodded to that.

Some Classic Dean Wesley Smith Stories
Available at your favorite booksellers.

"And our mission," Roscoe said, "is to crew and stock the *Morning Song* and head out from the Milky Way in a new direction?"

"That is the basics of it," Ray said.

Maria squeezed Roscoe's hand to signal there was more that Ray wasn't saying, but Roscoe had caught that as well.

"But you want us to go in a certain direction," Roscoe said, "that has some possible problems, correct?"

Ray and Tacita both sat there staring at them, then Ray nodded slowly. "Yes. We have heard that there may be another galaxy-spanning race in the direction we would like you and *Morning Song* to go."

Suddenly he and Maria being picked for this made sense.

He looked at Ray and nodded. "You picked Military and History and a lot of brains to lead this because you think we may need both in what we run into. And we are from a young galaxy still able to think without centuries of training into Seeder dogma."

Ray and Tacita nodded.

"After a time of growth and steady worlds, humans by nature are very pacifistic," Ray said. "We would stand little to no chance against an aggressive alien race who didn't like us. We don't even like large governments and when not needed, we disband them."

"Did you know this alien race might be out there," Maria asked, "when you sent the leading edge of Seeders and the *Morning Song* over a million years ago toward the Milky Way?"

"Yes," Ray said bluntly. "We need you to recruit fighters as well as workers and arm *Morning Song* for a fight if needed."

"The empty hanger," Roscoe said. "A fighter deck."

"Yes," Ray said. "And when the second ship arrives in forty thousand years, it will recruit from Andromeda and head out in a similar, but slightly different direction to see what it can find."

"And you have not scouted this alien race in any fashion?" Roscoe asked.

"We have some," Ray said. "From what we can tell, their main galaxy a million years ago was about thirty galaxies from the Milky Way, but we have no idea if they are now advancing or not in any direction. We really know little about them. All of this will be in the final educational session in ten days. One thing at a time."

Roscoe didn't much like waiting on something as important as that, but he understood. And Maria's hand in his helped him.

At that moment a table appeared between them, their seats on the couch lifted them to a comfortable dining position close to the table, and then food appeared.

Turkey, gravy, rolls, and more potatoes and dressing than any four people could eat in a week.

And it smelled heavenly. Until that moment Roscoe didn't realize just how hungry he had become.

"Eat," Ray said. "Then return to *Morning Song* and rest. Tomorrow will be another long day of learning."

"Can our minds handle this kind of information flow for ten more days?" Roscoe asked.

Ray and Tacita both smiled. Then Tacita said simply. "Yes, and you have only begun the learning. It will continue for life."

Then she leaned forward and grabbed a large drumstick as Roscoe just sat there until Maria pushed him to start eating.

Now Available
from all your favorite booksellers
in trade paper and electronic editions.

Section Three:
An Understanding of Power

Thirty-two

WHEN MARIA AND Roscoe returned to *Morning Song*, both Callie and Fisher came running down to the lower level of the Command Center to face them. They were both clearly very happy and relieved.

Behind them the big screen showed the open space and in the distance was the Milky Way Galaxy, filling a quarter of the screen with its billions of suns.

Maria felt like she was once again home and could feel herself relax.

She and Roscoe both did a quick scan of *Morning Song* to make sure she was doing all right. Everything seemed perfectly in balance and the big ship was still braking. After they got down far enough to allow other crew to come on board, they could start some of the major repairs that were needed.

Maria smiled at Callie and Fisher as she and Roscoe stood, continuing to hold hands. "We didn't know we were leaving like that or we would have warned you."

"Yeah, a surprise," Roscoe said.

"Where did you go?" Fisher asked.

"A long ways away to do a training session in the history of Seeders," Maria said.

"Every day we will be doing another," Roscoe said, "I suppose on different topics, so this will be normal. Are you all right here?"

"We are," Fisher nodded. "We're doing eight hour shifts and rotating."

"Great," Maria said.

Roscoe looked at her and smiled. "You up for a little exploring before we get some rest and go back to class?"

"I'd love that," she said, smiling, a surge of excitement running through her. Even though she knew the seeder history now and she really understood this ship, she wanted to see it all for herself.

Roscoe looked at Fisher. "Call if you need our help. And *Morning Song*, please help them and keep us informed."

On the image of space that filled the large front screen, the letters formed.

I will.

"Thank you, *Morning Song*," Maria said.

Then Roscoe squeezed her hand and jumped them.

As they arrived, the lights came up.

They were standing in a huge, multi-leveled room with a giant fireplace in the center far wall. It did not have furniture, but Maria could imagine this big room with art, furniture, and a crackling fire in the fireplace being amazingly comfortable.

It felt comfortable and like a home even without furniture.

The floor had a soft substance that felt like carpet on it, but she knew from her knowledge of the ship that it wasn't. It was part of the decking and could be altered to be as thick or as hard or any color that anyone wanted.

She knew exactly where they were. Roscoe had jumped them to the Chairmen's Suite.

Their suite.

"Wow," she said, looking around.

Hand-in-hand, they moved to look at the huge master bedroom and bath with a giant shower and a wonderful-looking tub that she knew she could spend hours in soaking and reading.

They both knew that the water systems in the big ship would need some major work to be up to full function after the long voyage. *Morning Song* had robots working on it, but they were making very little progress. So neither of them suggested using the big shower.

Each of them had their own office in the large suite attached as well, each office with its own bathroom attached.

There was also a huge kitchen and nice sized dining area that could hold a table for ten easily. And there was a larger dining area that could hold thirty people.

Even totally empty, this space felt wonderful and she knew, without a doubt, she could be home and very comfortable living here.

She turned and kissed Roscoe.

As with the kiss in the kitchen, the simple kiss took on entirely new levels of passion and intensity.

It felt like she was making love to him at that moment.

Through the kiss she felt even closer to him and more blended with him and clearly in love with this stunning man.

She pressed herself against him and he pushed back, standing there in the doorway of their future kitchen, kissing.

Kissing and so much more.

More passion than she had ever felt in her life.

Finally, he broke the kiss and stood there breathing hard as if he had run a fast mile.

She felt the same way. She felt like a schoolgirl getting a first kiss, excited and breathless, yet at the same time she felt like she had just made love to Roscoe for thirty minutes.

"Wow," was all she said.

He smiled and nodded to that, still breathing hard, his dark eyes staring into hers.

Finally, he turned and indicated the big suite with a sweep of his arm. "You like the place?"

"Do you?" she asked, holding his hand and pushing her shoulder into his arm.

"I do if you'll live here with me," he said, turning to face her again.

"Are you asking me to move in with you?" she asked, smiling at him. "We've only known each other less than a month."

"I am," he said, smiling right back.

"Then I love the place if I am living here with you."

She kissed him again, and once again it felt as if they were making love just standing there, pressed against each other, kissing.

When she broke the kiss that time, she laughed.

He was again breathing hard.

Then for the first time in hours, she let go of his hand and walked down the few steps to the area in front of the big fireplace, slowly taking her clothes off as she went.

Behind her she heard Roscoe say, "*Morning Song*, please do not allow scans of this suite."

In her mind she knew that *Morning Song* had agreed.

"Thank you, *Morning Song*," she said as she kicked her pants aside and turned to face the man she planned on spending a long time with.

He had his shirt off and he was staring at her naked body in a way that only a man could stare.

And she loved it.

She lay down on the fairly soft carpet-like flooring and smiled up at him as he struggled to get his pants off.

Then finally, he was on top of her and inside her.

And the passion was so great, she came almost instantly as the two of them melded both minds and bodies.

Thirty-three

FOR THE NEXT ten days, Roscoe and Maria went back to the big education and meeting room. Within minutes each time, Ray and Tacita joined them to prep them for the day's learning and answer questions and eat dinner with them when it was finished.

Roscoe felt like his mind was going to explode each day when the session was finished. One day was completely on the process of terraforming a planet. Another was on trans-tunnel mechanics, another was about political and governmental systems, the patterns humans took in growing cultures, and how to stop wars.

Ten topics total until the final day.

And every day he and Maria had gone back to *Morning Song* to check on the status of their ship, to help the tiring crew where they could, to make love, and then sleep.

They had used a few hours each day to explore their ship, including spending one hour just walking between the huge Seeder ships secured to one of the two major flight decks.

Even in an hour, they didn't get very far. There were so many ships and they were all so large. Even understanding it, the size and scope stunned Roscoe.

Finally they went back for their tenth lesson. Today it was about the coming mission.

This lesson worried Roscoe and Maria more than anything. They knew their mission on *Morning Song* was to seed new galaxies with human life, but they also knew they had to determine who the other major race was and that race's intentions.

So before they went under the bubble in the big room, Chairman Ray said, "We'll stay until you are finished this time."

And when they were finished, Roscoe finally understood why Chairman Ray had stayed. The aliens were very real and very powerful.

But they weren't aliens. They were humans.

It seems in the first education day, they had left out a pretty important galaxy-wide war that had happened in the first galaxy.

An off-shoot human culture from this galaxy called Lotus, after their first great, warlike leader, were the threats close to the Milky Way.

"That is not what I expected," Roscoe said after the bubble dropped and they could talk.

Maria squeezed his hand. He could tell she was as upset as he was. He would have rather been fighting alien spiders or intelligent raccoons or something.

Chairman Ray and Tacita were sitting across from them, worried looks on both of their faces.

"Now you understand why we could not scout them very well," Ray said.

"We could not allow them to know we were even close in any fashion," Tacita said, "you were given all the information we have about them and their culture."

Roscoe nodded. "Trans-tunnel flight, a desire to expand, they do not do terraforming, but instead leave planets the way they were and just take over and make bases and control the life there in a war-like way."

"Yes, when this galaxy's sane cultures finally cornered them and defeated them, we banned the survivors from this part of the universe," Ray said.

Roscoe nodded, the teaching clear in his head and starting to make sense.

"You built what was effectively the first Seeder Mother Ship called *Dark Night*," Roscoe said, "put the remaining four million members all in suspended animation, and sent the ship at full trans-tunnel continuous drive for six hundred thousand years."

"Yes," Ray said. "To a galaxy so far away, it never occurred to anyone at the time we would get close to it millions of years later."

"And you made sure *Dark Night* would never fly at top speeds again once it reached that galaxy," Maria said, nodding. "Thus trapping them in the one galaxy unless they made huge scientific jumps."

"Yes," Ray said. "And honestly, after so much time, we had basically forgotten about them until scout ships searching for alien life ahead of seeding realized how close they were to the target galaxy and pulled back."

Roscoe tried accessing a question he had and couldn't find it, so he asked. "You have no evidence that they have left their one galaxy?"

"That is correct," Ray said. "It is a hope we all share that they have not. The scout ships that realized where it was at in relation to the target galaxy came back into known space to report."

"But two million years ago they still survived in that galaxy," Ray said. "We will need you and your scouts from *Morning Song* to determine if they have expanded, very carefully."

"So we will not get near or seed any of the closest galaxies to theirs," Maria said.

"Again, a plan we think wise," Ray said.

Roscoe nodded to Maria. "We can deal with this."

"Can you see why we wanted new Chairmen with your abilities and youth?" Ray asked.

"We will need to maintain a military posture on *Morning Song*," Roscoe said, understanding completely. As Ray had said, advanced human cultures become pacifists and forget how to fight eventually.

"And I am needed to use my skills and talents," Maria said, "to map this area of the known universe in a way that makes sense and make sure all Seeders close are aware of restricted territories."

"Yes," Tacita said.

"But I have a question," Maria said. "Why do the Seeders have no historical memory past what we have been trained here? Why are entire galaxies of humans just left on their own to let the knowledge of Seeders drop into myth or religion?"

"Human nature," Tacita said. "When there is no threat to home or life, humans don't care about the past or what's even on the other side of their own planet."

"For a few hundred galaxies," Rays said, "when we first left this galaxy, we tried to maintain a cultural memory with those we helped start. But it never held and no one seemed to care."

Roscoe had seen that already at a much smaller scale, more than he wanted to admit. It was already happening in the Milky Way and Seeders were still everywhere in every culture there, helping them along.

"Well," Maria said firmly, "with the Lotus as neighbors, forgetting is not an option. So for the Local Group of galaxies and the ones we seed, we will change that practice."

Ray and Tacita both nodded, then smiled.

"They are smiling," Roscoe said to Maria, "because they are proud they picked us."

"We are proud," Ray said, laughing.

At that, the dinner table rose from the ground again and food appeared, steaming and smelling wonderful.

As they turned to dig into the roast beef and steamed vegetables, Roscoe decided he had one more question that he had been wondering about every day since he saw this big place.

"Do all the Chairmen meet at any point?"

"Once a year on the anniversary of the launching of the first Seeder Mother Ship," Ray said.

"And when is that?" Maria said. "How many standard days away?"

"Two-hundred-and-six days," Tacita said.

"How long ago did it launch?" Roscoe asked, wondering why all this information wasn't in the information flow in their minds.

"Just over six million years ago," Tacita said.

"Whose ship was that?" Maria asked as she dug into a pile of mashed potatoes that looked heavenly.

"Ours," Ray said, smiling as he took a second slice of roast beef with one hand

and reached out and touched Tacita's shoulder fondly with the other.

Roscoe had a first bite of roast beef almost to his mouth when Ray said that.

Eventually, the bite made it all the way.

Eventually.

Thirty-four

OVER THE NEXT ten days as they got *Morning Song* slowed enough to start taking on crew, Maria and Roscoe jumped to many various ships to start the hiring of crew.

Mother Ships worked just as any other Seeder ship. It was basically a corporation that hired crew and paid them. Any crew member could leave at any point and settle on a planet.

Living on the ship was cheap, far less than any salary working on a Seeder ship, so all crew members saved most of their income and often retired to a favorite planet after only a decade or so. Some were lifers, not caring much about the money, using it to help others where they could.

Maria had talked with Roscoe at different times about how he felt about spending such a long time with her, especially after they learned how really old Ray and Tacita were. The answer that Roscoe gave that finally satisfied her was "I'll tell you in a few thousand years."

She had really liked the sound of that and had kissed him and they almost hadn't gotten back to work.

But they had because of the amount of work they had to do.

They were faced with what seemed like an impossible task. They had an empty ship that was in need of some pretty extensive repairs after its million-plus years in space.

The warehouses were stocked with furniture, parts, and just about anything else needed on board the ship except for food. So bringing in food and getting the kitchens up and running would be fairly high on the list.

And the water system was a mess and had to be upgraded completely after so many years of lack of use. In fact, the ship had never been used, so many of the problems were new-built problems, even though the ship was so old.

Repairing water systems and major support systems was top on the list and could be done as the ship continued to slow, as soon as they got help on board.

Maria had come to love the ship, though, over the twenty days. She could feel *Morning Song* with her at every moment and loved that. She talked to *Morning Song* a lot and where possible, *Morning Song* would answer on a nearby screen.

But as the twenty days went on, she had also just fallen more and more in love with Roscoe. She felt she was blended with him, yet they were both very distinct people.

They often finished each other's sentences and they laughed a lot.

And they made love every day. With each lovemaking session, she felt even closer to him.

Making love, they became one person.

And one of them was always touching the other it seemed. They gained energy from contact.

On the day they decided to let the first ship try to dock with the *Morning Song*, she and Roscoe were in their command chairs. They had decided that Roscoe's former ship, *The Huntington,* should try first. It was the fastest of all the Seeder ships at sub-light speeds.

On the bridge beside them at one station was Fisher on Roscoe's right and on the other side Callie on Maria's left. The two of them just felt comfortable now in those third and fourth command positions. Maria liked them there.

All fifteen on board *Morning Song* were in the Command Center, leaving Fisher and Callie's ship, *The Lady,* empty.

"First, *Morning Song,*" Maria said, studying her heads-up display, "we need to move *The Lady* to one side of the big landing bay."

On the big screen in front of them was the image of *The Lady* sitting in the middle of the huge landing bay.

"A position close to Entrance 63," Roscoe said.

Maria knew that was the entrance they had used on their jumps to the Command Center the first time.

"Can we do that?"

The word "Yes" appeared in the middle of the big screen.

"Everyone, monitor your stations," Roscoe said.

"Go ahead, *Morning Song,*" Maria said.

The Lady vanished from its position on the big dock and appeared near one wall, still looking very small.

Maria could tell that all systems were stable.

"Very good, *Morning Song,*" Maria said.

The words *Thank you* appeared on the big screen over the image of the mostly empty landing dock.

"Power down engines to full shutdown," Roscoe said.

Maria watched the systems closely as the engines slowly powered down. They had decided it would be easier for a ship to match a constant speed than one that was changing every second.

"Engines powering down," Fisher reported, more for the rest of the crew, since she and Roscoe got the information slightly ahead of everyone through their big chairs.

"Atmosphere shield on the docking bay door seems to be functioning," Hudson said from a station behind her.

"Engines shut down," Fisher reported. "Everything stable."

Maria shifted the image on the big screen to show *The Huntington* matching speeds with them just outside the big bay door.

Red, who was now Chairman of *The Huntington*, came over the link. "Speeds matched. Engines off."

"Open the bay doors," Maria said.

The bay doors seemed to hesitate for a moment, then slid back in four directions.

Maria knew they would need to be serviced as well, but for the moment they were working.

"Atmosphere shield holding," Hudson said.

"*Morning Song*," Maria said. "Please bring *The Huntington* on board."

Maria knew a tractor beam had taken a firm grip around *The Huntington* and was pulling it in through the doors.

"Wow, some perspective," Roscoe said.

Maria was stunned as well. *The Huntington* was the biggest warship the Seeders had built in Andromeda, and yet coming in through the big bay doors, it looked almost like a toy hanging there.

"Middle of the deck is fine, *Morning Song*," Roscoe said. "They won't be staying that long."

The Huntington drifted over the massive deck and eased to the surface.

"Closing bay doors," Maria said.

"Tractor beam released," Roscoe said.

A moment later Red and Mattie's faces came across clear on the big screen. "Welcome to the *Morning Song*," Roscoe said, smiling at his old friends from Sector Justice.

"Wow," was all Red could say.

"Bring engines back to full. Let's keep slowing down," Roscoe said.

"Engines coming back up slowly," Fisher said.

Maria and Roscoe both stayed in the big chair until the engines were up and running smoothly and the ship was stable.

"Thank you, *Morning Song*," Maria said, standing and pulling Roscoe up as well.

"Very well done," Roscoe said.

The words *Thank you* again appeared on the big screen.

"Hudson, you have Command Center," Roscoe said. "Everyone stay to rotations for now. Help has arrived.

Hudson's head snapped up and his eyes were wide.

Maria squeezed Roscoe's hand for being so mean, and barely stopped a laugh at Hudson's look. He would be fine, just as Roscoe knew he would. Plus, *Morning Song* would warn them if something was going wrong.

Roscoe turned to Fisher and Callie. "Want to meet our first guests?"

"Love to," Callie said.

And a moment later Roscoe had the four of them in the Command Center of *The Huntington*.

And after the first twenty minutes of explaining the size and scope of *Morning Song*, Maria realized that they had one more important task that needed to be done very quickly. There needed to be an introduction video to *Morning Song* that everyone was required to watch.

Before coming on board.

Thirty-five

IT TOOK ANOTHER twenty days for the crew of *The Huntington* to take over some of Command Center duties and start repairs.

The fifteen original members on Fisher's ship remained there, sleeping and eating together, since they had all become friends. Roscoe liked those dinners since Fisher was such a great cook.

He and Maria had borrowed an extra bed and transported it to their suite on *Morning Song* because they just didn't want to keep everyone awake with their lovemaking. Besides, even without furniture, they loved their suite.

The crew of *The Huntington* bunked and ate on board ship, since repairs to the water systems on *Morning Song* were far from started, let alone completed.

Roscoe and Maria had been talking and wanted to offer the second-in-command to Fisher and Callie. But they weren't sure how to go about it. So one afternoon as things were calm, they jumped to Chairman Ray and Tacita's ship after asking the day before if they could.

They ended up back in the sterile meeting room and both Ray and Tacita were happy to see them.

"How is the learning settling in?" Ray asked as they all took seats, Ray and Tacita on one side, Roscoe and Maria on the other. As they always did, Roscoe and Maria moved so their legs would be in contact.

Roscoe shrugged. "I know the knowledge is there and I find myself knowing something suddenly when I need to know it, but I have no memory of knowing the information before. I'm no longer surprised at that happening."

Maria laughed. "Describes my experience exactly."

"It will get smoother with time," Tacita said.

Roscoe glanced at Maria and she nodded that he should go ahead. "We are wondering if we can offer the job of second-in-command of the upcoming mission to Fisher and Callie."

Ray sat back, smiling.

Tacita shook her head. "You can offer any job on the *Morning Song* to anyone you want, as long as *Morning Song* approves.

"We are not your bosses anymore," Ray said. "It is your ship, you have your mission, you do as you see fit on that mission. But you do need to ask your ship."

Roscoe nodded. That made sense. *Morning Song* needed to be able to work with them.

"Without sitting in the chairs," Maria asked, "is there any way *Morning Song* can give them the knowledge about herself she gave us at first?"

"Any panel will tell them," Tacita said.

"But I would do that in private," Ray said, "since they will have a lot of questions."

"Do you think Fisher and Callie will agree?" Tacita asked Roscoe.

Roscoe smiled at Ray and Tacita. "You put the four of us together for a reason, didn't you?"

"We did," Ray said, smiling. "If Fisher and Callie agree, can we ask one thing?"

"Certainly," Maria said.

Roscoe knew exactly what Ray was going to ask, so he said it first. "You want them in forty years to chair the next Mother Ship coming in."

Again, Ray laughed. "Yes. But I would suggest you not tell them that, not at first at least."

Tacita nodded. "Wait five or ten thousand years."

Again Roscoe just couldn't imagine living that long. But he agreed anyway.

Two days later *Morning Song* had agreed to their choice of Fisher and Callie, and Fisher and Callie had agreed and said they were honored beyond words.

Then they had gone through the scanner brain widening in the Command Center and been stunned.

"I can actually see and understand the ship now," Fisher said, looking off into the distance in his mind.

Roscoe laughed at that, since that was exactly how he had felt.

"*Morning Song,*" Callie said, "You are a masterpiece in construction and engineering."

The words *Thank You, Callie*, appeared on the big screen in the Command Center.

Maria hugged Callie at that.

That evening, in the kitchen of *The Lady*, while Fisher cooked a wonderful dinner in celebration, the four of them laughed and joked and then started to plan what was needed to be done over the next few years to get ready for the mission.

Ten days later, *Morning Song* had slowed enough to start bringing in more help.

The Huntington, with about half her crew staying, left to go start recruiting and setting up construction areas for the building of the warships needed.

Roscoe and Maria had put Red and Mattie in charge of the military wing of the mission and all the recruitment, since *Morning Song* had liked both of them and they both had agreed to go along when asked.

The plan that Roscoe and Maria and Fisher and Callie had worked out was pretty set. It would take almost five years to hire crew, do needed repairs, stock everything, and build enough ships to have a fighter fleet on board.

For Seeders, five years was a blink of an eye.

Chairman Ray thought that far too fast, but said he would wait and see.

For Roscoe, it seemed like a very long time.

But as long as he and Maria were together, time really didn't seem to matter.

The First Seven Issues
from all your favorite booksellers
in trade paper and electronic editions.

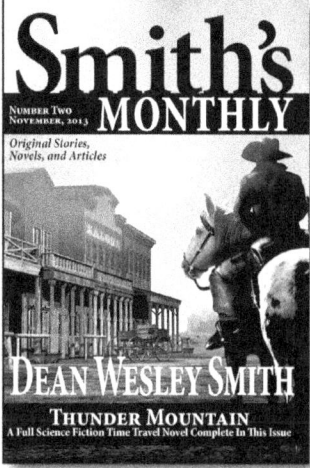

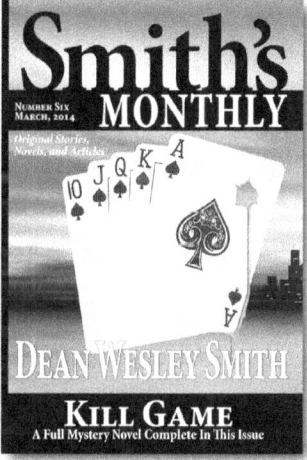

A subscription to *Smith's Monthly* saves you money and ensures you receive a monthly dose of diverse reading from *USA Today* bestselling author Dean Wesley Smith. Subscriptions are available in electronic and trade paper formats and begin with the very next volume. Subscribe today at www.SmithsMonthly.com. And if you missed one of these previously published issues, they're available from your favorite bookstore or online retailer.

Section Four:
The Mission Change

Thirty-Six

A MONTH LATER, more and more crew were coming on board and fanning out into different areas of *Morning Song*, doing repairs and bringing up stations. A promise of flowing water was still a ways away, something both Roscoe and Maria could hardly wait to have happen. Then they would be able to furnish and actually move into their Chairmen's suite.

They spent a lot of days, evenings, and often late into the nights in the command chairs, linked in with everything going on over the ship, working to prioritize what needed to be done first and helping the repair crews where they could.

Everything was going well, but over the last few days, there was something that had been bothering Roscoe as it became clear that their plan was soon going to be in full forward motion very soon.

Another couple of months, *Morning Song* will have slowed enough to actually trans-tunnel jump to a large Seeder base in a satellite galaxy on the way to Andromeda where all major repairs and crew recruitment would really start.

And those preparations included building a large military fleet.

So one night, after he and Maria had spent a wonderful hour in their suite making love, he brought what was worrying him to Maria.

She was naked, her wonderful red hair spread over the bed, her shoulder cradled into his side, her arm over him and her leg over his leg. They often slept just like that, feeling more comfortable touching as much as they could.

He couldn't even remember or imagine being alone as he had before meeting her. That just seemed like an alien time and memory.

"I'm bothered by something," he said.

"Nothing I did, I hope," she said, snuggling even closer against him.

"Oh, heavens, no," he said, laughing and hugging her. "I'm worried that we are planning for a mission with million-year-old scouting data."

She pushed herself up on her elbow and looked into his eyes with those wonderful, round, golden eyes of hers.

"You suggesting we send a scouting mission?"

"No, I think you and I need to do it," he said. "We need to see what we are taking over a million people on the *Morning Song* into."

Now she frowned. "How? The target galaxy is over thirty galaxies away from here. We can't be gone that long from the preparations here. That would take a decade to get there and back at top trans-tunnel speeds."

"I know," he said, smiling at her.

She shook her head and laughed. "You have a plan, don't you?"

"I do," he said, smiling at her, "but it will take being in the Command Center and the help of *Morning Song* to lay it all out."

She pushed away from him and stood, her wonderful naked body shining in the dim light of the bedroom in their suite.

"Where are you going?" he asked, enjoying the view of her toned body and smooth skin and the patterns of freckles.

"We're not sleeping until we work this through," she said, grabbing her slacks she had shoved off to one side of the bed. "You want to present this idea to Fisher and Callie as well at the same time? They are still in Command Center."

He stood, laughing. This was not what he expected, but he should have. "Might as well."

She pulled on the thin, silk blouse she had been wearing earlier without the exercise bra, then said simply, "*Morning Song*, please warn Chairman Fisher that we will be arriving."

Five minutes later, after one long kiss that Maria said was to hold her, they jumped to Command Center.

Thirty-Seven

THE MOMENT ROSCOE said that he was bothered by planning a mission on ancient scouting data, she knew he was right. And he seemed to have a way to scout the distant target galaxy without spending the years to get there.

Somehow. He was smart that way and could see patterns and solutions no one around him could see. One of the thousands of things she loved about him.

The overall mission was that *Morning Song* would seed galaxies along the way, getting close to the target galaxy in about one and a half million years. Maria was still having a very difficult time grasping those sorts of time spans, but yet it seemed very ambitious that they could completely seed an entire galaxy with human life in only fifty thousand years. But that was a normal time for Seeders.

In the Command Center, both Callie and Fisher stood as Maria and Roscoe appeared. They had both been working at their stations on either side of the big chairs. Both wore jeans and Fisher had on a dress shirt with his sleeves rolled up while Callie wore a white blouse with a necklace of freshwater pearls.

The Command Center felt like her home every time she came here. Even though it was a huge space, it felt intimate to Maria.

There were four other crew members in the room, so Roscoe turned to them and said, "Please take a break, everyone. Chairman Fisher will contact you when you can return."

All of them nodded and vanished.

"So what's happening?" Fisher asked, looking puzzled.

Maria smiled and sat on the empty chair for one of the environmental stations. "Roscoe has a plan he wants to run past the four of us and *Morning Song*."

"To do what?" Callie asked.

"We need to scout where we are headed," Roscoe said. "Before we make preparations we either don't need, or that are not enough."

Callie and Fisher both nodded.

Maria turned to face the big screen. "*Morning Song*, please bring up a two dimensional representation of the galaxies between the Milky Way and our target galaxy that are on the plan to seed."

On the screen the Milky Way was labeled. Then like stones crossing a river, the other galaxies and satellite galaxies along the way were marked, with a line from one to the other. The line stopped short of a galaxy marked with an X.

Maria had seen that image a number of times and studied it. If she really was as long-lived as it seemed she would be, barring accidents, that simple map represented the next million and a half years of her life.

Impossible for her to grasp, so she had made herself stop thinking about it.

"*Morning Song*, at a Seeder ship's fastest trans-tunnel pace," Roscoe said, "how long would it take to get to the target galaxy?"

The answer appeared on the screen below the map as a direct line appeared from the Milky Way to the target galaxy.

Seventy-one years.

"To your knowledge," Roscoe asked, "are there any Seeder ships between here and the target galaxy. If there are, explain what they are and show their locations."

Twelve scout ships.

Green dots appeared showing the locations of all the scout ships searching ahead for any sign of intelligent alien life.

Maria knew those ships were slightly smaller than Chairman Ray's ship and held a crew of a thousand or more. A couple of the scout ships were even larger and very fast. They were staffed with mostly scientists and explorers and their families, people who loved to push off into the unknown to see what they could find.

Those scout ships were very fast and only lightly armed, but had the best screens known to Seeder technology, so they could move around without ever being seen if there was alien life. She knew from the knowledge poured into her head that the scout ships often spent a couple hundred years or more in a galaxy.

The closest ship to the target galaxy was only two galaxies away from the target.

Suddenly Maria understood what Roscoe was thinking.

"*Morning Song*," Maria asked. "At full speed, how long would it take the closest scout ship to reach the target galaxy?"

Approximately twenty-three days.

Roscoe was smiling.

Maria went over and kissed him, then hugged him. "That's just brilliant."

Fisher cleared his throat and then said, "We might need a little more explanation here."

Maria turned to the big screen again and pointed. "*Morning Song*, please connect each ship with each other ship, starting from the Milky Way."

Green lines connected the green dots.

"Is any distance between ships too far for Chairman Ray to transport?" Roscoe asked.

No.
You and Chairman Boone could also make the jumps.

Now that shocked Maria. She had no idea she had that ability. She wouldn't even begin to know how to do it. Just the idea of transporting herself over an entire galaxy gave her the shudders.

Beside her, Roscoe was staring at the big screen, shaking his head. Clearly he had not known he could do that either.

Thirty-Eight

ROSCOE LOOKED AT Maria and smiled after he got over the shock of being told he could personally transport over distances between galaxies. He honestly didn't want to think about that at the moment.

Besides, he wanted Chairman Ray and Tacita to be part of this scouting mission as well.

But looking at the big screen, he suddenly realized something else that needed to be added to the upcoming mission, part of Maria's plan to help Seeders have more of a historical memory, even over millions of years.

"*Morning Song*," Roscoe asked. "Approximately how far can a person who has been given training as a Seeder transport under normal conditions?"

Over one hundred thousand light years is standard

"Why that question?" Maria asked, looking puzzled.

"A new addition to our mission," Roscoe said. "We add in jump stations along our path so any of us can easily return to the Milky Way at any time."

She instantly understood what he was suggesting and again gave him a hug.

"That will help with the Seeder historical records," she said.

"And help us return to our lodge at times for rest periods," Fisher said, smiling. "Thank you."

Roscoe could tell that Fisher and Callie really, really liked that idea. Leaving their lodge was one of the only hesitations they had about joining the mission.

"It will also make recruiting for this mission much easier," Callie said.

"We'll call it *Project Breadcrumbs*," Maria said. "Each jump station can have shops, sleeping areas, restaurants, and so on."

He loved that and they all laughed, but he knew the name would stick. And he had to admit, it would help a lot with recruiting. Someone knowing they could return home at any moment was much better than trying to convince someone to never return.

"So when do we talk with Chairman Ray and Tacita," Maria asked, "about this scouting mission and jump station idea."

"How about now?" Roscoe asked. "If there are objections, I sure would like to hear them before we go any farther."

"So would I," Maria said.

She took Roscoe by the hand and pulled him down toward their chairs. He knew what she was doing. In the chairs, they could talk directly to Chairman Ray and ask him to come here if he was close. As far as Roscoe knew, Ray was close.

They sat down in the chair and a moment later were melded even more than they were outside the chair.

Roscoe loved that feeling.

He loved everything about being close to Maria.

"Chairman Ray?" Maria said aloud, knowing her voice was being sent to Ray. "Would you and Tacita have a few moments to talk with us in *Morning Song's* Command Center?"

"Certainly," Ray said, his image clear in the reply. "Five minutes."

He cut off and Roscoe stood, pulling Maria to her feet.

"Well?" Fisher asked.

"Chairman Ray is on the way," Roscoe said, turning to look up at the images still on the big screen. He had no doubt this coming conversation was going to be interesting. He just wasn't sure how or in which direction it would go.

"*Morning Song*, please clear your screen for the moment," Maria asked.

The big screen cleared.

Roscoe had no idea what he would do if Chairman Ray said no to this scouting idea. There was no way he was going to spend years preparing a mission without knowing a little of what they were facing.

He had been in the military far too long to do that. He wasn't going to take millions of humans on *Morning Song* into some huge disaster or fight without being prepared correctly.

And correctly meant he needed to know what they were going to face, even a million and a half years in the future.

Thirty-nine

MARIA WAS HOLDING Roscoe's hand when Chairman Ray and Tacita appeared. Ray was in his standard gray slacks and silk dress shirt and Tacita had on dark pants and a white blouse that set off her black hair.

She looked stunning to Maria.

"Thank you for joining us," Roscoe said as Chairman Ray nodded to each of them.

They were all standing on the second deck behind the big chairs, Maria and Roscoe together, Ray and Tacita together, touching but not holding hands, and Callie and Fisher standing together.

"It is always a pleasure," Ray said. "So what can we help with?"

"We have two ideas that are linked," Roscoe said. "First, we hope to add into the overall mission the building of jump stations as we go along."

"Jump stations?" Tacita asked, frowning.

"Yes," Maria said, taking the lead with this idea, "stations on planets or in orbits or in deep space of some sort that we will design ahead that will allow any Seeder to jump back to the Milky Way and Local Group from any point along our mission. Or any galaxy we have left and recruited from as we move forward."

"Spaced about every one hundred thousand light years," Roscoe said, "a normal range that most Seeders can jump."

"It will help with my project of adding in a historical memory for Seeders," Maria said.

"And it will help in recruiting over the next few years," Fisher said.

"We call it *Project Breadcrumbs*," Maria said.

"Has that been tried before to your knowledge?" Roscoe asked.

Maria watched intently, her stomach twisting slightly as Chairman Ray glanced at Tacita, then shook his head.

"Such an obvious and good idea," Ray said, "but it has never been done to my knowledge."

"It is a very good idea," Tacita said. "Once the basic stations are designed, it could be fitted into the Local Group here as well, since all races in this area are still young and many Seeders would love to return at times to their home planets."

Roscoe smiled at Maria who squeezed his hand in excitement. She couldn't believe they liked the idea and that it had never been tried. Of course, Maria knew that if Roscoe hadn't thought of it, it still wouldn't be happening.

"I assume the second idea is the one that is in question," Chairman Ray said.

Roscoe nodded. "You recruited us because we were young and also had a military sense about our culture."

"That is correct," Ray said, nodding.

Maria was almost holding her breath she was so worried about this suddenly.

"So we need to act in a military fashion right now," Roscoe said.

Ray looked puzzled.

Tacita said flatly, "I do not understand what you mean."

"In any military situation," Roscoe said, "no army or soldier will ever go into a battle or mission without good advanced intelligence. Right now, we are planning this mission on extremely old data and that kind of reckless movement could well lead to disaster."

"What do you suggest?" Ray asked, his voice low and not cold, but not welcoming.

"We scout the target galaxy again, right now, so our preparations are in line with the threat we face," Roscoe said.

Maria turned to the big screen. "*Morning Song*, please put on the big screen the galaxies between here and the target galaxy."

The image of the Milky Way appeared with the galaxies between it and the target galaxy, again marked with a red "x" over it.

"Thank you, *Morning Song*," Maria said. "Now show the location of all Seeder Scout ships along that line."

The green dots appeared along the way.

"We can tell," Roscoe said, "at least from any reports coming from that lead scout ship, that the Lotus is not within two galaxies of that lead ship's position."

Ray nodded, looking up at the big screen. Then he frowned and shook his head.

Roscoe turned and looked directly at both Ray and Tacita. "I propose we jump to that lead scout ship and take a look at the Lotus galaxy before we go too much farther with large-scale plans to include a large military force on *Morning Song* when there is a good chance it won't be needed."

Maria could feel herself still holding her breath. This was one of those turning point moments and both she and Roscoe knew it. She wasn't sure how they had gone from making love to having a moment that might change decades and maybe centuries of work, but they had.

Ray stood there for a moment, then asked a simple question. "*Morning Song*, what is the name of that lead scout ship?"

On the big screen the words appeared over the images of the galaxy.

I do not know for certain, Chairman Ray

Maria watched as Ray nodded, then he said simply, "We will return in five minutes."

Tacita and Ray vanished, leaving the Command Center in silence.

Maria just shook her head and squeezed Roscoe's hand.

"When I'm that age," Fisher said, "I hope I explain my actions to the poor people around me a little better."

"When you're that age," Roscoe said, "you won't have to."

Maria laughed.

Fisher said, "Good point."

Then standing there in silence, Maria looked up at the screen and suddenly had a thought she didn't much like.

"*Morning Song*," Maria said. "How do you know the location of those ships? And do you know who sent them on those missions?"

The positions are their assigned projected positions at this point in time.

Chairman Ray sent them on the mission ahead of my being launched, ahead of the Seeder ships coming to the Local Group.

"Oh, crap," Fisher said softly.

Maria's stomach clamped up and she had a hunch their great idea to scout ahead had just been shot down.

"Are you telling me," Roscoe said, staring at the big board with disbelief, "that those scout ships have been out scouting for almost two million years?"

"Yes," Maria said softly.

"And that lead ship might not be there after all," Callie said, "or it might have been taken over by Lotus if they are expanding?"

"Yes," Chairman Ray said as he and Tacita appeared again. "That is exactly the result of using old data, as I have been asking you to do. That has been my problem and we need to correct that."

Maria stared at Ray for a moment, surprised at that statement.

"Do we even know if any of those ships are in those positions?" Roscoe asked.

"We do," Tacita said, "because being scout ships is their job and how they get paid. They scout and report back. Over the two millions years each of those ships has returned to a major Seeder galaxy many, many times for overhaul and updates of equipment. Scout ships always use the most advanced technology and have the best screens and speed."

"They also send a comprehensive report back every ten years," Ray said.

Ray turned to the big screen. "*Morning Song*, please contact my ship and update your records on this topic."

An instant later, on the screen about a third of the green dots vanished. But the ship two galaxies away from the target galaxy was still there.

"*The Horizon* is the name of that lead ship," Ray said. "It has over two thousand humans on board and is extremely fast and modern. Chairman Strong welcomes the use of his ship for such a scouting purpose you proposed, Chairman Mundy. He will have his ship under way at full speed toward the target galaxy in three hours. It will take just over twenty days for him to get there."

"How does he even know?" Maria asked, stunned, staring at the screen showing the incredible distance from the Milky Way over thirty galaxies to the solo green dot on the screen.

Ray just shrugged, as if that was a silly question. "I just spoke with him."

Forty

ROSCOE AND MARIA spent the next twenty days continuing almost day and night with the repairs to *Morning Song*.

And every day they found time to make love in their unfurnished suite. Maria insisted they spend that private time and Roscoe was not going to decline something like that with the most beautiful woman he had ever met.

And one he was head-over-feet in love with as well.

The crew on board had grown from the original fifteen to just over six hundred. And yet *Morning Song* still seemed completely empty to Roscoe.

Finally, after what seemed like an incredible task with more problems than Roscoe could ever imagine, the water systems on the ship had been completely repaired, recharged, flushed, and deemed safe. Having that system shut down and in near-zero temps had caused seemingly millions of problems. But now all the problems were fixed and it was functioning.

Finally, the original team could leave Fisher and Callie's wonderful ship, get their own places to live, and let Fisher and Callie have some peace.

So Roscoe and Maria spent a few hours in the morning in one of the huge warehouses, finding furniture for their suite.

And by that evening, it was furnished enough to live in. Even the fireplace was working. They had put very soft brown area rugs in certain places for contrast, and the kitchen was completely stocked. Maria had even found some incredible pictures of various worlds, framed in storage, and hung them on the walls.

She said as they visited new places together, they would replace them.

Roscoe had to admit, the place felt like home, a home he would enjoy for a very long time.

When Roscoe told Fisher that their kitchen was finally stocked and working, Fisher offered to cook the four of them the first meal in the new kitchen. Both Roscoe and Maria had taken him up on that instantly, since they had come to love his cooking and Fisher loved to cook.

Maria said it was better to start off their new kitchen with a quality meal instead of something either she or Roscoe could do.

And the meal had been wonderful. Great chicken dinner with great friends and lots of laughter. Nothing could have better for the first full meal in their new home.

Then next morning, Roscoe told Fisher and Callie to take good care of *Morning Song,* and he and Maria jumped to Chairman Ray's ship.

The Command Center there felt very small compared to *Morning Song's.* Roscoe was stunned he had been getting used to the huge size so quickly.

Ray and Tacita were standing there in front of the big screen. And both nodded to them as they appeared.

Roscoe had no idea what might happen. He knew that being so far away from known homes bothered him more than he wanted to admit. Sort of feeling like he was out in an ocean and couldn't see land.

Of course, over the next million plus years, all the galaxies they were going to jump over would be seeded with human life, by a ship and crews he controlled. But in the meantime, there just wasn't anything in any of them. All scout ships had come up completely empty for any intelligent alien life in any of the galaxies.

"We're only taking the four of us," Ray said. "And I'm going to jump us all the way to *The Horizon.* They are nearing the border of the target galaxy."

Maria glanced at Roscoe and took his hand. Clearly she was as worried about this as he was.

Roscoe just nodded and Ray reached over and took Tacita's hand in his. Then he smiled and a moment later the four of them were standing in a very modern Command Center.

There were seven crew in the room, four manning stations on the upper level, three at stations on the middle level. The place was pure white and what metal there was shined.

As they appeared, everyone stood and bowed slightly.

Then a young man with a beaming smile and short, blonde hair stepped forward from near the center command chair. "It is an honor to have you on board, Chairmen."

"The honor is ours," Chairman Ray said, bowing slightly.

Roscoe had no idea what all the bowing was about, but at some point he needed to ask someone.

Then Ray turned to Tacita. "Chairman Strong, you know Tacita?"

Strong bowed slightly again. "Always a pleasure."

Tacita bowed back.

Ray pointed to Roscoe and Maria where they stood holding hands. "Chairmen Mundy and Boone of *Morning Song*."

Strong's eyes got large and Roscoe was surprised at that kind of reaction. He bowed once again and said, "We are honored."

Roscoe didn't know what to say, so Maria jumped in. "We are the ones who are honored that you gave this mission such important attention."

"Yes, very much," Roscoe said.

With that, Strong nodded to one of his crew and turned around and pointed at the big screen. "Let me show you what we have found so far. We are within a few hours of the edge of the target galaxy at this speed and we are completely shielded."

On the screen a large mass of stars appeared. Roscoe knew the galaxy was a cluster galaxy that sat alone, with no secondary galaxies or satellite galaxies even close. It had about the same number of stars as the Milky Way, but there was no telling how many were suited for life. Cluster galaxies tended to have fewer on average than spiral galaxies.

"Long-range scans are showing no signs of any forms of extremely advanced cultures at all."

"Nothing?" Ray asked, sounding surprised.

"Nothing so far, sir," Strong said.

"That should not be the case," Ray said.

Roscoe wasn't surprised at all. But he didn't want to tell Ray that. Over the last few hundred years, and especially in the last forty working in the Sector Justice force, Roscoe had seen how short-lived dictators and totalitarian governments were. They often destroyed themselves quickly, even without Seeder help.

A huge ship full of humans had arrived here more millions of years ago than Roscoe wanted to think about. If they had managed to establish a stable, war-like culture, he would have been very, very surprised and worried. He was pretty sure a culture like that wasn't possible for more than a few hundred years.

But still, the chance of that was why they were here. And that fear was why Chairman Ray had sent the *Morning Song* and picked him and Maria.

But the chance was not great anything remained here.

"Any sign of where the *Dark Night* might be located?" Tacita asked.

"Yes," Strong said.

The image on the big screen focused in on a cluster of stars just inside the edge of the galaxy. "We located one of the beacons on it you said would be there, Chairman Ray. We will be in the same system thirty minutes after entering the galaxy."

Ray nodded and Roscoe felt stunned. Maria's hand gripped his tightly.

The big ship that had brought the Lotus here millions and millions of years ago was instantly found even from this distance. Amazing.

"How?" Maria asked.

"We planted numbers of signal systems in the big ship," Tacita said, "that would last and could not be traced."

"Is there a place we could wait and watch your scans and approach and not be in the way?" Ray asked.

Strong nodded. "Yes. I can jump you there if you don't mind."

Ray nodded and a moment later the five of them were in a large conference room with screens on all four walls and all sorts of stations around the walls.

Roscoe glanced around at the very comfortable space. In the center of the room was a white conference table with comfortable cloth chairs around it and doughnuts and other baked goods, along with fruit, on the table. There were also pitchers of water and glasses.

All the screens came up live at that moment and Strong pointed to one in the center. "You'll be able to follow us in Command Center there and all major scans and data will appear on the other screens.

"This is wonderful," Tacita said, looking around.

"Yes, thank you, Chairman," Ray said.

"My pleasure and my ship's honor," he said. "Now if you will excuse me."

At that he jumped away and appeared in the Command Center, quickly sitting down in his command chair.

Roscoe could tell that Chairman Strong was as excited as he was feeling, maybe more, since he and his ship existed to explore new places. And this galaxy was about as new and different as it got.

Forty-one

AFTER AN HOUR or more, Maria had given in and taken a doughnut and some water. The stress of watching and waiting was more than she could take. She wasn't sure if the chocolate-covered cake doughnut would help, but they had smelled so good, she had to find out.

More than anything else she wanted to get up and pace, but she forced herself to sit and eat instead. And luckily, the doughnut tasted as good as it smelled and was very fresh. And the dark chocolate was her favorite.

Roscoe sat in the chair next to her, staring at mostly only three screens, all showing visuals ahead. She could tell he was in his military mindset and not moving at all.

Ray and Tacita sat near the end of the table, one chair separating the two couples. They were also staring at the screens, swiveling around at times to take in other readings from other scans.

Maria was about halfway through the doughnut when Chairman Ray turned to them. "What did you expect to find here?"

Maria had had no expectations, but she knew what Roscoe had expected, so she nodded to him.

"Not much," Roscoe said. "But we had to know for sure, otherwise we would have prepared *Morning Song* completely wrong for her coming mission to seed."

"Why did you not expect any problems here?" Tacita asked.

"For the same reason you picked me and Maria for this task," Roscoe said. "I know military and dictatorships, and I know that is not a cultural structure that can sustain even over short periods of time, as you proved in the original galaxy. You won and sent the survivors here."

"Freedom of choice and a desire to make a profit will always win in the end," Maria said, then licked chocolate from her fingers.

"So what exactly are you expecting?" Ray asked after glancing at the screens once again.

"Ravaged and destroyed planets, maybe, that might be so destroyed as to not be overgrown with local plants. There might be small enclaves of humans, if any. Very low technology, if any."

Maria watched Ray nodding to that.

Roscoe went on. "Considering the millions of years they have been here, and logically spread out some at first, we might find a stable culture growing similar to what we plant."

"Seriously?" Tacita asked.

Roscoe nodded. "From survivors. But if they continued to develop without help, my gut sense is that they will just keep falling into the same patterns we all know so well that cultures go through."

"And thus end up destroying each other," Maria said, trying to decide to go for another doughnut or not.

Ray frowned.

"Seeding the planets is wonderful," Maria said, finally leaning forward to take another fantastic chocolate doughnut, "but it would be for nothing if not for the Seeders who remain behind for hundreds of thousands of years and guide the cultures up through the turmoil and the instability. That makes all the difference."

"Entering the edge of the galaxy now," Chairman Strong said over a ship-wide broadcast system. "Stay alert, everyone. Thirty minutes to first target."

Now that got Maria's full attention.

And made her even more nervous.

She bit into the wonderful chocolate cake doughnut, then grabbed a couple of napkins. Chewing, she put the doughnut down on a napkin and turned her full attention to the screens. Especially the one indicating the signal coming from the *Dark Night*, the huge prison ship that had brought millions to this distant galaxy.

Forty-two

ROSCOE STUDIED THE screens as *The Horizon* dropped out of trans-tunnel flight. On the screen beside the image of the Command Center, the dark image of the old ship appeared. Small at first, and then the image got closer and closer and larger.

He didn't know what to expect, but was surprised the ship looked almost round, with engines on one flattened side, not at all normal Seeder shapes.

But, of course, this was long before the idea of seeding outside the original galaxy had come about and the bird design of Seeder ships.

As the image got in closer, there was little doubt that the ancient ship was barely holding together. Giant meteors had smashed into it from all sides over the years. The only reason it still existed was because it was away from any orbit of any planet or large moon and no gravitational forces were pulling on it.

"Stunning any beacon still worked," Roscoe said, more to himself.

"Only one survived out of a hundred," Ray said. "We built them into bulkheads and in the metal walls of the ship itself."

"Wow," Maria said.

On another screen, it was clear that

what had been an Earth-like planet close to the big ship was nothing but a burnt and destroyed husk. Roscoe had no doubt something very ugly had happened on that planet, more than likely human-caused a very long time ago. No atmosphere remained at all.

"Chairman Ray, would you and the other Chairmen please come to the Command Center."

Roscoe glanced around at the other screens quickly before Ray jumped them to the Command Center.

"We are getting some very interesting scans from different areas of this galaxy," Chairman Strong said, not getting up from his chair.

The big screen focused on a star about sixty light-years away from where they had found the big ship. "A planet around this sun has a flourishing human society on it, early space age levels."

"Can we take a closer look?" Ray asked.

"There's something else," Strong said, "that you need to know before we move. We are showing preliminary scans of two different alien races in this galaxy as well. Both about the same technological level as the human society."

The image on the screen pulled back and Roscoe could see that one race was on the far side of the galaxy, the other only about four hundred light years from the young human society.

"We have no idea what kind of cultures they are from this distance," Strong said.

Ray was looking as shocked as Roscoe felt.

Ray looked at his wife for a moment, then turned to Strong. "We need to clear historical evidence that humans came to this galaxy from the outside. Can we bump the remains of *Dark Night* into a path that will take it into the sun?"

"We can," Strong said. "It will take a couple weeks to get it moving without tearing it apart."

"Can you consider that part of your mission now, Chairman?" Ray asked Strong. "And destroying any other historical evidence of the Lotus coming from outside this galaxy."

Strong nodded. "That is no problem."

"Can we take a look at the advanced civilizations safely?" Roscoe asked.

"Please," Ray asked Strong, who nodded and then indicated that his crew jump to trans-tunnel flight.

Within minutes they were back in real space, approaching the human population.

"Early space age," Strong said, nodding.

Roscoe noted that Strong glanced around at one of his crew on the bridge. The brown-haired woman shook her head and looked back at her board.

"Without help," Strong said, staring at his screen at his command chair, "they will destroy themselves and this planet in the next decade. If not sooner. They are in the standard human society growth pattern almost perfectly."

"Then we need to get some help here quickly," Maria said.

"Why would we do that?" Tacita said, frowning and looking at Maria. "They are Lotus."

Roscoe actually laughed. "Millions and millions of years ago their ancestors were Lotus. But now they are just a new human planet trying to get started and they need help to survive and follow a path to stability."

"We're Seeders, aren't we?" Maria asked, staring at Tacita. "Helping young human cultures get started on the right road is part of our job description."

Tacita started to open her mouth, then closed it. Roscoe could tell that Maria's words had hit home and got through the millions of years of thinking anyone in this galaxy would still hold the beliefs from so long before.

Chairman Ray had a slight grin on his face, but said nothing.

Strong looked between the four of them, then said, "Many of my people were trained in planetary cultural growth. We're going to be in this galaxy giving it a good scouring for a good two hundred years, if not more. We can help them until better help arrives."

"Thank you, Chairman Strong," Ray said, bowing. "You and your crew will be justly rewarded, I can promise."

"Thank you, Chairman," Strong said.

"Please send regular reports every month for the next few years," Ray said. "I'm going to be following this very interesting galaxy's progress with great attention."

"As am I," Roscoe said.

Strong nodded.

"And I really am curious as to the other alien races," Ray said. "A very unusual find. Thank you for your ship's work on this. And your time. It is very much appreciated."

A moment later the four of them were back in the Command Center of Ray's ship, over thirty galaxies away.

Roscoe still couldn't wrap his mind around how that was done. He was just glad Ray was good at it.

Chairman Ray turned to Roscoe and Maria. "It seems we have a mission statement to change."

"Thankfully, yes," Roscoe said. "And I have some ideas."

"As do I," Maria said, smiling.

Tacita actually smiled at that.

Chairman Ray stared at both of them for a moment. "Nothing can substitute for the excitement of youth. I will be looking forward to the new ideas."

Roscoe took Maria's hand. Then with a nod, he jumped them back to the *Morning Song* Command Center, much to the surprise of Fisher and Callie, who expected them to be gone much, much longer.

Section Five: The Future

Forty-three

MARIA JUST COULDN'T get enough of Roscoe, and forced them to spend private time together every day, even though they had a million things to get done and worked together all day.

She felt they needed the time.

And they both enjoyed it. She was stunned, but she kept feeling closer and closer and more in love with Roscoe every day. She didn't think this kind of depth of love was even possible.

Since the scouting missing, she and Roscoe and Callie and Fisher had spent many meals planning what exactly to do with all the extra space that Ray had designed into *Morning Song* for a huge fleet of military craft.

Part of the space, Maria was happy to see, would be converted into making jump stations for the *Breadcrumbs* project. But that took up such a small part of the huge space that Ray had planned for a military fleet, it didn't seem to really dent the empty areas.

Ten days after they returned, while having dinner in their suite—a wonderful dinner Fisher cooked of stream trout, garlic potatoes, and steamed vegetables—she and Roscoe decided to tell Fisher and Callie about the *Morning Breeze*, the second big empty Mother Ship coming into the galaxy in forty years.

"Ray and Tacita hope you two will be the Chairmen of *Morning Breeze*."

Fisher just blinked.

Callie said simply, "What?"

Both were stunned.

Maria loved it, since Fisher and Callie knew what being joint Chairmen of a Seeder Mother Ship meant.

They had just finished eating and were talking about the next day's major tasks as they cleaned up when suddenly Maria had an idea.

"You guys want to indulge me for a moment in the Command Center?"

Roscoe looked at her and raised his eyebrows.

She punched his arm. "Not that kind of indulge. I got an idea that will take help from *Morning Song* to figure out if it is even possible."

"Last time we did this, we ended up thirty galaxies away from here," Roscoe said, smiling.

"I don't think this is that far," Maria said, smiling at the three laughing friends.

They jumped into Command Center, much to the surprise of the crew working the evening shift.

"Would everyone please take a break until we call you back?" Callie asked.

The five who had been on duty nodded and vanished.

"*Morning Song*," Callie said, turn-ing to the big screen that at the moment was totally blank. "In your updates from Chairman Ray's ship, have you pinpointed the location of *Morning Breeze*. If so, would you show us?"

On the big screen the image of the Local Group of galaxies appeared, clearly showing the Milky Way and their position.

A dotted line extended backwards and ended with a green light labeled *Morning Breeze*. It seemed to be numbers of galaxies away. And at mostly sub-light speeds and only short trans-tunnel jumps as *Morning Song* had been doing, Maria could see how that distance would take forty thousand years.

"At the top speed of *The Lady*," Maria asked, "how long would it take to reach the *Morning Breeze* in trans-tunnel flight?"

The stunning words appeared on the screen.

Thirty-one days.

Maria turned and looked at the shocked expression on the other three faces. Then she said simply, "Now we have some real planning to do."

FORTY-FOUR

OVER THE NEXT week, while still slowing *Morning Song* and getting more and more help on board to work on the major repairs and getting areas of the ship staffed, the four of them met every evening over dinner to plan.

Roscoe enjoyed those dinners more than he wanted to admit.

And they often ended up in the Command Center of *Morning Song* using the big screen to get some scale of the different galaxies where their seeding mission was heading.

On the seventh night of dinner meetings, Roscoe was thinking about the paths of future seeding missions when a different image appeared in his mind.

A balloon.

And he said that out loud.

At the moment he had been handing dishes to Maria to put into the dishwasher in their suite and Fisher and Carrie were still sitting at the now cleared table.

Maria looked at him with a puzzled frown? "Balloon?"

He nodded and handed her the last plate he had rinsed, then dried off his hands and moved over to his spot at the table.

"You know how we are always saying that Seeders think big."

Fisher made an arm gesture. "I think *Morning Song* is an example of that."

"And the fact that they have been doing this for more millions of years than I care to think about," Maria said.

"What happens if they aren't thinking big enough?" Roscoe asked.

"Now you are starting to scare me a little," Callie said.

Maria looked completely puzzled.

"Time to head for the Command Center," Roscoe said, smiling. "There is something that Tacita said at one point that has haunted me and I think I might have an answer."

A few minutes later they were there and the regular crew had taken a break.

Roscoe pointed to the big screen. "*Morning Song*," he said, "please put the Milky Way at the center of a sphere and slowly expand out the sphere until the edge of the sphere hits the closest galaxy outside the Local Group."

On the big screen that image appeared, with a dotted line circle. It hit a galaxy that they all knew had been seeded already.

"Thank you, *Morning Song*." Roscoe said. "Now please expand that sphere exactly one hundred thousand light years in radius."

"The distance of a jump station," Maria said and Roscoe smiled at her and nodded.

"Are there any unseeded galaxies in that sphere?"

"No," appeared on the screen.

"Please keep expanding the sphere by one hundred thousand light years in radius and put the number of unseeded galaxies at the bottom with every expansion. Stop at five expansions."

At two hundred thousand light-years, the numbers of unseeded galaxies was finally three.

At three hundred, it jumped to eight.

At four hundred it jumped to fourteen.

At five hundred thousand light years in radius from the center of the Milky Way, the number of unseeded galaxies jumped to eighteen.

"What exactly are you saying?" Fisher asked Roscoe.

Maria studied the image on the big screen for a second and then turned to Roscoe as well.

"We have been snaking our way outward as Seeders," Roscoe said. "Always just jumping to the closest galaxy ahead without a lot of thought. With the *Breadcrumbs* transport stations, why do that? Why not make the Milky Way the center of this expansion and move outward in a consistent sphere pattern."

He looked around at his friends and

at the woman he loved. All three of them were blinking.

He went on. "The second deck can be a complete construction deck for building more Seeder ships as we go. We can have an entire factory working on both *Morning Song* and *Morning Breeze*. With the hundreds of frontline Seeder ships now working Andromeda, the frontline Seeder ships we have here, and the other Seeder frontline ships on *Morning Breeze*, we can do this easily if we keep building."

"And with the transport system, the entire bubble of Seeded galaxies can be held together," Maria said.

"Exactly," Roscoe said. "Tacita said that they needed so many more Seeder Mother Ships. Why not have a base here building more Seeder Mother Ships as the bubble expands and we need more?"

"And each Seeder Mother Ship would have a factory on it as well," Fisher said, nodding.

Maria moved closer and kissed him, sending shivers through him. Then she held him at arm's length and looked at him with those huge golden eyes. "That mind of yours continues to amaze me."

"Scares hell out of me," Fisher said.

Forty-five

MARIA LAY NAKED, tucked under Roscoe's arm two hours later. The lights of their wonderful suite were dimmed and they had made love and then settled down to get some sleep. She felt relaxed and satisfied and completely at ease with her life and her world.

She loved just being against Roscoe, touching his skin, listening to him breathe, enjoying his faint musky smell. She could never seem to get enough of him, and when they were in the big command chairs and linked through *Morning Song*, it felt even better.

She opened one eye and looked at him. He seemed to be sleeping and she

needed to sleep as well. But she just couldn't turn her mind off yet.

She was trying to remember not knowing Roscoe Mundy, her life before the last two months. And even though that had been hundreds of years of living, those times seemed like distant memories now compared to the last two months.

How was that possible?

And if the idea of expanding out in a sphere was accepted, with the transport stations, they were going to start an inter-galactic culture that would stay in touch, learn from each planet, each culture, each galaxy, and continue to advance into lev-els she couldn't begin to imagine.

Just the idea of that had her excited beyond words.

And she and Roscoe and *Morning Song* would be on the leading edge of the building.

"Are you all right?" Roscoe asked her, hugging her closer.

She snuggled down even more against his smooth skin and hard muscles of his chest. "I'm about as all right as I can be," she said, softly.

"So what were you thinking about?"

"Honestly," she said, "about what we are going to build and about how much I love you."

"I really like both of those thoughts," he said, hugging her even tighter against him. "You know, we've never really talk-ed about that we are committing our-selves to each other for a very long time."

"Does that bother you?" she asked.

He laughed softly. "It actually is one of the things I love about doing all this. I'm going to get to do this for a very, very long time with you."

She kissed him on the chest and said, "I like that thought as well."

"How about you?" he asked. "Are you bothered by us being together for such a long time?"

"I'm worried about one thing," she said, snuggling down against him.

"And what's that?" he asked.

"I'm worried that a very, very long time won't be long enough."

"Then we'll make it even longer," he said, squeezing her. "I promise."

"I promise as well," she said.

And with that she kissed his skin one more time and snuggled down close and went to sleep with the man she loved and planned to love for even more than an eternity.

~

Coming Next Issue in Smith's Monthly
A New Novel Series.
The First Novel in the *Ghost of a Chance* Series

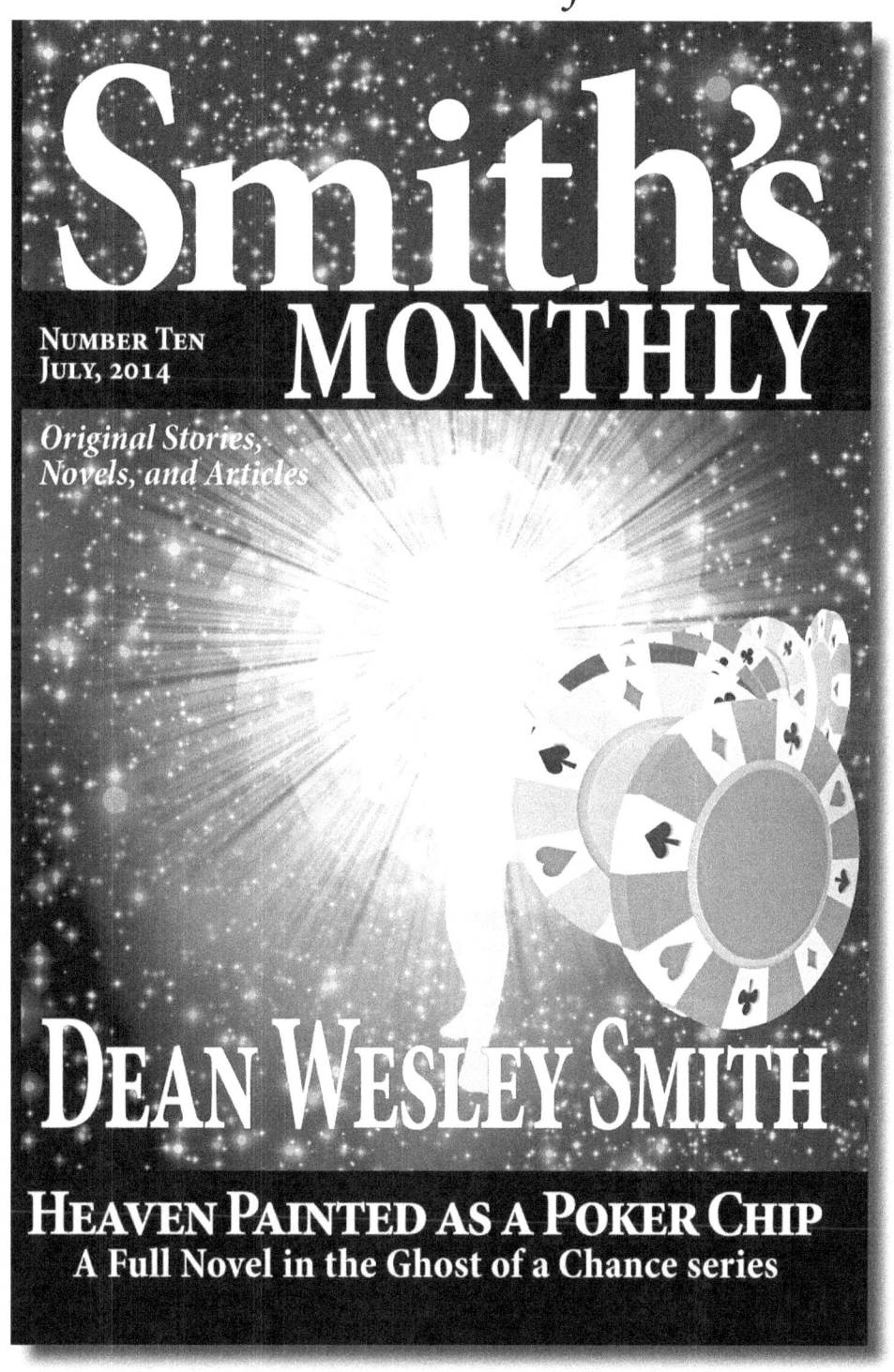

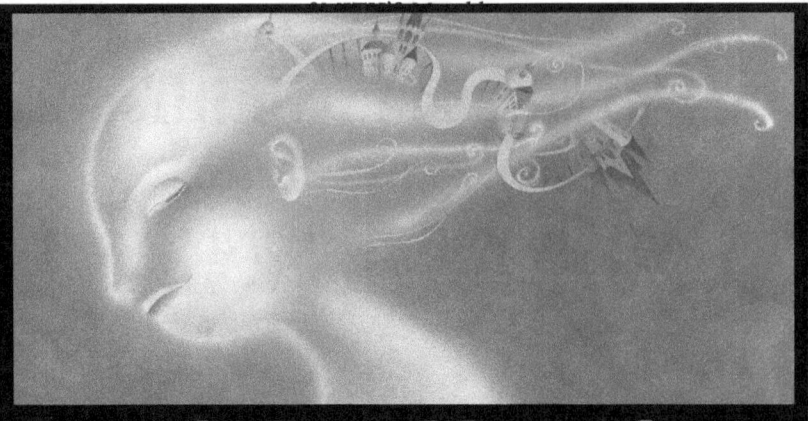

Poems by DEAN WESLEY SMITH

So You Want to be a Writer

It has been almost eight months
since my fresh resolution to a new year
broke with a snap that no one heard
and I didn't notice.

Somehow, I filled those eight months
with getting ready to start the resolution, again
hoping it hadn't aged like fruit
in the sun.

Now, tonight, I ignore the ripe smell,
the stench of fear,
and the drips of sweat
that make my fingers slide off the keys.

Two weeks on, eight months off.
Tonight I restart the resolution to write,
grinding my creative engine
like a car that needs a complete tune-up.

The engine sputters, the tires need air,
everything smells of mold and burnt oil,
yet there is a jerk forward, a few words, this poem.
I call it progress.

I hold my breath and work to keep typing,
waiting for the impulse to choke and die,
since there never seems to be enough time,
even with a good resolution.